Rhonda,

Happy Reading

Thanks for your support

DANNY AND MJ

A STORY OF FORBIDDEN LOVE

Suzanne Casey

ARCHWAY
PUBLISHING

Archway Publishing books may be ordered through booksellers or by contacting:

Archway Publishing
1663 Liberty Drive
Bloomington, IN 47403
www.archwaypublishing.com
1 (888) 242-5904

ISBN: 978-1-4808-8553-0 (sc)
ISBN: 978-1-4808-8554-7 (e)

Library of Congress Control Number: 2019919531

Print information available on the last page.

Archway Publishing rev. date: 12/11/2019

*à **Mme Justine***
The influence of a good teacher can never be erased

to pc

CHAPTER 1

♀

met Danny through work. He was a product representative. He'd come to City Hall, where I work, to showcase his latest babies: top-of-the-line printers. As City Manager, I avoided attending any product presentation. But something told me to go to this one.

I heard Danny before I saw him. His deep voice carried all the way down the hall as I walked up to the conference room he'd been assigned to. I'm not sure if it was his husky voice that captured me or the laughter of my fellow coworkers, but as I approached the room, I saw myself as enthralled by this salesman's enthusiasm as my colleagues were.

I walked in, but nobody noticed I had entered. He had my people's full attention. The more he spoke, the more they craved him. Danny was a true salesperson, knowing exactly what his audience desired. I couldn't make out where he was among the dozen or so men and women huddled in the left corner of the room. No matter, his charming voice had snaked itself around my ears, and I was as intrigued as my coworkers.

This was so not like me. My entire career path had been led by my friendly, yet business-comes-first attitude. My fellow associates never feared my presence when I walked into a room, but they knew I expected a certain level of professionalism, whether it was the way they answered emails, or how they dressed. Yet I wasn't one to enforce my beliefs. They just learned that being on my good side would be beneficial for each one of them.

I cleared my throat, letting everyone in the room know that I had arrived, and that business was to begin. It took a few more seconds to finally see this man who'd captured everyone's attention. The group slowly dissipated, some more reluctant than others. And only at that point did I see Danny. That's when my so-called professionalism went down the drain.

I was thankful the conference table was within reach. When I made eye contact with Danny, my legs buckled. Literally. Never in my entire life had I experienced such strong emotion in seeing someone for the first time. And I'm the mother of two children! His eyes were mesmerizing, beyond blue. Now that I've gotten to know them better, I like to describe the colour of Danny's eyes as the colour of the sea. They changed tones, like the ocean does with the weather. In his case, the depth of blue changed with his temperament. When he was moody, his eyes darkened to a shade of charcoal grey, reflecting his emotional self at the moment. And when in the build-up of lovemaking, his eyes turned a toe-curling royal blue. But on the day Danny and I met, this fateful May day, a day that he was in his prime, happy to be doing what he loved doing, his eyes caught me off guard. Those gorgeous eyes toppled, and took my breath away. They would lure me all afternoon to sneak glimpses at them. They were the colour of a mid-morning sky, sapphires with a twinkle of silver.

There was no Armani suit. He had arrived wearing a thin grey-and-black-wool-blend sports jacket, which was resting on one of the twenty-two desk chairs surrounding the conference table. Danny's black pants were tailored for his fit, and they fit him perfectly. His yellow shirt showed a few signs of wrinkles. His tie had grey and yellow stripes over a black background, picking up all three colours of wardrobe. I also noticed his shoes. He sure chose to invest in good shoes, being on his feet a lot.

Nevertheless, that was not what had brought me to my knees, so to speak. It was his eyes. They were piercing, looking straight at mine as if he could see what I was thinking.

Annie, my right-hand girl, leapt to help me stand straight again, and I casually blamed losing my balance on a loose shoe. Having caught everybody's attention, I asked everyone to please take their seat so Mr Russell could start his presentation. I sat the farthest away from Danny, facing him from one end of the table to the other, hoping that distance would protect me. Everyone shuffled their way around the table, getting to their individual swivel chairs, soft whispers being shared, and thank goodness nobody noticed the heated glances this latest salesperson and I were sharing.

It made me blush throughout his entire presentation. My heart raced for no apparent reason. I felt heat on my neck, perspiration in my palms. I was embarrassed by my reaction, unable to stop. I bit my nails, a nervous tic of mine.

Danny made his pitch, capturing his hushed audience with his enthusiasm and his knowledge of his company's products. His best tool of all, however, was his baritone voice that resonated slightly beyond the room, the same voice that had caught my attention earlier.

I was pleasantly surprised that at the end of his presentation Danny made his way towards my end of the table. He opened the door to let people out, thanked them individually by name for coming. And as he shook their hands, he gave them each his business card.

"Thank you for giving me your time, today," he told them. "And if you're interested in hearing more, I'd love to share my knowledge over a cup of coffee." Corny, maybe. But this little touch got to me. And when the room emptied, the two of us remaining, I found myself speechless. It was like I was meeting a celebrity. Words escaped me, and blushing became my downfall. As a true gentleman, Danny did all the talking.

"Again, Ms Taylor, I appreciate your hospitality in letting me come over, this afternoon. And like I've offered your colleagues, I am ready and willing to discuss more of the line of products I represent."

Then he handed me his business card, his name embossed on the top right corner. The electric charge that transferred as our hands touched startled me and I dropped his card to the carpeted floor. Danny knelt down to pick the card up, and as he slowly stood back up he brushed oh so lightly my right calf, making my knee twitch. How weak he made me. How weak I had become.

Danny stood up, straight as a board. There was no expression to show whether touching my leg had been accidental or intentional. We did not exchange another word, only a nod goodbye. Danny walked over to his sports jacket, casually putting one sleeve on then the other. He reloaded his briefcase and headed for the elevator down the hall. Not once did he look at me, and I'm thankful he didn't. I looked like a pitiful puppy waiting to be acknowledged, one more time, and not like the CEO of my city.

I walked back to my office and flopped myself into my white tufted-leather chair. I knew I was flushed. The heat radiating from me was intense, yet tingling. I'd exhausted myself that past hour, trying to behave around this man who, in society's standard, was far from a god. Danny was roughly 5'3", had a wiggly belly and a shaved head. Yet, my heart fluttered at the sound of his voice. My knees buckled at the sight of him. And my engines roared when he dared to touch me.

What had he done to me? How had he gotten himself wrapped around my heart so quickly? Who was this man? I felt like I was in junior high, writing my name on a sticky pad. Not MJ Taylor, but MJ Russell. Snap out of it!

I could no longer concentrate on anything. I left the office a half hour early, which was rare for me. As I passed people, making my way to the parking lot, they all took double glances at me. I ignored them. I had to get this man out of my head before the kids got home. He was, after all, just a charmer looking to make a sale.

I headed home and went straight to the shower. I needed to cool down. I needed to rinse my thoughts away. I had hoped this would be the best way to get Danny Russell out of my head. Instead I found myself sobbing uncontrollably. My nerves were shot.

♂

I watched MJ stumble, wondering what she had tripped over. I hadn't seen anything in her path. Perhaps it was just a new pair of shoes. Then I saw it. MJ sneaking in glances. Just like Cathy had. Just like Tina had. MJ was crushing on the colour of my eyes. I hadn't had that kind of effect on a woman in over a decade. I'd added on a few pounds over the years, and women noticed the size of my jacket before anything else. MJ's reaction brought back good memories. I found it rather exciting.

Over the course of my presentation, I gave equal eye-contact to all, both men and women, making sure they felt important, that I valued their presence. Some preferred looking at the smart board, others writing down points or questions. But most looked in the general direction of my face. MJ was different. She turned away each time I looked at her. And every time I did, I caught her looking straight into my eyes.

Usually, I wouldn't pay attention to such behaviour. She seemed to be uncomfortable, out of character. With every glance she intrigued me, perhaps much more than she should have. It was exciting. Made me feel young again.

Tina and I have been together for thirteen years. Her daughter Emma sweet sixteen. Alex fifteen. I have always treated her children as my own.

Tina remained a waitress, but after hopping from job to job she'd found a boss who respected her need to be home when the children arrived from school. And I was okay with that. She worked four hours a day, four days a week. She kept Fridays open to run errands for our family.

Tina is an amazing cook and has fed me a little too well over the years. But that's my issue, not hers. With my career affording us a nice cushion to live on, she in return has given me a good life of stability and happiness. And despite an absentee father, Emma and Alex have thrived, doing fine, both at home and at school. Not once have they called me Dad, even though I had been raising them both since they were still in diapers.

As surprised as I was by MJ's reaction, and her lack of professionalism for the rest of that presentation, I was just as surprised at how I reacted to the attention. I was a happily committed man. I had nothing to complain about. I had enjoyed, over the years, mostly behind sunglasses, the array of women walking by. I'd glance at them, enjoying the view. But never to the point of making Tina jealous. I just appreciated nice curves when I saw them.

So why MJ? Why at this point in my life? In hindsight, I realize now that every time I made eye contact with a person in the room, I glanced quickly at MJ before focusing back on the smart board. Not sure if I was doing that to tease her, or for my own benefit. I'd look away, but I couldn't get her out of my mind. She quickly became ingrained into my brain.

The only reason I had come to City Hall that day was that Kevin, who was supposed to do this presentation, had called in sick. Well, not sick - his wife was in labour. I quickly grabbed the information off his desk, and headed to Main Street, conferencing with him on the phone on last minute details. I wanted to be on top of my game for this potentially huge contract. Fate brought me to that building that day. Fate brought me to her eyes.

Again, in hindsight, I see that, perhaps to fuel my ego, I chose to continue to tease MJ, to see how I could break her bravado. I even kept this possible contract to myself, instead of returning it back to Kevin. I insisted that only MJ work with me. It became a game. I was enjoying the renewed interest in my self, sparked by MJ's body language around me. She was such an easy target. And the more I pushed, the more she caved in.

At first, it was a great boost to my ego. Then I lost respect for her, questioning if she was the right type of person to represent our city in such an important position. Mayors and councils come and go. But rising to the top as City Manager, that required skill, knowledge, poise. And poise was something I did not see from her. Over time, however, I saw that MJ could fake her poise. The politics of her job required her to be pleasant, but firm. She just couldn't do it with me. I was a stumbling block for MJ.

It had been such a long time since anybody other than Tina had been attracted to me, that I'm surprised I recognized the signs. Here was this middle-aged woman, in a prominent position, wedding ring on her finger, who kept herself in pretty good shape, and for reasons neither one of us could pinpoint, she was developing a crush on me.

I, a forty-three-year-old man with a shaved head and a beer belly, tipping the scales at over 200 pounds, a smoker with a boring job, was crush-worthy. I felt rejuvenated. I felt sexy. I had to know more about MJ Taylor, and business meetings weren't going to cut it.

CHAPTER 3

♀

A week passed before Danny called my office, wondering if I had read his brochures. I hadn't. I had his business card in my possession, and had even transferred his contact information into my phone, which was an idiotic thing for me to do.

"I appreciate your eagerness to get a contract with the City of Holliston, Mr Russell," I answered. "I may be in a high position, but the Purchasing Department deals with these procedures."

"I respect that, Ms Taylor," he voiced, "but I was hoping to deal with you directly. Mostly because it would be financially advantageous for the City to upgrade all their equipment at once. I'm ready to offer you a deal you cannot refuse."

"Again, Mr Russell, I appreciate your persistence, but-."

"Ms Taylor, I understand your position. We both have jobs to do. All I want, really, is just a few more precious minutes of your time, in your office. Or perhaps over coffee. Or even cocktails. You decide what works for you."

Despite my better judgment, I agreed to see Danny in my office, two days later. We could've had a luncheon meeting, but I didn't trust myself. I was afraid of my behaviour. I was afraid of his. I was still lightheaded from the first meeting.

So here I was, thirty-eight hours later, fishing through my walk-in closet at home. I was looking for the perfect outfit. Business-like and weather appropriate had always been my go-to attire. And if I was to speak at council meetings under the glare of television cameras, I always brought an extra pantsuit to change into, prior to my appearance.

This was different. I found myself scurrying among my thin blouses, those that required matching camisoles, and then my selection of skirts. I also looked for a work- appropriate pair of heels. I didn't want to get the wrong attention from my team. But I did want today's skirt to give a slightly more defined curve to my derrière. I was dressing up for the man. What was I thinking?

I realize now, years later, what exactly had been happening in my head, my heart, my loins. At the time, however, I was oblivious. I was a married mother of two teenagers, busy with my career and my household. Danny was a crush. A crush that defied all previous crushes I'd ever had.

I loved my Rick. Life got in the way of pure intimacy, but we still had an active love life. And we made the effort to go out on dates. Although lately, those dates consisted of going to the theatre, or teaming up with friends, which suited me fine. As parents, one-on-one conversations persistently focused on our children and family, rather than us as a couple. Cracks were forming, and yet we took it simply as a part of being parents.

I ended up choosing a tulip-shaped skirt. It was one of my favourites and when I slipped into it, I wore it with pure confidence. Its rich, amethyst colour highlighted my svelte hips, and its overlapping in the front hid the slight belly I was never able to get rid of after my two pregnancies. "Badges of victory" was what Rick called my belly. The skin-coloured sandals lifted my heels a few inches, just enough to give a curve in the back since I was *blessed* with my mother's non-existent backside. I paired this all off with a lacy mauve blouse, wearing a mauve camisole beneath. To make sure I wouldn't raise any eyebrows, I added the matching blazer to my skirt. And off to work I went.

My meeting with Danny was not scheduled until 3 p.m. I'd allotted him one hour to pitch his product at me. I found myself extremely unproductive, all day. I wasn't daydreaming, per se, I was mostly coaching myself to react better to him. Better than I had last week. He was just a man, after all. He was no different than any other male equals I had at work. He was a salesman. It was his job to charm himself into my head, and he had succeeded. No, I had not been prepared to see my knees give out under me. But I was now writing that off as a weak moment, and nothing more.

I accomplished only half of the tasks I usually would, a thousand thoughts racing through my head. I prepped myself to a much more poised second encounter with Mr Russell. Half an hour before, I found myself edgy, looking at the clock above my office door every minute or so. I resolved to step out of my office and get some fresh air. There was a trendy coffee shop across the street that created my favourite skinny latté. The walk felt wonderful, even in delicate heels.

As I got off the elevator, I saw Danny chatting up with Annie. His persona was wrapping itself around her head as well. He was *good.* They both turned and smiled simultaneously. My eyes fluttered at his smile. I'd hoped Annie hadn't noticed my behaviour. I was trying to make sense of it myself.

"Good afternoon, Ms Taylor," Danny said as he extended his hand. My arms full with a pocketbook and a coffee cup I ignored the handshake. "Annie and I were discussing last night's ball game. It's not every day one finds a Blue Jays fan as passionate as her."

"Annie," he added. "It's been a pleasure. Next time I'm at a game, I'll buy you an authentic souvenir."

I unlocked my office and reached for the brushed-nickel handle to the glass door. Danny skipped ahead and opened it for me. I thanked him, putting my latté next to my laptop. I stored my handbag in the bottom drawer of my desk. Finally, I looked up and gave him the floor, so to speak.

"I'm truly grateful to speak with you, one on one, Ms Taylor. Now, is it Ms Taylor? Or Mrs Taylor? Or may I call you MJ?"

Sly move on his part, was my thinking. Get into my comfort zone so he'll find my weaknesses and I'll fall for his tactics, draw up a contract with his company on the spot. I've always preferred keeping business contacts professional. But to me, Mrs Taylor was my mother-in-law.

"MJ is fine," I grinned, staring into those same eyes I'd lost myself into, last week.

Hate to admit it, but from that point on I got into a trance, and barely heard a word Danny said. I had no doubt setting up a contract with his company would be beneficial in the long run. I just could not retain any information he was giving me. My eyes had glazed over, and I found myself nodding at him with my mouth slightly open. Danny had, once again, succeeded in making a fool out of me.

"I believe I've taken enough of your time, today, MJ." His voice dropped, his damn eyes locked with mine. "It's time for you to go home. I'll write a summary of my suggested prices and email it to you. How about I call on Monday to see if you require any additional information. Or if you'd prefer, I can address council myself directly."

"Thank you, Mr Russell," I stuttered as I got up to smooth my skirt and adjust my blouse.

"Danny, please," he grinned. "Mr Russell was my father."

"Well then, thank you, Danny," I replied. "It's been a full week, and I apologize if I seem a little distracted. I look forward to your email and will contact you by the end of the day on Monday. These purchases do not require council approval. It is my budget to balance. The Purchasing Department and I will be making this decision."

I extended my hand towards him while taking a deep breath,

concerned of how my body might react. It failed me slightly the last time. Danny reached out to take it, but he also positioned his left hand to grab my right elbow. How did he know my knees would tremble again? Was it written on my face? I caught myself, but the damage was done. Danny pretended not to notice, mostly to keep my dignity intact. But he and I both knew.

He had a brief chat with Annie, waved at her as the elevator doors opened. And as the doors started closing, his ice-blue eyes looked straight through my glass-walled office, straight through into my own eyes, and he smiled a knowing grin. I immediately felt heat climb through me. He knew. He knew I knew. He knew I knew he knew. My cheeks flushed. My loins warmed up. My breasts perked. I had been caught twice with my hand in the cookie jar, and there would be a price to pay for that.

CHAPTER

4

♀

All weekend, I contemplated on how to handle Danny. He was offering the City of Holliston a deal we could simply not refuse. Some of our equipment was starting to show its age. Between the tune ups and repairs we were paying for, for the sake of my allotted budget, my department heads, my beautiful town, I could not let this deal fall through.

I also knew I had to remove myself from the negotiations of this contract with Danny's company. I had to let one of my subordinates handle those details instead of myself. I was not fit to negotiate anything with Danny. I was barely fit to be in his vicinity. I was unable to shake off my feelings for him. His hold on me was tantalizing, leaving me in a pool of saliva, awakened hormones, and moistened underwear. It was not professional of me, nor the behaviour of someone else's wife.

Monday morning, I headed for my weekly meeting with the mayor and all my fellow department heads. Typically, this gathering in the conference room adjacent to the mayor's office would last a few hours. This day, it ran a little bit longer. All present seemed to have a little bit more to share. I, for example, brought up the presentation Danny had given two weeks previously.

"I am definitely in the works to strike a deal with Juno Electronics," I announced.

A strong round of yes's and applause erupted in the room. I grinned. I guess everybody had gotten fed up with our antiquated equipment after all.

"All right then," I smiled. "In the next forty-eight hours, if you could gather the items each one of you will need in your individual departments, I would appreciate it. Have it on my desk by the end of day Wednesday, and I'll see what I can do."

After I left the meeting, I took my morning coffee with Annie, casually asking how her weekend had gone. Once my mug was empty, I went into my office and emailed an invite to Danny.

> *Good morning, Mr Russell,*
> *After some reflection on my part, and a brief mention of your offer at a department meeting this morning, the City of Holliston is looking forward to going into business with Juno Electronics. We are currently gathering information on the equipment needed. An assigned member from the Purchasing Department will be in contact with you within the week to draw up a contract.*
>
> *Sincerely yours,*
> *Marie-Josée Taylor*
> *City Manager*
> *City of Holliston*

I pressed "send" and then dismissed Annie for lunch while I settled myself into my office chair. I started reading and addressing the posted mail that Annie was unable to deal with herself. Then I went back to my laptop and looked at the emails that had accumulated over the weekend. The most recent communication received came from Danny, having been sent five minutes after mine.

> *Good morning to you, Mrs Taylor,*
> *Juno Electronics looks forward to furnishing the City Hall offices with our latest equipment. You will be captivated with our line of fabulous products, and even more pleased with our guarantees and fantastic customer service.*
>
> *I have no doubt your Purchasing Department staff members are well educated in addressing this contract, but I insist in dealing directly with you, Mrs Taylor. Once the equipment is purchased and installed, then your people can communicate with my people.*
>
> *Thank you for your business, and I look forward to meeting with you, soon.*
>
> *Sincerely yours,*
> *Danny Russell*
> *District Manager*
> *Juno Electronics*

I was lost for words. When responding, I wanted to have the perfect vocabulary in place to end this charade he and I were playing. But I chose to ignore answering his email, continuing on with my other work. Reports had to be written. Decisions had to be made. Budgets had to be balanced.

Enveloped in my work, my lunch hour came and went. Annie knocked at my door at 1:45, startling me. She pointed at her trendy watch, indicating I was overdue to stop and take a break.

Annie was an absolutely phenomenal asset to my well being. Beyond the required skills as my administrative assistant, she was a walking calendar of my life, and a mother figure to me. I wouldn't have expected any less from Annie. Buying the perfect gifts on Christmas, or her birthday, or Administrative Assistant Day, never seemed to cut it. I could never repay her and I've always found it rather humorous that she adopted the role of mothering me at work, even though I am twenty years her senior. I guess it's just her nature to be that way. I made a conscious note to invite her and her fiancé to come have dinner with Rick and myself, knowing it will probably never happen.

I cracked a big smile while pushing my chair away from my glass and chrome desk, grabbing my office keys. I locked up, thanked her with a kiss on the top of her blonde head, and walked up to the staff lunch room down the hall. I didn't always bring my lunch, often having a working lunch down Main Street with whoever might need my attention. Mondays though were always hectic. Between meetings, catching up on weekend communications and monthly budget presentations at our televised council meetings, a bagged lunch was safest.

I settled down with my egg salad sandwich and cherry tomatoes, plugging in the kettle to make myself a cup of peppermint tea. I was two hours away from clocking out, so I didn't see the need to fuel up on coffee that late in the afternoon. However, I did treat myself to a handful of chocolate-covered almonds purchased from a dispenser in the lunch room.

I picked up after myself, joyfully tossed an almond up in the air to catch it with my mouth. And succeeded. Rick had taught me that while in college. As I reached my office, I flung another one up, and caught it again. I've still got it, I chuckled to myself.

I checked with Annie if there were any messages. There were none. I sat in my chair with a few almonds left in my hand. They were starting to warm up, slowly melting, so I laid them next to my keyboard. I swished my mouse to reignite my screen, and three emails had since come in. Thank goodness I loved my job. It was one of those positions that was never, ever done. I played the game of tossing another chocolate-covered almond into the air every time I answered one of those emails. On the third one, as the almond briefly floated in the air, there was a knock at my door. It took my focus away for a millisecond. I felt it land on my chest, but did not hear it fall to the ground. Not wanting to keep the Deputy Mayor waiting, I resolved to look later. He noticed what I'd been doing and smirked.

"MJ, sorry to bother you this late, but I'm gonna need an updated written report on the renovations at the zoo hospital, ASAP. The Premier is dropping in tomorrow, and I'd like to be well informed."

"Absolutely, George," I answered. Dread came over me. My four o'clock departure had just gotten delayed by half an hour. "Do you want it emailed? Or would you prefer I text it to you? This way, you could read up on it this evening, versus in the morning."

"A text would be fantastic," George smiled. "MJ, you're a peach!"

And with that, he turned around and left my office. I immediately sent a text to all three members of my family, saying I would be late coming home. I noticed a slight commotion behind George, quickly realizing it was Danny coming off the elevator. They shook hands as Danny introduced himself. Tucked under Danny's left arm was a box the size of a toaster, wrapped in brown paper with a small bright blue bow in one corner. As I walked towards my door, feeling my core temperature rise as I approached his aura, I saw him give the box to Annie. Her squeal was almost deafening. Instantly, the adult in her had left the building, replaced by an adolescent.

"Look, MJ!" she expressed with tears in her eyes. "Mr Russell got me an autographed Jays jacket!"

I was stunned. That could not have been an easy thing to get. What was he up to? "That's a... a generous gift, Mr Russell," I said, frowning. "And of course, Annie cannot accept it."

Danny smirked at me then continued speaking as if I wasn't there.

"I just happened to be going to Toronto this weekend with my brother-in-law, and I always try to catch a game when I'm there," Danny answered. "I used to share an apartment with the Jays' equipment manager. He was able to get this jacket signed by all the current players. Took a bit of work, but seeing Annie's reaction was all worth it."

"What can we help you with, Mr Russell?" I asked curtly, cutting short any more small talk. The workday was coming to an end for the entire building, except security and eventually cleaning crews. I wanted to go home.

"I simply wanted to touch base with you, *Mrs* Taylor," he answered, croaking the word Mrs slowly. "I wasn't sure if you'd had the chance to read my reply to the email you'd sent earlier today. And since I was in the neighbourhood, I thought I'd drop in. Killing two birds with one stone," Danny concluded, his delicious eyes keeping a steady hold on mine.

"Again, I appreciate your persistence, Mr Russell. But as my communication with you this morning indicated, I will be appointing a member from the Purchasing Department to negotiate a contract with Juno Electronics, as you can appreciate how full my calendar must be."

"I understand, Mrs Taylor," Danny smiled. "But as I indicated to you in my previous email, I deal directly with the higher ups only. Once we're in, then my subordinates can communicate with yours. All I ask is a moment of your time."

"Mr Russell, I'm a very busy woman. It's the end of the day, and I have a report to prepare and send to our Deputy Mayor before I can leave the office. I don't have time to entertain you right now."

"I can wait," Danny persisted.

"What report, MJ?" Annie cut in.

"George wants me to have an updated report on the zoo hospital renovations texted to him as soon as possible," I sighed.

"I received one today!" Annie smiled, pulling it out of a folder yet to be filed on her desk. "I'll email it to him."

"No," I breathed out. "He insisted I text it to him so he can review it this evening." I was starting to feel defeated by not getting rid of Danny. He was making me jittery. But I also felt relief that Annie was, once again, there to save the day for me.

"I'll have that done in a jiffy!" she cheerfully exclaimed. "It's three minutes to 4. It'll be in George's phone before he reaches his car in the parking lot.

"Annie, what would I do without you?"

"I guess MJ has time to see you now, Mr Russell," Annie said, smiling as she ushered Danny and myself into my office.

We walked silently to the majestic window, featuring a spectacular view of the Sevy River two blocks away. The mayor's office had the same scenery, but one storey above. I was edgy. I nervously made small talk with Danny, pointing at several buildings surrounding City Hall, giving the history of them all. Not once during my rambling did Danny take his eyes off of me.

The lights dimmed behind us, indicating Annie had completed her task and was now stepping into the elevator. It was ten minutes after four, and my entire floor of colleagues had gone for the day, leaving me alone with Danny. A smirk remained on his face from what I could see from my peripheral vision. He made me nervous. I didn't dare look him straight in the eye. My voice trailed off, no longer able to fake small talk. We weren't touching or I definitely would've crumbled to the floor, had that happened. But Danny was standing so close to me my hair fluttered whenever he exhaled, a trail of goosebumps following behind.

And then it happened. Our bodies touched in the most unusual way. Danny startled me so, I gasped. His stubby fingers plunged in between my awakened breasts, plucked out the semi-melted chocolate-covered almond that was resting in my cleavage. He examined it from side to side with a queer sense of amusement, then plopped it into his mouth.

"Very sweet," he proclaimed as he licked his fingers clean. From there, Danny let himself out of my office, leaving me stunned and motionless.

I was mortified. I was shocked. I was angry. I was turned on. I was moist. I was so ashamed of my behaviour, I couldn't look at him. Any other person touching me like that, I would've slapped their face, charged them with sexual misconduct, called security. But this man, this piece of flesh, he's done nothing but torment my soul since the day he walked into my life. He's turned me into mush at the sound of his voice, sight of his face, touch of his skin. I somehow welcomed his inappropriate gesture. And this time, my knees stood straight.

5

♂

My mind was awakened by this woman, even though I was happy at home. MJ's clumsy reaction only fuelled my desire. I struggled with the need to know more about her. I requested a meeting with City Hall for the following week, wanting to know exactly how many of my products they were interested in buying. My inventory was not kept in the Maritime provinces. I needed to order them, and then have the product shipped from Montreal. If the City of Holliston was desperate for my products, we couldn't continue stalling these negotiations.

I received an email from MJ CC-ing a bunch of other people, confirming a scheduled meeting between Juno Electronics and City reps for the following Tuesday, herself included. I was glad to see this was starting to progress. This contract was going to be a humongous one. I could definitely use this bonus, and the recognition that came with it.

I was also glad that I would be able to see Marie-Josée Taylor a bit more. But why was I torturing myself? She was a beautiful creature with curves at the right spots, but I'd seen many beautiful women in my travels. What was it about her? Maybe it was how naive she was about it all. MJ had no idea how much of a knock-out she actually was. I chose to ignore my own behaviour for the time being. I was playing a stupid game with her. I felt alive again doing so, though.

I showed up the following Tuesday a bit early, wanting to touch base with Annie, and I had a little gift for her. I'd learned, over time, that buttering up the right-hand person to the higher ups was like getting the red carpet rolled out in front of you. Figuring out what made Annie happy would give me full access to MJ Taylor. I couldn't bring Annie autographed jackets every time. That would be overkill. But even something as simple as a fancy coffee, or movie passes, which I had today, could make me waltz my way right back into MJ's office.

Today, however, I came off the elevator to find Annie absent. I helped myself to her sticky notepad on the corner of her moon-shaped desk, and wrote a brief message. From there, I went back down to the lobby of the building, officially announcing my presence, and was escorted into the conference room outside Council chambers. I walked in to find a small group of people mumbling amongst themselves. The meeting was scheduled to start in the next few minutes. I eyed my lawyer guy, Jim Williams, in the corner and started walking his way.

"Would you like some coffee?" one of the male City representatives offered.

"No thank you," I answered, having just drunk one while driving over. MJ wasn't here, yet. This was too big of a contract for her to sabotage it by not showing up, so I wasn't worried.

Watching the last few people filter in, I went into panic mode. She was not amongst them. Why did I deem her presence so important? Why did I need to see her again? Why was this gnawing at me so much?

As they all sat with coffee mugs in hand, one young man with a white shirt and flowery tie cleared his throat in order to begin the meeting. I found out he was Tommy Jones, a member of the Purchasing Department, and was going to conduct the proceedings.

"I thank you all for being here today, especially Mr Russell and Mr Williams," he said as he pointed us out with an open hand. " We hope to make this afternoon go smoothly and quickly," Jones stated.

Mr Jones asked for everyone to introduce themselves, like a roll call, and we went around the table. We were only six people, but I kept wondering about my prized #7.

"I've noticed the City Manager is absent," I casually added as I introduced myself to the room. "Will she be joining us?"

"Mrs Taylor had planned to be here," Mr Jones answered, "but she was called away to a more urgent situation. My apologies."

I felt trapped. MJ had understood that I wanted her here, that I wouldn't seal the deal without her being there. Yet, here I was, fending for myself, not able to plead my case without sounding suspicious. So for the next hour or so the people present and I went through each line of the contract Tommy Jones and his department had drawn up. My man Jim modified a few words before two employees from the Purchasing Department and I agreed on a set price for the contract. We would then reconvene at the same time in three days, on the Friday, to sign the deal.

I left pleased that I was going to profit dearly from this deal. My commission alone was going to be substantial. But I was still bummed out in not seeing those legs, and her full D-cups. I made a mental note that I would not sign on Friday if she wasn't there. And I would let her know that, today.

I shook hands with Jim in the parking lot as we parted ways. Lo and behold, in pulled MJ as I was heading for my car. She parked a row away from me, and didn't seem to notice I was there. I trotted to her passenger door and opened it as it unlocked itself when she killed the engine. I didn't mean to scare her, but I did want to surprise her by hopping into the front passenger seat. Her hands flew to cover her face in shock as I jumped in, and I regretted my move.

"Didn't mean to scare you, Mrs Taylor," I explained as I reached out to her. She backed away.

"Too late for that," MJ stated, even though she was already softening up to my presence.

"I missed you up there," I said, pointing to the building across from us. "I told you I would not be selling you anything if you're not part of the negotiations." I then brushed her right knee slightly, making it twitch.

"It couldn't be helped," MJ squirmed, starting to feel the heat building between us, once again. Man, she was easy!

"We meet on Friday afternoon to finalize everything. If you're not there, I walk out," I threatened.

I'm not sure what got over me, but I rested my left elbow on her seat, letting my fingertip go up her blue dress, tracing her right hip, then her rib cage, and finally stopping on the side of her breast. I left my finger there to see what she would do. MJ looked out the window, sunglasses still on. From outside, it just looked like she was looking straight out. But from my view, her eyes were darting from side to side, watching to see if people were noticing what was happening inside her car. Of course, nobody could see. Her tinted windows blocked an immediate view for anyone that might have glanced over. And during the whole time, MJ never moved or pulled away from my touch.

We didn't speak for several minutes, and I was begging to feel more. I didn't want to push my luck. I finally brought my finger up an inch, making it stroke a bit more of her tit. MJ remained motionless. I put my index finger on the higher part of her tit where her nipple might be. That's when she pulled away. Damn!

"I won't be here Friday," were the words MJ broke the silence with. "You'll have to do without me."

"Then the deal is off," I blurted out, startling her, startling myself.

MJ turned her hips to face me. I reached up and removed her sunglasses. I wanted to see her eyes. I wanted to see them struggling as they looked at mine. And they were.

"You can't do that," she said. "You just spent your afternoon ironing out the details. It's a done deal!"

"It's not a deal until it is signed. I'm not signing if you're not there."

This is not the behaviour of a district manager, yet here I was flirting with a client. And what would my superiors think if they knew? And Tina? My ego was stronger than my head at the moment.

"Don't be ridiculous. This is a huge deal for your company, and you'll lose it all because of your obsession of me?"

"Obsession," I laughed. "And you're not obsessed?! I will not be there if you're not. It's that simple. If I show up and you're not there, then I walk out. Understand?"

I challenged her, and she blushed. "I will not be there Friday," MJ repeated.

"Then it's up to you to reschedule this meeting. One that works for all involved. I want you there."

"You're being difficult," she tried to argue. It was cute. "It's not a good sales tactic."

"Maybe, but watching your nipples pop through this dress, I still think this deal is a go," I smiled as I nodded at her chest. Now I was being crass. Get it together, man!

MJ's eyes grew wide, her arms crossing immediately to protect her dignity. I laughed as I left her car to stroll over to mine. I knew I had gotten to her, once again, and she didn't know how to react. When I rolled out of the parking lot, MJ was still sitting in her vehicle.

♀

I was mortified. I had, once again, played right into Danny's hands. I should've kicked him out of my vehicle the second he stepped in. I should've gotten out. I should've gotten the commissionaire's attention to escort Danny from my car. I should've shooed his stubby fingers off of me. I should've done many things. But I let him touch me. It felt good to be touched. It felt good to be wanted again. And maybe he was doing this for other reasons. But at the moment, I wanted to think that Danny was doing this because he actually desired me. I questioned why that should matter.

We were playing a cat-and-mouse game, and it took years off of me. I felt like I was in my twenties. It was an awful way to act as a wife and a mother. But to think I was under somebody's radar was rejuvenating. I felt naughty and silly at the same time.

I was startled by Danny jumping into my car. But I have to admit, it was a lovely surprise. I just couldn't let him think it was. I had pride to upkeep. I did like his sense of humour, his forcefulness, his boldness. And he was easy on the eyes. I was inches taller than him. But when sitting next to each other, we were shoulder to shoulder.

I was fearful of looking at him, afraid of my reaction. I heard him catching his breath. I could smell his musky aftershave. I smelled tobacco on his sports jacket, and I surprisingly liked it. But to look at his eyes, that would've been disastrous. It would have been the end of me. So I chose to look away.

Then Danny challenged my resistance even further by putting his arm on my seat, and I almost lost it at that point. I was thankful I still had my sunglasses on, shielding me from his stare. I am an educated, middle-aged woman with years of experience in dealing with all sorts of characters, his included. I've risen to my position with dignity and self-control. But this man who sat next to me, he was causing me trouble with it all. And I was letting him!

When his fingertip reached over and touched my dress, all I wanted to do was whimper. I was so vulnerable. I wanted to turn, and let him have his way with me. But it was unprofessional, unfathomable. I believe I managed okay. Once he left, I remained seated and waited for my body heat to cool. I concentrated on my wedding vows to Rick. Yes. Rick my husband. What a fool I was making of myself with this salesperson. He wanted a sale, not me. Right?

Back at my office, I called Tommy Jones, seeking a summary of what had been agreed upon.

"That is an incredibly good deal Juno is offering."

"I agree," Tommy said. "But where's the catch?"

I wasn't about to tell him that I was the catch. "Mr Russell has some peculiar wants," I answered. "And he'd almost cancelled the entire contract, today, just because he wanted me to be there. I couldn't make it, unfortunately."

"Why you?" Tommy asked, sounding confused. "Why the City Manager?"

"Simply because I was there from day one," I lied. "And like

I said, he's peculiar about certain things, so my presence will be required from now on."

"That's not a smart way to run business," Mr Jones continued.

"I'm not arguing that," I smiled. "But look at the contract we are about to sign. Unbeatable!"

"Alright, then. So Friday, we will see you at the meeting?"

"Well, that's why I'm calling you. I can't make it. I'll be away on business. Can we reschedule for a week from today? Mr Russell is available, as am I."

"I'll make it happen," Jones answered.

Good boy! He had rearranged this gathering so that we could all be present for the signing of this darn contract.

The following Tuesday morning I came in early, wanting to be on top of my game. Danny would not deter me from being the organized person people knew me to be. I rolled in at seven, way ahead of everybody else in the building. Annie had yet to leave her house at that time, so I was able to get all my emails read and answered before she would even pull into the parking lot.

The signing of the contract wasn't scheduled until eleven, so I had hours to get my paperwork done before psyching myself up. Eight o'clock came, and still no Annie. It wasn't like her to be late, but I continued typing away. I figured she'd walk in at any moment. Minutes later, Annie stepped out of the elevator with two cups of coffee from the shop across the street.

"How sweet of you, Annie," I exclaimed. She had her hands full so I walked over to help her.

"One of the employees from Charlotte's Coffee Shop was waiting in the lobby. He had strict instructions to deliver these lattés to your office at eight a.m., sharp."

"Who are they from?" I asked. Danny came immediately to my mind.

"Sorry, MJ. It was anonymous."

I knew it would be. I was going to have to let this pass. It was a conflict of interest to accept gifts of any kind. But for this moment I feigned ignorance so Annie and I could enjoy the lattés.

Around ten, I was getting fidgety. Why was I reacting so strongly to this short little man? Deep inside, I knew why. I just didn't want to face it, yet. Rick was hardly ever home. Our children were getting ready to fly the coop. I was lonely. Danny gave me attention. Male attention.

Fifteen minutes before the meeting, my nerves got the best of me and I chose to slowly make my way to the meeting room. Wanting to burn some of my pent-up energy, I took the stairs, pacing myself so as not to create perspiration. I had four sets of stairs do descend, and I enjoyed the peaceful quietness the area offered, despite the echo my shoes made as they hit the metal grates. But there were no phones ringing, no people mumbling, no keyboards being tapped.

I reached the first floor. There was a large *1* on the door next to the small window. I peered out of the glass. It was no bigger than the size of my hand. I could see my people shuffling into the meeting room. Among the crowd was Danny. He was wearing a pin-striped navy blue suit, accentuating his beautiful eyes. Very dapper. I presumed it was a brand new suit for the occasion. It was, after all, a fairly big contract. It would be a good occasion for him to celebrate. I wondered if this suit was worn for my enjoyment.

His eyes sparkled as he made small talk with Mr Jones. In return, Tommy laughed at whatever Danny said. Tommy then extended his hand, pointing at the conference room door for Danny to enter. Danny nodded. But just before Danny took his first step, he looked at the door I was hiding behind, smiled and winked. He knew I'd been watching. Caught with my fingers in the cookie jar again. All the meditating I'd been doing these last few minutes, deeply breathing in and out, was thrown out the door.

I braced myself and opened the steel door. I joined Gary, our top IT guy, as he entered the conference room. I surveyed the table to see what chairs were available. It was a large table with plenty of empty seats. Gary and I opted to sit in the front part of the room, near the smartboard. I then looked to see where Danny was. I saw him at the refreshment table, vigorously stirring his coffee, smirking at me.

I ignored his flirting, and sat at the first chair available on the right side of the table. He wasn't going to influence me. So what did he do? He bolted to sit in the chair opposite me. I felt my body temperature climb and I drank half of the glass of water in front of me. I needed to survive this next hour without making a fool of myself.

CHAPTER 7

usiness-wise, I'm not sure why I had to be present during this meeting..except I seemed to enjoy torturing myself. Heaven knows I had plenty of other things to tend to at the office. I'm thankful my colleagues never questioned my being there. I served no purpose to the proceedings.

I craved to be in his presence even though I did everything to ignore him. I looked down on my papers, or up above at the smartboard that projected the contract. I even looked at the people around me. From time to time my eyes betrayed me and would look Danny's way. And every single time, he was looking straight at me. He was no longer smirking. I should have been alarmed. But instead, I smiled as well. Danny was no longer flirting with me. If that step had been accomplished, what could be next?

I felt his foot rub my panted leg under the varnished table. Danny's legs may have been shorter than mine, but his feet could still reach across and touch my knee. I jumped, but not enough to disturb the proceedings. I brushed his foot away, but then felt the other foot touch my other knee. This time, I didn't brush it off. I was warming up to his game. My thighs separated slightly. I was heading towards a dangerous fantasy.

I had no business being in that room. So any conversation happening, it was of no concern to me. I let my guard down and studied this adult-child. Danny seemed amused by playing footsies with me.

Against my absolute best judgment, I decided two could play at this game. I surprised him by having my other foot reach over to his side and touch his other leg. It was rather fun to watch *him* startled. His blueberry eyes immediately opened wide.

He slid his hand under the table and grabbed a hold of my pantyhosed foot, and started massaging it. It was not what I had expected. It was getting sensual, and it needed to stop. I was encouraging him. I was encouraging myself. I didn't know where it would end. I pulled my foot away but Danny held on, I pulled again and he let it go. I had done damage. I was now showing interest in him, and he was going to nurse that as far as he could.

Once the reading was over and the papers signed, hands shaken the half dozen people sitting in that boardroom left, leaving Danny and myself alone.

"Have lunch with me," Danny said.

"No, thank you," I answered firmly.

"Have lunch with me," he repeated.

"I don't think that would ever be a good idea," I said, blushing.

"Have lunch with me," he kept repeating. And every time I answered with a different way of saying *no*.

"I'm too busy today," I said as we exited the room.

Danny left without saying another word. Deep inside, I had wanted him to keep trying, even though I would've said *no* every single time. I just didn't trust myself. I didn't trust him, either, for that matter. I couldn't pinpoint what was so attractive about this man, that I would forget I was married, that I held an important position. His magnetic force scared me.

A little over an hour later, I looked up from my desk to see a delivery man deposit a couple containers of chicken chowder on Annie's desk.

"What's going on?" she asked. "First, lattés this morning, now a catered lunch. I wonder who our secret admirer might be."

I figured if Danny was going to include Annie in his charade of showering me with gifts of food, I needed to let her know who these were from.

"I'm not swearing you to secrecy, but I want you to keep quiet," I said.

"Okay," Annie answered, puzzled.

"Danny Russell from Juno Electronics is behind these...these gifts. I'm 95% certain of it. If these become too frequent, or too lavish, I will talk to him about it. Otherwise, enjoy the treats."

"It's okay to accept these?" Annie asked.

"I'm only presuming these come from Mr Russell," I answered. "If you're uncomfortable accepting them, please throw them out. But this soup smells delicious, and I'm going to have it for lunch. You're welcome to join me in the lunch room."

CHAPTER

♂

A few weeks later, the City's shipment arrived, and my technicians were ready to install. I was not going to miss the opportunity to be at MJ's vicinity. That woman was gonna get me in trouble if I continued chasing her skirt, but oh so worth it. I volunteered to supervise the crew, even though it had never been my duty to supervise. I sent an email to MJ, CC-ing the mayor's office, as well. I wanted to suggest a time-frame that might work better for City Hall, one with the least amount of disturbance to their day-to-day work.

> Good Morning Mrs Taylor,
> As indicated from the very beginning, we at Juno Electronics pride ourselves in offering the best customer service to our clientèle. Seeing how huge this project is for us all, we would like to suggest coming in

after hours. We would like to cause the least amount
of disturbance possible during your business hours.
        We are more than willing to accommodate you,
knowing how important the everyday business at City
Hall needs to be upheld. So with your permission, our
company is ready to come in on a Saturday to make
the install.
        Please let me know at your earliest convenience
if this is an option you'd like to explore. I am always
available to be at your service.

With regards,
Danny Russell
Juno Electronics

By the end of the day, I had yet to hear back from MJ, but I let it slide overnight. The next morning, though, I sent her another email. And I again CC-ed the mayor. I wasn't trying to get her in trouble, I just didn't want her to ignore me.

Good Morning Mrs Taylor,
I am making certain that you have received an email I had
sent yesterday. Your shipment is safe in our warehouse. I
presume you are as anxious as we are to get it installed.
This way, you and your colleagues can enjoy this new
and updated, reliable equipment, as soon as possible.
        I look forward to hearing from you at your earliest
convenience.

With regards,
Danny Russell
Juno Electronics

My phone rang minutes later.
"Are you trying to get me in trouble?"

"I'm trying to give you the best service possible, MJ. I like you too much to purposely cause you any trouble."

What the hell was I saying? *Like* her too much? Was I hitting on her? Get a hold of yourself Danny Russell! This flirting is not worth my job. Or my home life.

"Well now the mayor's on my back because of you," MJ snapped. "I didn't respond yesterday because I was trying to coordinate having someone from each floor to be present on whatever Saturday works for us all. I cannot let strangers roam around City Hall unsupervised. And now I had to explain to the mayor why I had yet to respond to your email."

"It's okay," I answered.

"It's not okay. Now he's upset I didn't reply as a courtesy. And he's right. So officially, I am apologizing."

"Wow!" I expressed, feeling like a heel. "I'm the one who needs to say I'm sorry. I just thought you were ignoring me."

There was a silent pause.

"Can we start this conversation over?" MJ asked.

"Sure," I said. "Wanna have lunch with me?"

I heard her chuckle. My teasing was being well received. She was warming up to me.

"No, Mr Russell. I cannot have lunch with you."

"Danny. My name is Danny. Just call me Danny," I sighed.

"Well, then, *Danny*, I cannot have lunch with you."

"You realize I'm going to ask you until you do," I said.

"Don't waste your breath," MJ replied, but I could hear amusement in her voice. "It will never happen."

"We'll see about that," I chuckled. "I will lay off the emails. I will wait for your official answer as to when you want my people to be there."

"I will get back to you today," MJ answered. "Chances are, we will take you up on your generous offer to come on a Saturday. But it won't be this one. If I can get all my ducks in a row, your technicians can probably come the following Saturday."

"Oh, and MJ..." I added, waiting for her to respond.

"Yes, Danny?" she finally spoke.

"You need to be there, too. I'll be waiting for you." MJ was silent. I couldn't even hear her breathing. "Are you there?" I asked. There was no response, so I repeated my question. "MJ, are you there?"

"I'll be there," she finally answered in a whisper.

CHAPTER 9

♀

I tossed and turned all night. Rick two feet away from me. I was playing with fire. I was encouraging Danny to play with me. I had no idea how far this would be going. I was ashamed of my response. I didn't want to let Danny know I was crushing on him. I didn't want to fuel him in any way. I was, I admit, enjoying the excitement of these exchanges. I was falling into his trap, or maybe jumping in with both feet.

The next morning, I showed up at work to a smiling Annie brandishing a steaming latté in her hand. She pointed at the other one on her desk.

"He's at it again," she smiled. I sighed.

"I'm going to have to address this," I said, unlocking my office door.

"Honestly," Annie smiled, lowering her voice, "I'm enjoying these."

I smiled back. I was, too. I enjoyed the treats. But I mostly enjoyed what they meant. "I know," I said, "but we are threading on thin ice."

"But are they *really* gifts?" Annie questioned, lowering her voice. "I mean, it's food. There's no evidence of them within minutes, and I'm kinda enjoying this pampering."

"I'll still have a talk with him." I went into my office, and settled myself in. Latté in hand, I called Danny.

"Good morning, MJ," he answered joyfully. "What do I owe the pleasure of hearing your voice?"

"You have to stop with the lattés," I said.

"What lattés?"

"And the soups," I answered. "You have to stop. They are definitely a conflict of interest, and we can't accept them anymore."

"I'm not sure what you're talking about," Danny answered with a chuckle.

"I believe you do," I answered. I turned to look out my window, my back at Annie. I didn't want her to see the flush coming through me.

"All this can be cleared up over lunch," Danny said, which made me laugh out loud. He was taunting me.

"I'm not having lunch with you, Danny. It's inappropriate."

"It won't be after the installation," he laughed.

In no time, Installation Day was upon us. I left my family in their slumber while I drove to work on a foggy Saturday morning. I tried to arrive ahead of the others, but some early birds were already there waiting for me to open the door at the back entrance. Danny was among them.

"Good morning everyone," I said loudly as they gathered around. Danny didn't move. He just kept his arms crossed and his delicious eyes on me. I struggled to fish out the key to unlock the door and let them in. "All of you, thank you, once again, for giving up part of your Saturday to get this done."

With doors unlocked, alarms diffused, and everybody accounted for, I guided Team Juno to the fifth floor and the mayor's office. I spent most of my morning standing in the main hall of each floor as Team Juno went about their business, guided by members of City Hall to each area in need of new equipment. I made sure that all involved stayed on the same floor at the same time. I did not want to deal with any strays.

Danny also stood in the hall near his teams as they worked, making himself available for any question or issue. His focus, however, was on watching my every move. I was technically at work, and on duty. But my clothes were more casual than my usual business attire. I was wearing a loose-fitting extra long pink t-shirt and grey yoga pants. Every time I caught Danny looking at me, he was looking at my pants. I regretted my choice of clothing, yet I knew I would be seeing him. What were my hormones up to?

Two floors and two hours later, I sent one of my team members to go get a tray of coffee and the largest box of donuts. When he returned, I called everyone to the third floor staff room. I had everybody stop for fifteen minutes. Danny started a conversation as he stood way too close to me.

"What kind of music do you like?" Danny asked, throwing me right off.

"I like old soft rock, I guess," I answered. "Chicago, The Eagles. That type of music."

"That really dates you," Danny snickered.

"It's the music I grew up on. My parents had those records. That, and Ginette Reno."

"Who?!?" Danny shook his head.

"My father loves her voice. She's a famous Quebec singer, but you wouldn't know that."

"Well, I like country music. Old and new. Thanks for asking."

"Timbit?" I offered, bringing the box of the colourful array of bite-sized donuts to his reach.

"I'd rather have lunch with you," Danny answered, causing me to laugh out loud. It made most of the people in the room turn and look at us. I waved my hand at them to indicate that there was nothing to see.

"Persistence is certainly one of your stronger features," I said. "And no, I will not have lunch with you, Danny."

"My business with you ends today," he replied. "Except for maintenance, of course. We are no longer in possible conflict of interest, here. Have lunch with me."

"I don't think it's prudent for the two of us to be having lunch together," I said.

"Why are you so afraid of me?" Danny asked, stepping closer.

"I'm more afraid of myself," I finally spoke the truth. Then I blushed, my body heat rising again.

Danny nodded and walked away, content.

An hour and a half later, having completed both third and second floors, I suggested having lunch brought in. Almost unanimously, the men voted to work right through the installation, wanting to go home earlier. I was outnumbered, so I agreed. I helped myself to some water and brought a bottle down the hall to Danny. I handed him the cool bottle as a peace offering.

"Thank you," he responded, his hand brushing mine as he took the water. My mouth fell open, then closed it immediately. However, the damage was done. Danny had seen my reaction, and I couldn't take it back.

"Your installation crew is quite efficient," I expressed. "Kudos to you and your company."

"You get what you pay for," Danny responded. "We only hire the best. We should be out of here in an hour."

We rode the elevators down with his team, and at this point, I sent most of my people home, leaving one staff member to stay with me. And what was left to be equipped was the Finance Department, the front desk, and the Council Chambers with the adjoining conference room. I figured between my colleague and I, we could handle it.

I found myself nibbling on my fingernails, a bad habit that popped up whenever I was overly stressed. I forced myself to put my arms to my sides with my hands fisted as I walked to the Finance Department, where they were working. I supervised their progress until completion. I locked behind them, and led them to the Council Chambers. I asked my colleague to keep watch while I used the washroom. Danny watched me leave, and followed behind into the main lobby. I came back out to find him waiting for me, and I froze.

"Why are you so afraid of me?" Danny asked.

"I told you why," I answered, embarrassed by my honesty.

"I saw you, the other day. You were watching me behind the window in that door," he murmured, nodding. "Show me what was so interesting."

I trembled, not trusting where this was going. I feared him touching me, like he'd done when he removed the chocolate-covered almond out of my bra. I should've listened to my instincts. It's an ability I seemed to have lost the day I met him. But in order to have control of this, I had to show him that he didn't influence me. I lunged to push that stairway door open. I walked in, with Danny right behind me.

"Show me how you looked out," he taunted. "Stretch your head out like you'd done then."

I listened, and did as told. My body betrayed me.

"Was your body contorted?" Danny asked. "Or was it leaning against the door?"

Like a robot, I showed him how I'd stood slightly on the side, and had my face a few inches from the window. I had hoped not to be seen.

"Did you like what you saw?" he continued, enjoying my uneasiness. "Did your pretty knees buckle again? Did your mouth fall open like it always does? Did your body get warm?"

Danny was being very inappropriate, and I had to end this. I stood up straight, abandoning the position I had been showing him for his obvious pleasure.

"That's enough," I commanded, pulling my t-shirt over my Lululemons.

"Is it, now?" Danny smiled, looking me up and down. "Is this what you were wearing that day? Oh, obviously not. You choose to wear church-lady clothes at work. But this...this outfit that you're wearing right now, it's a sweet piece that fits you rather well. You put this on for me today, didn't you?"

I was melting, but didn't want to show him. So I stood firm.

"I believe that if you'd worn these clothes," he smirked, "I may have jumped you."

My eyes opened wide, startled by his brute honesty. I was shocked by my reaction.

"Oh please," he said in amusement. "You knew you were seeing me today."

"There is nothing revealing about a t-shirt and some pants, Danny," I answered in anger.

"MJ, you dressed in clothes that follow your curves like this," Danny said as he touched the side of my breasts, like he had done in my car.

I pulled back, mostly to retain some level of dignity. Danny continued talking.

"That t-shirt is following every delicious curve your tits have to offer."

I was mortified. I covered my face in shame.

"And when you leaned over to that window, just now, and stuck out your ass my way, I just wanted to have a feel. He patted my derrière. Shamed to the core, all I could do was walk away to join our group in the Council Chambers. Danny followed behind. No other words were spoken from either one of us.

CHAPTER 10

♂

I had her. I just needed to find the right bait for MJ to finally agree to have lunch with me. She didn't know it yet, but she was going to be mine to play with. And soon. Why did I want this to happen? I wasn't ready to go there, yet. I enjoyed the hunt, but MJ, she wasn't making it easy for me.

I had to court her, but not the old-fashioned way. I had to shock her with moves she'd never encountered. Moves like touching her butt cheeks, or the sides of her tits. Even simply talking dirty to her. She may have been hard to get through, but it was fun trying.

The following week, I sent both MJ and Annie a small bouquet each to brighten up their desks. MJ sent me a text with a photo of the flowers thrown out.

These flowers are gifts, and we cannot accept them, she wrote. *But thank you. They were lovely.*

Note to myself: obviously I could only gift them food. They needed to get rid of the evidence, almost immediately. Flowers were harder to explain.

So from that moment on, I started an account with the coffee shop across the street from their office, the café she liked so much. I had them deliver a new concoction every Tuesday morning.

I'd get a thank you from them both, but MJ still refused to budge. I needed to surprise her. Since I had no reason to hang out at their office, anymore, I found myself struggling over what else I could do. And then I asked Annie if she knew which radio station MJ listened to while driving. For the following eight weeks, I requested a song for her, every single work day. I knew the station manager, and he played along with me. He also didn't question my reason, thankfully. But maybe *I* should've. What was my goal at the end? How far was I willing to go?

On Week Seven, MJ texted me after hours, at suppertime. I was at home, so I quickly put my phone on silence after it dinged while we were watching some old reruns.

Should I be intrigued by these very lovely, but suspicious, songs being requested every single day on the radio? Those from Juno to Josée? Or am I simply being silly?

Good! At least she took it with humour.

It's about frigging time you figured it out, I wrote back. *Did you like them?*

I'm not quite certain what you're up to, Danny Russell, she answered, *but your buttering me up is starting to take effect.*

All I want is lunch with you, I answered back.

Maybe, she wrote.

I put my phone away. I was jumping for joy. MJ was no longer saying *No*. Her shield was starting to crack. It was time for me to go full force.

My cocky grinning caught Tina's attention.

"Who was that?" she asked as she was mending a pair of pants.

"Oh, just a reminder from Denise for dinner at her place this weekend." I tried to sound casual. I should've had my phone shut off, never thinking MJ would make contact outside of business hours.

"That reminds me," Tina said as she put her needling away, "I should ask her what we can bring."

"I'll ask her right now," I panicked as I texted Denise, preventing Tina from finding out my lie. "She says to bring rolls." I answered as I put my damn phone away.

I tossed and turned that night, as well as the following two nights, reflecting on my insane obsession for this married woman. But after a few days, I still ended up calling MJ at work.

"Remember that Saturday? Installation Day? Did you ever take your day off?"

"No," MJ answered. "I usually don't bother. Or I'll tack it onto a vacation week."

"I propose you come spend it with me," I said with ease. I crossed my legs on my desk while toying with a company pen in my mouth. It was more important for me to see her, than to not.

"Why would I do such a thing?" MJ whispered, the request having taken her breath away.

"I just want to have lunch with you."

"I'm not sure about that..."

It felt like the idea was cooling down, and I needed to think quick.

"You sound like you could use some coffee right about now," I suggested.

"No-o-o," she laughed. "No more coffee. No flowers. No song request. You really are a sweet man, Danny, but our business together is done."

"That was harsh!" I tried to soften up. "If our business together is done, as you're suggesting, then anything you receive from me is no longer a conflict of interest. Right?"

"Well..." MJ answered. "Technically, until the warranties expire, we are still in business.

"You're a tough cookie to crack, Marie-Josée Taylor," I said, defeated. She chuckled.

CHAPTER 11

♀

never knew what Danny had up his sleeve, but the intrigue got the best of me. I started anticipating surprises from him. He would not do something every week, but when he did, my heart skipped a beat. It felt like I was being courted by him, and I started feeling less and less guilty of my feelings.

The sporadic delivery of tasty gifts was enough to make my week. And it pleased Annie as well. But unlike her, I got extras, such as the song requests.

I found myself taking a different route to work, passing by his office building. I'd look up to see if his building was lit, or look out for his car in the back. And the longer the stretch between his gifts, the antsier I became. I'd go by his workplace, morning and night. It was starting to trouble me. Yet, I couldn't help myself. I missed his presence. His smile. The twinkle of his eyes. The magnetic force of Danny.

I started talking myself out of my feelings. I'd tell myself this whole dynamic Danny and I had created, it needed to stop. At least for the sake of my marriage, my family, my career, and whatever family life Danny may have had at home. I'd prep myself up, trying to forget about Danny Russell. And then, out of the blue, steaming sweet coffees would show up on Annie's desk. My reserve kept being blown, and I was back at square one.

Then I got a telephone call from Danny.

"Good morning, Sunshine," his cheerful voice greeted me across the wire.

"Good morning," I answered back, happy to hear his voice.

"I see what you've been doing." His voice rumbled, it was so low.

"Meaning?"

"I noticed a little while back that you changed your route getting to work."

Oh no! I was embarrassed, and wasn't quite sure what to say.

"Next time you drive by, just drop in," he continued. "I'll gladly give you a tour of my office. Not quite as fancy as yours, but it serves its purpose." Danny then hung up.

I didn't take him up on his offer. The good girl in me kept fighting with the newly-discovered, adventure-deprived woman. The battle was tiring. My heart told me one thing while my head said the opposite. My goody-two-shoes spirit disciplined myself into not responding to him. But the part of me that was attracted to Danny's persona and his breathtaking eyes, that part kept driving by and taking peeks towards the windows. The fact he was no longer coming by my office made me miss him. Crave him. I enjoyed his surprises, but I wanted more of his presence. Much more. And that scared the daylights out of me. I was married, for God's sake! I had made vows to Rick, until death do us part. Yet, my heart deceived me and I kept detouring in front of his work.

Then one morning, as I drove by his office, I was stopped in traffic right across the street from the front door of his building. I glanced over, out of habit, and there was Danny in a second-storey window. He waved and laughed wholeheartedly at my antics. I immediately looked away and faced forward. My cheeks turned crimson as the chain of cars finally started moving again.

I pulled into the City Hall parking lot, and killed the engine of my vehicle. I crossed over to the building. I barely acknowledged the people I encountered. I needed to address my behaviour to the one person that mattered, once and for all. I rode the elevator to my fourth-floor office lobby, greeted Annie quickly as I unlocked my office door. I didn't want to dismiss her. I just needed to deal with the matter at hand.

I hung my blazer and locked up my pocketbook before heading down the hall to the single-stall washroom, locking the door behind myself. I stood there, face to face with my best friend and my worst enemy: myself. What was I doing, flirting with danger? Flirting with a man while trying to live my marriage? This was not how I had been raised. This was not the behaviour of who I knew me to be.

Yet, it felt so right. Danny made me feel so alive. So young. So free from all my responsibilities. When I spoke with him or communicated with him, or even better, be in his presence, all those worries went away. I no longer had work or family issues. No mortgage. No feeling of abandonment. Danny was there for me, and I latched onto that fact a little too strongly. For goodness' sake, I didn't know a thing about Danny Russell. Yet, here I was fantasizing about him.

I stood in front of that mirror, and looked at the person looking back. Despite what my loins were saying, I liked what I saw. I saw a woman who was discovering a part of her she didn't even know existed. Marie-Josée Noël Taylor was more than the titles she carried. I was more than Nicole and Marcel's mom. Or Rick's wife. Or my parents' daughter. Or even MJ Taylor, City Manager. I was a woman in my prime, who only now was discovering that I still had *it*. I was still desired, and that I loved being me. I wasn't ready to curl up and shrivel as I aged. I still had lots to give, and Danny had made me discover this.

I came out of the washroom a new and improved version of who had entered there. I had a new step in my walk, and a glowing smile to boot. Annie took a double look at me as I went by her desk while she was on the phone. Her being busy gave me the opportunity to call Danny at his office, uninterrupted.

"Good morning, sir," I tried to sound professional, but I was quickly losing my grip on that.

"Did you enjoy your drive to work today?" he asked, not really questioning me.

"Are you in the office all day?"

"Why?" Danny chuckled. "You coming over?"

I stayed quiet. I was starting to think twice about all this. Then he spoke when he knew I wouldn't.

"Listen, MJ," he started. "I will be here all day. I'll even eat lunch at my desk. The building empties around five. You can come visit my office any time. It's been a while since we've seen each other, and we could catch up a bit."

"I'll see," was my answer. I was no longer feeling as brave.

I actually went back into the washroom, telling Annie I'd be right back. I found the MJ that had slightly escaped after my conversation with Danny. I was still in awe of the person I was becoming. I was just not a good receiver of being made fun of, like I had felt with Danny's teasing.

For the next few days, I took my original way home. I'd stopped detouring onto Plains Road where Danny's office was. But I also missed him. I was spending my nights trying to fall asleep while having visual snippets of our times together dance in my head. His touches. His words. His laughter. His incredible eyes. I was obsessing over him, and I didn't have the capacity to know how not to.

The following week, I found myself back on Plains Road once again. I'd look up the windows to see Danny, with no luck. Then on the Wednesday, on my way home, I detoured onto his office's road, and again got into a bit of traffic next to Danny's building. I avoided looking on my right where Juno Electronics was. I looked straight ahead. I was startled by a rap on my passenger door window. I looked, and there was Danny, leaning on my vehicle, motioning for me to roll down the window. I did as told.

"Pull in," he said as his head motioned towards the parking between myself and the building. Danny waited for me at the main entrance of his office building while I fed the parking meter some change. My fingers struggled with the coins, they were shaking so much.

"Welcome to my home away from home," he said as he opened the door for me. I went in and acknowledged the front desk girl as she was heading out for the day.

"This is my version of Annie," Danny smiled. "Her name is Lucy." I nodded.

"In back, we have parts and tools for the installers. In front, it's our staff room and conference room, all in one. And over there is the one and only washroom in the building. It's not a very big building, but most of our business is on the road."

Danny motioned for me to go ahead of him as we climbed the stairs to the second floor. I stopped on the landing to find out which direction to take. I caught Danny trying to look up my skirt. I felt flush, but I didn't call him on it.

He had a corner office, which was minimally decorated. As he'd pointed out, most of his work was not concentrated within those four walls, but rather on his laptop while on the road. His office was responsible for all Juno sales throughout Eastern Canada. I noticed a couple of photos on the other window ledge, pictures of what I presumed was his family. Danny caught me looking at them. I sucked in my lower lip. For this flirting to happen, our families couldn't exist. Yet, here was proof his did. We both ignored answering the unasked questions.

"And here is the view I have from my window," Danny spoke as he waved for me to join his side, away from the pictures, and look out. "I may not see the Sevy River from my office, but I do keep getting glimpses of this pretty lady driving by."

I dropped my chin down to my chest, nodding in agreement. I'd been had, and I needed to enjoy the jab he was throwing at me. We didn't speak in what felt like minutes. We stood in silence as the traffic dissipated in the now-darkening evening. Danny and I stood next to each other, me looking at the horizon while he looked my way. My hair was again fluttering at his exhaled breaths. But unlike the first time, I wasn't quite as nervous. It was still uncomfortable to be stared at, that way. But I trusted the fact that these large windows, with the blinds open, would protect me from any of his attempted moves.

I started getting restless. With his eyes never coming off of me, I felt his left hand rest oh so softly on my lower back. I exhaled a held breath I didn't know I was holding in. I purred out a moan. It was just enough to encourage him, which was never my intention. Or maybe it was.

Danny's hand lowered to the curve of my buttocks, and those cheeks squeezed automatically. Again, I was encouraging him when I didn't mean to. But I also found myself not brushing him off. It's not that I couldn't. I just wasn't. I was enjoying his touches. It brought shivers down my spine, and I let it happen. His hand lowered and my knees weakened. I kept facing away. But I could see his reflection on the now dark cool pane. He was smiling. Danny had me where he wanted, and I was losing my reserve. I needed to get out before I got in any deeper.

I bent down to pick up the pocketbook I had dropped during those few moments of silence. His middle finger felt me further down, touching my mound under my skirt. I gasped. Danny couldn't see my reaction since my face was still down between my knees.

"Thank you for the tour," I stuttered as I stood up and headed for his office door. I ran down those stairs, out the door, and straight to my car. Danny stood at the top of the stairway, watching me leave. His arms were crossed. His grin exuded success.

CHAPTER 12

♀

Over the next few weeks, my shell began to open up. The shell I grew up in. The shell my parents taught me to live by, with all the rules of society. The rules that expected you to be proper, and dress the part. The rules that told you to keep your knees together at all times, and which cutlery to use. I was such a prude. Based on what I knew, it was a given I'd meet, fall in love with, and marry Rick.

To say Danny was not my type would've been an understatement. His physique. His crass vocabulary. His bold sense of humour. Even his education. They were all inferior to what I had been taught to look for. However, put them all together, and Danny as a package threw me off my path. It made me question everything I knew. It opened my eyes to a world that surrounded me, a world that I remained cocooned away from. Danny was my bad boy.

I finally gave in, and he suggested we meet for coffee at a Mom

& Pop restaurant near my home in Holliston North. I arrived first to a mostly deserted restaurant. They were in between meals. An older lady was sitting in the booth closest to the exit. Her long white hair was knitted into a bun. Her beige all-weather coat was pooled around her bony hips, and a crumpled Sudoku magazine was being studied by her ailing eyes. She had a pen in one hand. Her other set of fingers kept polishing the rim of a lukewarm cup of tea at her disposal, the logo of the restaurant printed on the front of the mug. At the opposite corner of the restaurant was a man sitting very comfortably. Too comfortably. His legs were sprawled across the red pleather covered bench. His cheeks glowed from the cell phone he held close to his face. He was enjoying whatever his screen projected. He was due for a haircut and a shave, but his priorities were obviously different from mine. I chose to sit in a corner away from them both.

I was glad Danny had chosen this location. But I still questioned my sanity. Several times over the weekend I composed an email in my head, wanting to bail out of this coffee date. I wasn't ready to be in a social setting with him. I don't think I would ever be. But by Monday, I had changed my mind, again. I was going to face this man, and prove him wrong about me. I was going to prove it to myself as well.

I ordered a coffee when the waitress appeared. I fished through my pocketbook, and felt the sleek metallic tube of lipstick between my fingers. I debated on touching up my appearance, opting not to. Perfecting my appearance would only encourage this game of his.

I felt the waitress's presence and looked up to welcome the hot beverage she was bringing me. Strolling right behind her was Danny. He was wearing a charcoal colour suit that fit him to a T. I jumped when I saw him. He still had that power over me.

"Oh, sorry Hun," the waitress apologized in her smoker's raspy voice. "I didn't mean to startle you." She deposited the cup in front of me, turned to Danny to get his order, and walked away.

"You look lovely, today," he smiled as he draped his blazer on the chair he was going to sit in. He held his tie against his protruding belly as he slid onto his seat. He knew my surprised reaction had been caused by him, and not by the waitress. Yet, he said nothing. He didn't have to. He just knew. He knew I knew. And I knew he knew I knew.

"Thank you, Mr Russell," I said. "You look very dapper yourself."

"Danny. My name is Danny. I want you to call me Danny. And only Danny."

I tried staring him down. He reciprocated. It ended with our waitress delivering him his coffee and a piece of coconut cream pie covered with many inches of meringue.

"Their desserts are to die for. Especially their pies," he said as he brought a forkful into his mouth.

"Why are we here, Danny?" I asked as I sat on my hands. Anxiety was welling up in my body, even if I loved being with him.

He took another bite before looking up at me with his mesmerizing eyes. I felt I was losing my strength.

"You're way too wound up, MJ," he smiled. "You need to relax and chill. Have some pie." And with that, he extended a forkful across the table.

"No, thank you."

"It wasn't an option. Eat it!"

Without arguing, I did as I was told. I opened my mouth slowly. My eyes closed. I looked up to find him reaching over with his left index to wipe some meringue off the corner of my mouth. His finger's touch created a hot current between our two bodies. I was failing horribly in trying to prove him wrong.

"I just want us to be comfortable together," Danny said, taking a sip of his black coffee. "I like that you react to me. I haven't had that effect on people in a very long time. You, MJ. You are a ray of sunshine to me. I want you to know how special that makes me feel."

My mouth fell open, unable to respond.

"And let me tell you," he continued, his hand waving towards me, "getting this reaction from such a beautiful, intelligent, vibrant woman like you...well that's the icing on my cake."

I could feel my cheeks blushing, flush creeping up my neck. I knew my cover was blown. Danny simply took it in stride.

"This tension that you have around me," he added, "I believe we can get rid of it by getting to know each other better. I like seeing you."

I was starting to believe him.

"Tell me five things about you," Danny said as he crushed the remaining pie crumbs on his plate with his fork before licking the back of the utensil. I stared at him, captivated by his simple movements. I hated myself for being so weak. "Well, I'll start," he continued, in what was turning into a monologue, since I remained speechless. "I live with my life partner Tina and her two children. I like fishing. I love football. Watching it. Playing it. Betting on it. You name it. I have three sisters. And both my parents passed away."

Every sentence fascinated me. The words he chose. The order he put his five truths. It said so much about him. I was warming up to him, my anxiety gone.

"How long ago did your parents pass?" I asked, finally able to speak.

"My mom died about fifteen years ago. And I was five when my dad died."

"Heavens! Five?" I exclaimed, unexpected tears welling up.

"It was a long time ago," was his response. "Life goes on."

My hand reached across the table to him, squeezing our fingers together. I later realized that that was the moment I fell in love with him. My future was going to change drastically from that point on.

"Your turn," Danny smiled. He adjusted his sitting position. With his elbows on the table, and his chin resting in his palms, he looked as if he was about to hear an amazing story.

"Pretty boring, really," I sighed. "I grew up comfortably in a very conservative home with both my parents. My mom passed a little while back. I got my university degree at Mount A. I met my husband Rick during my studies. I have two teenage children. And I bake to relax."

Danny took another sip of his coffee.

"I told you mine was boring."

"Tell me more about you growing up."

"My life was boring and predictable growing up."

"Tell me anyways," Danny insisted.

"My mother grew up on Village Road when houses were further apart, with beautifully manicured gardens. My father grew up behind the hospital he still runs. They were an odd couple of sorts, at the time. Holliston was divided between the English and the French. Yet, my parents met, fell in love, and got married. They made it work. My father graduated from Dalhousie University, and is quite fluent in both languages. My mother never learned French."

"Where did she work? What did she do?" Danny was full of questions. And I kept answering him.

"She was a nurse at the hospital. My parents conceived several times, but my mother kept miscarrying. I was pregnancy number seven. I was born healthy and kicking."

"That must've been tough on them," Danny cut in.

"I'm sure it was. They never talked about it with me. They just kept me on a pedestal."

"So you're an only child?"

"Yes. My father insisted on giving me a French name: Marie-Josée, after his father Joseph. I don't mind. But it wasn't ideal to have such a French name, and going to English schools."

"So why go to English schools?"

"My mother became a stay-at-home mom after my birth. She devoted herself to me, hoping to fulfill all her expectations through me. Being raised by her, I spoke mostly English, only learning the basics of French for my dad's side. And I haven't learned much, since. Mom and I spent most of our time together. Even after I started school. She'd drop me off and pick me up. I never took the bus, as it was supposedly *beneath* my family.

"I realized later, as an adult, that all the dreams and hopes my mother had had for her unborn children, she expected these dreams to be fulfilled by me, myself and I. That was a heavy burden to carry.

I had to be the perfect child, all the time. I was always competing academically to be the best in my class. I wanted to have top honours to make my parents proud. In return, I never had the chance to click with anybody. I never had a best friend."

"I can be your best friend," Danny said sweetly, his eyes turning a shade lighter.

I laughed.

"When it was time to apply for college, I had my mind set on Mount Allison. I didn't want to be far from home."

"What did you study?" Danny seemed truly interested in what I had to say.

"At first, I thought of following my parents into a medical career of some sort. But one day, my dad showed up on campus, and took me out for coffee. He saw how miserable I was. And he guided me towards a Bachelor of Arts, where I would be happiest. I wasn't meant to be in the medical field. And my father showing me that, that was the first time one of my parents looked at me as an individual, and not as an extension of themselves."

"Your dad was smart," Danny added.

"He still is," I smiled. "But I wish my father would have taken control earlier. I loved my mother. And she was very devoted to me. But to a fault."

Danny excused himself to use the facilities. It gave me a moment to reflect. Was I sharing too much with him? Was this conversation getting too deep? Or too personal? In truth, I enjoyed talking to my newfound friend. And he seemed interested in what I had to say. So when he returned, I continued talking about myself. I had never had such a captive audience.

"I met Richard Taylor at Mount A. Rick was the one who showed me how to be a little more independent. He taught me that a woman who fended for herself in this world would be a lot happier. Otherwise, I would end up like my mother. Which I didn't want. Rick pushed me to pursue my studies. And he veered me unintentionally towards an office management career. He also encouraged me to stop going home every single weekend, like I had been. Instead, we started having daytime dates together."

I chuckled as I welcomed a refill on my coffee. "My mother brought me up as a well-spoken, well-dressed young lady, and I practice all of those manners to this day."

"I noticed," Danny intercepted. I blushed. I was having fun.

"I dress conservatively, even at the gym. My mother would be mortified if she saw me squatting in these contraptions. Anyways, once I graduated from Mount A, I came back to Holliston as a real grown-up. I was no longer the *daughter of.* I applied at several places in town for work. I was accepted in the Finance Department at City Hall. My foot was in the door, so to speak. And I never looked back."

"So when did you and Rick move in together?"

I looked at him, questioning if I should go there. We were now treading towards my sex life. "I moved in with him after we got married."

"So you were a virgin until then?" he asked, shaking his head. I paused before deciding to answer such a personal question.

"Having been raised by an overprotective mother, I had no intention or opportunity to sleep with anybody before getting married. It's what was expected of me. And honestly, I wasn't that impressed by it."

"So Rick is your only one," Danny stated, shaking his head. "Wow..."

"We purchased a house in the developing north end of the city. And within a few years, we were blessed with Nicole. And then Marcel. We are the perfect nuclear family. Rick and I pursued careers in our chosen fields. We have a beautiful home. Two well-behaved children in tow. We are living a perfect life."

Danny frowned. "I hear a *but.*"

"Rick got bored. He wanted more action. More fun. Sort of like a mid-life crisis, but ten years early. He chose to go back to school. And he opted to learn to drive an 18-wheeler. He was gonna be on the road and see the world, leaving us behind."

"This obviously upsets you."

"I've said enough," I said, shaking my head.

"MJ," Danny pleaded. "I'm here to listen."

And for some unknown reason, I continued. "Rick loves us, but as a package. He's never really been involved in our children's lives. He brings home the bacon, but doesn't cook it. And now that I think of it, I'm describing my home, growing up."

"Is he still trucking?"

"Yes, he is. And he's happy about it. Anyway, one day at work, our Mayor approached me to become the next City Manager. I was honoured to be asked. The former one was retiring at the end of the year, and I was promoted to the position seven months later. I got to pick the former City Manager's brains during that time."

"Do you still like your job?" Danny asked.

"I felt overwhelmed at first, despite having been coached for over half a year. Now, the job is great. But I've also felt a resentment stirring within me. I've grown jealous of Rick's independent life. The selfishness of my husband's choices. His leaving the child-rearing on my shoulders alone, no matter their ages. I had been too busy working, raising Nicole and Marcel, and keeping house to notice my feelings."

"Until now," Danny whispered.

"I've said too much," I answered as I nervously got up. "I'm sorry to cut this short, but I have to pick Nicole up from volleyball practice."

"Can we meet again?" he asked. I couldn't refuse. I was now as interested in this man as he was in me. I guess I had always been.

"Sure," I answered a little too enthusiastically. "Here again?"

"No. I'll text you."

CHAPTER 13

♂

had gained some momentum with my pursuit of this woman. But I was now living a double life. I felt the heat that came with that secret kept. MJ was worth it, so far. I had so much to teach her. So much to learn from her. I found myself jerking off in the washroom, before going home to Tina and the kids.

But there was another side to this that I had not considered. MJ's grace and independence was something new to me. Tina, Ellen, and all the others in between these women. They all wore make-up and jewellery, skirts and heels. But not like MJ. There was this subtlety in how MJ presented herself. Her clothes were a higher quality than what I had known. Her clothing was more structured. They lay better on her skin. Her jewels and make-up were more subdued. MJ was classic. She wasn't trendy or harsh. Even in high heels, she could walk in them as if they were slippers. All of these factors put together, it's probably what made her that more sexy to me. She was different from all the other girls I'd known. And MJ, unaware of how attractive she was, made her that much more hot to me. She carried herself well. She dressed without knowing how voluptuous her curves really were. Mother Nature was very kind when she gave MJ her tits. And they were begging to be kneaded by my hands. Her perfectly rounded shoulders. Her tight calves. Those were a result of her workouts. And now that I'd had a feel of her ass, I wanted to be nasty to those cheeks. I knew that I could no longer stop this chase until I banged her.

So for the following two weeks, forgoing my own need of caffeine, I spent a fortune having coffee delivered daily at Annie's desk for both these women. On Sunday evening, at the end of the second week, MJ finally sent me a text.

You are determined, aren't you, MJ wrote.

You can't blame a guy for trying, I answered. *Have lunch with me.*

I'll think about it, was her answer.

I'm not sure how much more my budget could afford this pursuit. After all these efforts, it went from *Maybe* to *I'll Think About It.*

Have lunch with me. Thirty minutes of your time is all I ask. One on one. Your choice where. My treat.

MJ didn't reply. I tossed and turned that night. I wanted release, but Tina was sound asleep with her mouthguard in place. I let it ride. The next day came and went. No reply from MJ, again. I was finally starting to lose hope. It made me question what was so tantalizing about seeing this woman naked. Then, on the very next morning, I opened up my laptop at work, and found an email from MJ.

Good Morning, Mr Russell,

Would you be so kind as to call me at my office at your earliest convenience? It's not urgent. But the matter is pressing.

Thank you, and have a great day.

With regards,

MJ Taylor
City Manager

I called her office immediately.

"Hello," she answered with no indication in her voice of what was so pressing.

"What's up?" I asked curtly, slightly peeved. She was starting to play my game. And I didn't like being on the receiving end of it.

"I am gifting myself a day off, tomorrow. If you can keep up with me, I'm going to take a ride down to Fundy National Park and do a few hikes. We can have lunch. So, yes, Danny. I will finally have lunch with you," she chuckled.

I was speechless. MJ had finally agreed to share a meal with me. It wasn't quite the setting I had in mind. But this also meant having more than a half hour with her. It was more than I'd expected.

"I am in!" I declared. "Meet you at work?"

"No, no," she spoke up with concern. "Socializing with you remains a major conflict of interest. Meet me at the mall near the grocery store entrance. 8:30 sharp. Wear something comfortable and warm."

CHAPTER 14

♀

had a difficult time sleeping, that night. I had committed myself to spending most of my day with the one man I couldn't fathom eating lunch with without feeling constant attraction to. I showered, soaping up twice to make myself smell prettier. I stood in front of my full-length mirror, trying to decide how to wear my hair. I wanted to be practical, yet not frumpy. I realized I was treating this as a date. Yet, it wasn't. Yet, it was.

I ended up wearing tie-dyed leggings, my best running shoes and the loosest fitting t-shirt I owned. I didn't want my breasts to tug on the cotton. I didn't want to encourage Danny's eyes on me. A zip-up hooded fleece jacket stuffed with thin gloves in the pockets in case, finished my ensemble. I didn't wear any extra jewellery. And of course no cosmetics. I did mist my favourite perfume on my throat, wrist and cleavage. I tied my hair in a ponytail, and off I went to pick up some coffee and a bagel. I didn't want to be late meeting Danny.

I arrived about twenty minutes before my suggested time. I sat and read the news on my phone while taking large bites of my bagel. I ignored the large steaming coffee in its holder. I'd have plenty of time to sip on that during the long morning drive ahead. I was so consumed in the article that I didn't notice Danny had arrived. He walked up to my window, his shadow getting me out of my reading trance. He was dressed for work. I lowered my window. My eyebrows formed into a questioning frown.

"I couldn't find an excuse not to dress this way when I left home, this morning," he said as he hopped into the backseat behind me. "I will change while you drive."

"No, Danny. You change. I can wait two minutes."

The door had barely closed behind him before he started taking his clothes off. He may have been behind me, but my rear-view mirror gave me glimpses of his body. I had so much to learn from him. Unlike me, Danny had no body-image issue. His belly wasn't large, but it did exist. And it was hard. I noticed his chest hair curls were minimal. He stripped down to his dress socks and underwear before redressing himself into the casual clothes he had brought in his briefcase. Once fully ready, he left from the backseat door, and entered into the front passenger door. Danny Russell sat next to me for the next hour or so.

"I saw you sneaking glances," Danny smirked.

"Hard not to," I answered casually, trying to sound aloof. My body was in heat but I couldn't let him know. "If you're going to flirt with me, or tease me, then you can leave right now."

"I'll behave," he laughed as we rolled away, and headed off to an adventure together.

We arrived at the park. The gates were no longer tended by staff. It was late in the year, so I had to go pay for the daily fee inside. We stopped in the main building and used the washroom facilities. We also got tide information.

Our first few hikes were small trails, just to warm us up. Dickson Falls was always so pretty, no matter the season. I was also watching Danny's tolerance level. He was not in the best of shape. But he kept up. Once back to the parking area, I went into the trunk and got us some drinks and snacks in the small cooler I had stocked up earlier that morning.

"If you do this next trail with me - the Three Vault Falls - lunch is on me."

"I said I'd pay for lunch," Danny insisted.

"Yes, but this trail could kill you," I laughed, seeing how he was still panting for air from finishing up the Point Wolfe trail. "I promise I will go at your pace, as long as we do the entire trail. The view is worth it."

"Sounds difficult," Danny grimaced.

"It can be," I warned. "Again, I will pay for lunch. Or you can stay in the van while I go do it on my own."

"I'm coming," he said.

Once back to the vehicle, we were both wet from perspiration despite the cool air. We were also hungry and tired. I pulled out more bottles of water, and some granola bars to refuel until we could reach an eatery to have a suitable meal. I felt tired. I had hiked for hours while holding onto the stress of being in his mere presence. It was becoming exhausting holding up appearances. I debated on suggesting a nap, but was fearful of his reaction.

"I don't know about you," I finally said, "but I think I could use a nap more than a meal, right now. Fifteen minutes, tops."

"Sounds great," Danny panted. He was still out of breath. We lowered our seats into a horizontal position. We fell asleep facing each other, the sun being our blanket. I woke up to him looking at me. I felt embarrassed.

"How long have you been awake?" I asked, putting my seat back into its upright position.

"Long enough," his baritone voice made my nipples twitch. "You looked so peaceful."

"Buckle up," I declared as I started up the van. I pretended ignoring the lovely words he had just spoken. I couldn't fall into his trap.

I put my Toyota in gear, and off we went to this wonderful little eatery outside the Fundy National Park gates. I had a bowl of their delicious chowder while Danny had a submarine sandwich. We walked over to the bakery next door where we each had our own sticky bun for dessert. Danny got some of the brown sugar topping on the tip of his nose while taking a big bite. I swiped it with my fingertip, and licked my finger clean. He, in return, purposely smeared some on my mouth. We laughed. Danny leaned over the picnic table we were sitting at. He grabbed my chin with his fingers, and licked the syrupy goo off my mouth. It wasn't quite a kiss, but it might as well have been. My heart was racing, my loins inflamed. It was time to stop this exchange before it got more heated. I headed for the van, and Danny followed.

As we returned to the mall, shortly before four, I waited for Danny to dress into his work clothes. I found myself sneaking in more peeks, more than I should have. I was attracted to him. I dreamt about him. He was also turning out to be the first true friend I'd ever had. He hopped out of the backseat, and slid himself back into the front passenger seat.

"Today was a good day," I breathed out. "I enjoyed your company."

"I did, too," he smiled. "I thought you were trying to kill me, at first."

I laughed out loud.

"Those pants, though..."

"What's wrong with my pants?" I frowned.

"They don't leave much to the imagination, and my imagination is wicked."

And with that, he rubbed my thigh while looking straight into my eyes with his own sapphires, and then left my vehicle to walk over to his.

I wanted to be angry. I felt embarrassed. But I knew when I was getting dressed that morning, every item I put on, it was to impress Danny. I could not be shocked by his words if that's what I'd dressed to get.

I watched him drive away before I drove myself home. I couldn't wait to see him again.

CHAPTER 15

♂

'm not sure what changed her mind of meeting me one more time, but I'm glad she had. I had never worked so hard to get a woman. Why this woman? I had no real answer except she intrigued me. She was smart. She was shy. She was hot. She was a new toy to play with. And why was I doing this when I had a family waiting at home? Beats me!

A week later, I suggested a bar in a three-star hotel off the highway. We would be away from faces we'd know, able to speak our minds. These types of hotels usually hosted sports teams for the many tournaments Holliston planners organized. This particular hotel was clean and had a quiet pub-style eatery. They served things like pulled pork sandwiches, nachos and BLTs. Their coffee was not something to brag about. It was simply a quiet place that might allow me to finally penetrate this woman's shield, and see what exactly this game we had been playing these last few months might be about. Was she into me?

Or was she just not seeing how provocative her glances had been? I was going to get to the bottom of this, once and for all.

Unbeknownst to MJ, and not 100% sure I was thinking with the right head, I had checked into one of the rooms upstairs. Just in case. Obviously, I had bigger intentions than she did. But if this get-together was going to start any steam rolling, I didn't want her to back down during the process of us checking in. I just had to woo her to this room, three floors above the pub. My body was ready for hers. It had been for some time. But in my head I struggled, knowing my actions could hurt Tina and the kids.

I debated during the last hour, while sitting in my car, whether to wait for MJ, or have her wait for me. At the end, I chose to sit in the deserted pub. While sipping on their god-awful coffee, I had the perfect view of the entrance. I wanted to see MJ strut those hips towards me.

Our chosen hour was 3 p.m., and I had arrived at 2:15. I checked into the room, prepping it for any possible action. Mostly, I closed the curtains, and laid open the bed in case we got feisty. That took mere minutes. I now had to kill half an hour until her possible arrival.

I didn't question what I was doing. My intentions weren't pure, and I truly believed neither were MJ's. The attraction was real. The glances were real. The energy was definitely real. The question was: were we capable of crossing that line? Were we willing to throw to the wind what we each had at home for a romp in the hay? I apparently did the moment I paid cash for the room, and took the key from the desk clerk.

As I patiently waited for her arrival, I passed the time looking around the pub. The decor was minimal. The round wooden pedestal tables were stained an oak colour, with plexiglass protecting the tops. Black pleather club chairs hugged them all. All tables were aligned in rows of two, leaving plenty of space for patrons and servers alike to co-mingle. Including the stools at the bar, there was seating for fifty. Muted flat-screen televisions covered the white crown mouldings. They were all projecting different stations.

I had settled into the last table on the right side of the establishment. I started my tab by ordering a whisky on the rocks. I needed to settle my nerves a bit. I no longer fooled myself into thinking this was a game I played with this woman. I wanted her. I've wanted her since the day we met, and I was going to let her know today. I just had to convince her that she felt the same way I did. The liquor went down smoothly. Much too smoothly. I ordered a second glass, and sunk that one down pretty quickly too. At the rate I was going, I would be sloshed under my chair before MJ even pulled into the parking lot. I had to slow down. That's when I got a taste of their coffee. I was not expecting a barista masterpiece. But drinking tar wasn't my idea of coffee, either. This would work in my favour if she showed up. Instead of sharing coffee together, MJ and I could go for something stronger.

Two chickadees were keeping me company on the other side of the window. They were battling for ants that ran around frantically on the dirty sill. That's when I saw MJ's Toyota pull up. Relief released itself from my shoulders, a tension I didn't know was there until it left my body.

She was mere feet away from the window I had access to. I saw her shut the engine off, but stay in her car. Her head bent down slightly, and I figured she was texting someone. I put my hand on my own phone in my back pocket, hoping it wouldn't be me she was texting. My phone never vibrated by the time I saw her put her phone in her purse. Relief!

Having one last peek at herself in her rear view mirror, MJ stepped out of her car. She locked it, headed for the hotel entrance. The doors slid open as she approached the sensors, and she stepped into the lobby. What a view I had. She was dressed for work. She had a blue skirt and blazer with a silky cream blouse peeking underneath. She wore her red hair down, and it was curling slightly at her shoulders.

MJ looked briefly on each side, trying to locate the pub. She looked a little scared. But she still walked confidently into the bar with long strides, flexing her calf muscles in the process. My hands fluttered at the thought of touching their silkiness.

She slowed her stride and stopped at the bar. She ordered herself something from the bartender while letting her eyes adjust to the dark. Seeing me in the corner, MJ waved and gave me a warm smile. She took the glass of wine the young lady handed her, and then headed my way. It was a sight I will never forget. Everything about MJ was genuine. She was finally comfortable in her own skin around me. MJ took a spot on my right, her back at the bar with the many silent flat-screens glowing behind her head. Her entire attention was focused on me. My cock flickered.

"Hello there," I greeted her. "Glad you showed up."

"Hi," she answered. Her smile never left her face the entire time we sat there. We each ordered another glass and did small talk for the next ten minutes.

"May I show you something?" I bravely asked. I was seeing the minutes tick tocking by without accomplishing what I had come here to do. I wanted her to be true to herself. I wanted to see if she liked me as much as I liked her. All we were doing was stalling the inevitable.

"What's that?" MJ asked curiously.

Without saying a word, I got up from my surprisingly comfortable chair and sank the rest of her red wine. Her eyes showed surprise by my bold move. I took her by the hand, and led MJ to the elevator, which was located between the pub and the front desk. She looked as stunned as I felt. We were surprised for where this was going, knowing where this was leading to. And neither one was stopping the chain of events unfolding in front of us.

What seemed like forever to arrive, the elevator door finally opened. And when the box started moving up, MJ threw herself at me! Her lips melted on mine, her mouth accepting my tongue down her throat. My hands struggled to decide where to land: in her hair, on her boobs, or her butt. MJ made the decision for me when she intertwined her long fingers into mine, and nailed me against the wall of the cage, as if I was being crucified. She was passionate, needy. And she was mine to explore for the next hour.

As the elevator shaft slowed to the fourth floor, MJ backed away.

She readjusted her clothes and straightened her hair. Then she stepped off the elevator floor as if nothing had happened. I found her amusing. Refined and ladylike on the outside, but a tigress waiting to come out from the inside. I couldn't wait to get to the room and unleash her.

We walked the deserted hall of the fourth floor. I walked ahead as I knew which room I'd booked. 429. I had purposely booked a corner room so we'd have as much privacy as possible to make her comfortable. It wasn't much of a view, but I doubted we'd be looking out much.

I swiped the card into the slot of the door, and pushed the handle down. I opened it for MJ to go in. She hesitated. MJ looked back at me, a worried frown developing on her forehead.

"Don't cry," I begged, myself now frowning as well.

"You weren't supposed to feel good," her voice croaked.

"What?" I asked, confused.

Her frown disappeared, and a smile formed on her reddening face.

"Just now. In the elevator. You weren't supposed to feel good."

And with that said, she walked into the carpeted room. I didn't even wait for the door to click shut. I grabbed her arms with enough force to take charge, and pinned her against the wallpaper.

Hearing her shoulder blades thump against the wall, I released her arms and took her spread out hands into mine. Her purse dropped on the multi-shaded brown carpet. I pinned her fingers above her head, and made her spine arch. It pushed her delightful tits against my chest. My cock could no longer stay contained. As my lips took a hold of her bottom one, I zipped down to release my shaft that was aching inside my pants. It sprung out and slapped itself against the bottom of her belly. MJ's sigh let me know she felt it. I started biting that lower lip of hers and watched her eyes roll in her head. I let go of her left hand to be able to cup her tit.

"Don't move," I commanded when I saw her hand come down from above her head.

MJ quickly put it back up. Her mouth was open, and she was breathing heavily. Her reaction I would analyze at a future date. For now, I was busy destroying her composure. Her hands were both back above her head, with her tits at my reach. My left knee flexed itself to spread her legs apart. I brought that same knee up to her crotch, putting pressure on her pussy I'm sure was getting wet. No longer needing to hold her down, my hands were now free to feel her up.

"Close your eyes," I said in the most gravelly tone I could conjure. Her big brown eyes stopped rolling, and focused instead on my own. Her mouth slowly peeled a grin, and she closed her eyes shut.

I unbuttoned her blouse, revealing a bra-covered cleavage I wanted to bury my face in. But not yet. I had to make a lasting impression on this woman. I wanted MJ to want more from me than just a one-afternoon stand. I wasn't risking everything I had for a one-shot deal. I had to make her beg for more.

"Take your bra off," I whispered in her ear, bringing a trail of goosebumps down her neck. Her nipples hardened through the satiny material holding her tits up. Without opening her eyes, MJ did as she was told. Her blazer, blouse and lace-trimmed bra pooled on top of each other around her long, lean legs. "Hands back up," I commanded. And just like that, MJ did as she was told. I could get used to this.

My fingers traced the outer rim of her heavy breasts. They were slightly peppered with freckles, perfectly round and soft like deflated balloons. The skin was blazing hot against her ribs. I made them jiggle. They fit my hands perfectly. Her tightened nipples were almost transparent. And they tasted salty when I took a lick.

I let go of her hands, and took all my clothes off. Except my socks. MJ was watching me. I again stepped toward her. My belly was touching her stomach. I went in for a lasting kiss. She tasted so sweet, I could've kissed her for hours.

Not losing her stare, I looked straight into her eyes as I sucked her right tit with all my might. MJ moaned hard, and her knees gave way. Her bum landed on her blouse on the floor.

I picked her up, and walked MJ up to the bed. I pushed her shoulders on the bed. I undid her zipper on the side of her hip, and quickly removed her skirt, exposing the matching panties to her bra. I took both my index fingers, hooked them on each side of her panties, and pulled the satiny material off. Her honey-coloured curls greeted my fingers.

My right finger decided to explore more, and opened her barely hairy lips. My left finger was looking to get wet, going in as deep as it could. I pulled back, standing in front of her. I was waiting for her to look at me, but she was still recovering from my finger. That was a woman in deep need of a hard fuck.

"Are we really doing this?" she asked in a whimper.

I never answered. There was no turning back. I had her fully exposed to my view, and I was going to have a taste. I knelt between her legs, and my tongue went for a lick. I felt her tense up, but I didn't care. I kept giving her oral. I wanted to hear MJ come. She eventually did, scaring herself in the process. The second time she came, she took a hold of my ears and held me hostage between her legs. I watched her hips ride out the wave going through her body. I lapped up her juices as they reached my tongue.

As MJ retook control of her body, I fucked her, pumping eight times at full force. I didn't apologize for my early release. It's what I was born with. All my other conquests learned and accepted this downfall of mine. I simply learned to please them with my hands and mouth. Fucking my partners was for my benefit, only. MJ would learn that, too.

CHAPTER 16

♂

Unbeknownst to MJ, I had charmed my way to her floor after she had left the office one morning. I walked the few feet separating the elevator from Annie's desk, and started chitchatting about her day. She was telling me about her plans for the rest of the week. Casually, I asked Annie if I'd be able to see Mrs Taylor that day, knowing very well that MJ was on her way to Edwardsville. I knew Annie was breaching privacy by telling me MJ's schedule, that she was in meetings all day.

"What if she gets stranded," I asked. "It's announcing foul weather."

Again, Annie breached the privacy clause, disclosing that she had already booked a room for MJ. Just in case.

"You are one valuable person, Annie," I answered. "I would snatch you in a jiffy if you chose to leave here. You think of everything."

I got what I had come for. I hugged her goodbye. Yes, Annie and

I were now on hugging terms. I went back home to quickly pack a bag, telling Tina I needed to go to Mayne overnight. I had to throw her off my scent. I would be back by supper tomorrow, I told her. Tina didn't question my reason. She never did, as this was a norm for me. I was often sent on road trips, here and there. The life of a salesman.

And off I went in pursuit of some MJ pussy. I had had a lot of reflection time these last few weeks as I was off to Halifax earlier in the month, and our headquarters in Montreal at the end of last week. Spending a lot of time travelling and sleeping alone, I found myself wanting MJ. Not just her body, but her company. Her mind. Her smile. Of course, her eagerness to please me, and to be pleased was on my list, too.

Making MJ discover her deprived self was beyond a turn-on. I was in for the ride, ready or not.

As I drove to Edwardsville, I realized that my absence these last few weeks had probably cooled her down somewhat. I would need to charm myself back into her life. To surprise her in Edwardsville, I hoped that getting stranded there overnight would not go against my plans. Only time would tell.

I arrived shortly after 11 a.m., and snow had already started falling. The wind had blown the clouds in earlier than expected, and by 1 p.m. it was a full blown blizzard out there. RCMP were strongly advising travellers to stay off the Trans Canada Highway. Route 1 and Route 2 were dealing with white-out conditions from Edwardsville right through to Hilda. Offices, schools and shopping centres were closing at noon, leaving MJ stranded in Edwardsville. I was here to keep her company...if she wanted.

I sat in the lobby with my laptop open, but I was working distractedly. I was looking out for her while trying to get some work done. Who was I kidding?! I would accomplish nothing on that day. I was simply hoping to have her to myself.

My back was against the outside wall, so my view was facing the front desk of the hotel. I hoped for her safety that she would come in, soon. It was nasty out there.

A cold gust of powdery snow swirled through the lobby when MJ came in. The double set of doors tried to minimize the amount of the white stuff coming in, without much success. The long welcome mats with the hotel's trademark logo sewed on them were soaked with January snow. Guests dusted themselves off as they walked in, almost breathless.

It was shortly after two o'clock. MJ came in with a briefcase and purse in one hand, and her cellphone in the other. What a sight to see, her hair windswept, and her face damp from snow melting on her high cheekbones. MJ was speaking on the phone to a nameless person on the other end.

"Honey, I'll be fine. I'm checking in to the hotel now. I'll send you the room number as soon as I have it. I have my cell phone with me. And I'll be on the road as soon as it's safe to travel, tomorrow morning."

She paused as she listened to the response on the other end. Before MJ could muster another word, she locked eyes with mine. She dropped her bags on the floor. Her mouth was ajar. She blubbered a few sounds before focusing on her phone again.

"Okay, Nicole. Go in my top drawer. There's a pair of pink socks on the left. Take a twenty from it, and get a taxi to drive you to Jillian's for the night. Marcel can stay next door at Mark's. Dad is safe on the road. And we will all meet up for supper tomorrow night. Sleep tight, Honey. I love you."

And then MJ was all mine. Her eyes weren't readable yet. I wasn't sure how she felt about my presence there. But I was about to find out.

"What are you doing here?" she whispered loudly. She looked a bit frazzled as she sat in the chair next to me. She straightened her skirt around her knees.

"A little bird told me I might find you here," I answered, "and I thought it would be an interesting opportunity to get you for the night."

"I can't be seen with you," MJ whispered again. "My colleagues and I are all staying here."

"Discreet is my middle name," I whispered back. "You do what you need to do with them. But please let me into your room so we may have some privacy to talk...and whatever."

I was surprised at how MJ didn't question the fact that we were about to share a room together. As if it had already been agreed upon, ahead of time.

MJ got up and walked to the front desk to check in. One of her colleagues approached the counter at the same time, and they chatted briefly. I heard MJ answer him that she was feeling a little under the weather, and that she was going to retire early in her room.

"But thank you Barry for inviting me to dinner," she said kindly as they shook hands. "Maybe next time."

MJ then focused on the desk clerk, signed for her room card, and headed for the elevator. Seconds later after the door had closed behind her, my phone lit up. A text vibrated.

429, our favourite #. Give me 5 minutes.

With that message, my cock sprang to life. I had to cool it down. I needed this evening to be perfect. I wasn't about to waste it with a five-minute fuck. I took a brief walk around the block in the storm, chilling myself good. And like a man on a mission, I walked confidently back into the hotel, straight to the elevator. I made my way to the lady hiding behind Door 429 with my hands full of goodies.

CHAPTER 17

♀

y first reaction to seeing Danny, casually sitting on the lobby sofa at the hotel, was of pure disbelief. The Who What Where When Why and How travelled through my mind in the few seconds it took my brain to register that I was actually staring at him. I had just found out a half hour earlier, through Annie, that she had been booked me a room. And now, obviously, Danny was also going to be stuck here. I knew from the morning text exchanges that this was no coincidence. Annie and I would have to have a conversation. And sooner than later. I was positive Danny had pumped some information out of her.

In the meantime, I had to make an immediate decision about how to express my shock. I quickly ended my conversation with Nicole before walking confidently towards Danny. I wanted him to know that this wasn't the right time, or the right place to figure our things out. But as usual, my hormones deceived me, and they made my body tingle at the sight of him. I thought I was on my way out of being under his charm, but I stupidly fooled myself. I so wanted to jump on his lap and lose myself in his kisses.

I remained the professional MJ Taylor throughout my entire time in the lobby, since I was surrounded by fellow colleagues. We were meeting the Edwardsville version of us. They had recently hosted the annual Canadian Association of Municipal Administrators conference. And we, in Holliston, were working ourselves up to host the CAMAs in two years. We were in town to work with their team to iron out all the details that would make our hosting this event as smoothly as they had.

I wanted to make a quick exit to my room, as I knew what my heart desired. But I stayed the professional. I chitchatted a few minutes with these people before saying my adieus for the evening. These men and women headed towards the bar while I went the opposite direction, walking in the strides I had learned from my mom. Be confidant, she'd say. Stand tall and proud.

However, when I entered that sleek elevator, I became all mush. I craved Danny's touch. His breath on my skin. His penetrating words in my ears. His lips on my mouth. His damn eyes baring down on mine. As soon as the door closed behind me, I texted Danny my room number.

I anticipated the moment that I would open that door to him. Being stranded in a hotel during a snowstorm, I needed to keep my clothes presentable for tomorrow morning at my departure since they were the only clothing I had. Thankfully, there were a couple of fluffy white terry cloth bathrobes folded neatly in the bottom drawer of the bureau. I immediately put one on, and hung my wet clothes on hangers to dry. Then I waited for Danny's arrival. What made me presume he would want me half dressed? I suppose I just wanted him to.

I didn't want to sound desperate by texting him again. But I did wonder what was taking him so long to come up. Maybe he chickened out. Then again, no person would be crazy enough to drive two hours out of their way on a winter day, only to bail at the end. Maybe Danny ran into someone he knew, and now had to think of a plan b. Or at least shake these people off his track. Maybe...

Then that's when a knock rapped on my door. I sprang up from the edge of the bed where I had been sitting anxiously, waiting for his arrival, and leapt to the door. My heart jumped for joy at the sight of his face. I was about to spend an entire evening with this man. My guilty conscience was in hiding. This was surreal, like a dream. Rick escaped my thoughts, as did the children. I wanted Danny in this room. In this bed. In me.

I undid the latch bolting my door, and opened it to greet a cold and soggy Mr Russell. He was carrying a few bags of food with him.

"The city is shut down," Danny trembled as he stepped in. "I went around the block, looking for a corner store that might be open. I have brought frozen pizzas, some chips, Coke, chocolate. And a can of whipped cream. Just in case. I figured you didn't want to be seen with me at the restaurant downstairs."

As he pronounced the last five words, a mischievous smile developed on his face, making his eyes turn ocean blue. He was up to no good. And I welcomed it.

CHAPTER 18

♂

ignored, to the best of my abilities, the fact that MJ was naked under that robe. I could easily have my way with her, then and there. The fact I had the entire night with her to explore all her crevices, and turn her every which way but loose, made me slow down. I just wasn't sure my cock would handle that long of a wait.

I took my overcoat and hung it next to her clothes in the open closet. I then peeled my boots off. I placed them next to her black leather ones. I deliberately took my sweet old time undressing. I wanted to see how fidgety she would get. It made me chuckle inside. I now knew that MJ was as deep into this affair as I was. There was no more denying it. There was now no turning back.

I continued the process of removing my clothes. Next were my socks, which I hadn't taken off the last time. I trusted the cleanliness of this hotel much more than our previous one, I suppose. I undid my tie and laid it on the bureau. I then took my watch off, the only piece of jewellery I ever wore, and put it on top of the tie. Next came my shirt, which I pulled out of my belted pants. I chose to have my back at her. I wanted her to become desperate for me. And it worked. I heard her get off the bed. I didn't bother looking to see where she was heading. I knew.

"Sit!" I commanded. And MJ did as told. Why was I doing this!? This wasn't like me. Both times I've had her in my reach, and I took charge. And she let me.

I continued my slow process of undressing. I was standing in front of this magnificent woman, making her want me more by the minute. I would have her eat out of my hands by the snap of my fingers. If I wanted to. Before I could undo my belt, I had made a tent in my pants. My cock was hot and bothered for her.

I dropped my pants on the floor with my underwear still on me. I turned around to greet MJ with my knob trying to poke itself out of the slit of my underwear. I placed my hands on her two shoulders, and pushed MJ down to the floor on her knees. Her back was against the foot of the king-sized bed. Her robe untied itself. One of her nipples came to view. The skin of my cock was as tight as it had ever been. It was painful, but in a good way.

Without thinking twice, or asking if she was comfortable with oral sex, I held her head in place with both my hands. I grabbed her wavy hair just above her ears, and jammed my entire rod in her mouth. I heard her gag as I reached her tonsils. She grabbed my bum in approval. She wanted me to continue. MJ guided the depth my cock went in by pushing my ass cheeks towards her. My cock wished to go further down her throat. But I respected this woman, and my heart said to let her have some control.

With my cock still in her mouth, I let go of her head and let my hands go search and find what they were looking for. I grabbed a hold of her two perky pink nipples. I felt the weight of her tits as I pulled them up. And that's when my spunk released itself into her mouth. Shot after shot, the build up of the entire day came out. Like a true sport, MJ let my milk pool itself into her mouth. I pulled back to let her spit it out. Instead, she swallowed me. She swallowed me! Her body itself receiving zero sexual satisfaction. I would have to fix that, and soon. But first, I needed a drink. A stiff one.

CHAPTER 19

♀

What came over me, I'm not quite sure. I quickly found out being a bad girl was intoxicating. I could feel myself getting moist down there while he overpowered me with his voice and his actions. I liked being told what to do. Maybe that was the angle my mind was thinking. I needed to not be in command. I didn't have to control everything. Between home and work, I ran everything. Or so it seemed. This was an outlet for me to be able to let go. I could enjoy the ride for a change. It was an interesting ride, one I never pictured myself being on. But here I was, sharing my hotel room with a man I wasn't married to. I was secretly hiding him while we had our way with each other. I wanted to uncover all my secret fantasies with him.

Rick and I had had a conservative sex life. We had not stepped far from the missionary position, and always in the bedroom. It's not that we were stuffy or boring. Well, maybe we were. I just never thought we were. Rick and I were just satisfied with the life we led. Porn was never a word in our home. We had a loving, full life together. Romance included. I never realized I was in need of anything more. Until Danny came along. He introduced me to a whole new side. I welcomed everything he had thrown at me. The good and the bad. It's like he brought out the best in me, and the worst, sides that I didn't realize existed. And he alone held the key to this whole new part of my persona. All I knew was, I had never felt more alive than I did with Danny.

Watching his reaction to my swallowing his sperm made the acrid taste go away much faster. It was not enjoyable. And I planned to never taste it again. It was not something Rick and I had ever tried, and I planned to keep it that way. This was definitely a one-time only moment. I would share my opinion if Danny tried to do it again.

I rose to straighten up and retie my robe while Danny used the washroom. He came out completely naked. I was struck by how comfortable he was with his nudity. Never had I ever felt that way about myself. I was super critical of my flaws. And I was less than generous to myself when it came to look at the beauty of my body. It's probably why I found it amazing that this almost forty-four-year-old man, two years my junior, would find me attractive after all these years. Time had taken its toll on my body. You would never see a magazine cover model with sagging breasts and a muffin top. I even had the beginning of a second chin developing. I could simply not help being over-critical of myself. Yet, here was this younger, chubby man who was developing his own set of breasts, and with more hair on his back than on his head walking around naked without a worry in the world. It didn't phase him a bit. I was going to have to learn from that.

But not at that moment. I had to go freshen up, as well. I went in and gargled some mouthwash from the sample bottle. I took a facecloth to cool down my face and neck. I even took a swipe down at my sex.

I came back into the bedroom to find Danny setting the small round table next to the window with paper napkins. The paper cups already had Coke poured into them. The microwave oven next to the coffee machine was buzzing with hand-sized pizzas cooking for our mid-day supper. We had developed an appetite after our encounter. We were famished, despite the early hour.

"It smells delicious," I said. I would've eaten anything. So even cardboard pizza was better than nothing.

He handed me my glass. My eyes widened at the taste.

"I had a sample of rum in my bag," he explained. "Thought I'd add some into our glasses."

I sat on one chair while he brought the hot pizza to the table. Danny sat opposite me, and we ate without a single word exchanged. Either we were both very hungry, or we were lost for words. Maybe both.

"Would you like another one?" Danny asked as I put my last bit of pepperoni into my mouth.

"Maybe later," I answered as I was licking the crumbs off my fingertips. It was a bad habit I only practised in the privacy of my home...and now with Danny. "I would like more to drink, though."

He leaned over to his side, and picked up the large bottle of cola parked next to his right foot. He opened the plastic bottle and refilled my glass. As Danny reached for the mini rum bottle, I started to protest.

"I don't want to drink anything stronger than wine," I said. He ignored my request.

"I want us to stop ignoring the white elephant in the room," Danny said. "I want us to talk about our fantasies. What we are willing to do. And not do. I know the conversation will be less awkward if we have a little help from Mr Bacardi." He proceeded to spike my drink. "What I just did, I have never done to anyone. This forcefulness. It's not like me," he protested. "But it is a major turn on. And I am positive that this is all new for you, too, MJ. Correct me if I'm wrong."

The heat of the alcohol was turning me into a speechless woman. I was facing the man that was going to be a significant piece of my life puzzle. He was right. We needed to clear some things up. We had all evening to discuss it. But at the rate I was going, I was going to be under the table in ten minutes. So I pushed it away. I wanted to pay better attention to him.

"Honestly, Danny, I'm not sure where this is heading, either," I answered. " I'm not sure what I want from this. I just know that I don't need to be drunk to enjoy your company. So no more rum please."

He looked me deep in my eyes. His sapphires were melting my chocolate eyes. He took my glass away from my hands, and sunk down the rest himself.

"Okay," he said, licking his upper lip. He then smiled back at me.

"As for fantasies," I continued, "I am green. I am completely clueless as to what I desire. I never felt deprived with Rick. How can I know what I want when I don't know what I'm in need of?"

Without even thinking twice, Danny shared his. "Well, I suppose my ultimate fantasy would be a threesome. I'd love to watch you with another woman."

Without a mirror nearby, I still knew just how red I had turned following his words. Oh my goodness, it was disgusting and embarrassing to think of myself being with a woman. And then watched! This was a conversation I had to end immediately.

"Alcoholic drinks or not, I am not comfortable having this conversation with you. I'm feeling very vulnerable. So please excuse me."

I got up and walked as calmly as possible to the bathroom. I closed the door behind me, and started pouring myself a bath. A bath always soothed me, ever since I was a little girl. And as the water flowed, filling the tub, it also drowned out my sobbing. I knew Danny was more experienced than me when it came to making love. But I felt hurt. It was just a matter of time before he'd dump me and move on. In the meantime, I had committed adultery twice with him so far, putting my family on pause, at risk. What a fool I was. And now I was stuck in this room with him until further notice.

I was mortified at the thought of even seeing another woman naked in a romantic way, never mind touching her. This evening had quickly soured, and I had to save face. Hiding in the bathroom for the next half hour would help. I disrobed, and placed the plush garment on top of the counter. I slowly lowered myself into the steamy water, waiting for the fog to take my thoughts away for a while.

CHAPTER 20

♂

hit. Shit. Shit.

I went too far. I went too fast. I was finding out the hard way that MJ may have been adventurous in spirit, but her thoughts were still controlling her body. I knew she wanted more. I could see it. I could feel it. I could taste it. The more I did, the more she took. MJ was definitely craving new adventures with me, but her conservative side was continuously in a battle, constantly pulling her back. I had to pace myself better.

I gave MJ fifteen minutes of being alone, to let her gather her thoughts and self esteem before I joined her. Thankful she hadn't locked the door, I tapped lightly on it before turning the knob, just in case she may have fallen asleep. She hadn't.

I found MJ stiff as a board when I walked in. A hand towel was modestly hiding her breasts. She was embarrassed exposing herself to me. I fought hard not to react. I returned to the bedroom, and came back in with two glasses of wine as a peace offering. Without saying a word, I grabbed a facecloth on the metal shelving above the toilet, and knelt down at the foot of the tub. I lathered some soap onto the now wet cloth, and washed MJ's back and neck, softly pushing her body forward to ease my task. Strands of her hair were kissing her lower neck. I wanted to kiss it, also. For the first time since I had met MJ, I wanted to make love to her. Not fuck her. She had always been vulnerable to my touches. But this evening, I saw her as the delicate flower that she had always been.

Not a peep came from her. No protesting. No shooing away. MJ had had a long day, and she needed to relax. I saw and heard the stress come off of her. She breathed out loudly. Tears trickled down her cheeks. I wiped them away with my thumbs as I held her head and kissed her forehead. Her shoulders slumped forward as I continued washing them. Her breath intakes came in deeper and longer in between, as if she was falling asleep.

Without letting go of her, I guided MJ back to rest against the back of the bathtub. I started lathering up her arms. I avoided touching her boobs. I wanted to express my level of caring for her, not initiate sex again. Twice, my forearm came into contact with the side of her left tit. I pulled away immediately. I didn't know where else I could wash her without MJ thinking I was doing a move on her. So I stopped washing. That's when she opened her eyes and looked up at me.

"I have seen the many shades of your eyes," she exhaled, her words almost sultry. "And I can almost always read the emotion that comes with those particular colours. What I see now is regret."

"It is, MJ," I answered. "I didn't want to hurt you, or scare you. I'm so sorry."

"Don't ever be sorry," she answered as she sat up. She reached for her glass of wine, and took a sip before continuing. "This is all new to me. I don't know what you want from me, and I feel overwhelmed. This....this is a fantasy world we're creating here. It's exciting, yet stressful. I like how I feel when I am with you. I do! I really do. I just don't know how to balance it all. And I certainly don't know what I want from this. Can you understand?"

"Of course I do," I replied, shaking my head. With that said, I stood up and left the bathroom. I closed the door behind me, and let MJ be with her thoughts. I gave her the space and privacy she needed.

I was shuffling through the many channels on the wall-mounted tv when MJ walked into the bedroom. Her robe was tightly knotted around her waist. The ends of her red hair were curling, wet from touching the bath water. She looked serene. MJ played the part of a woman in charge at her office, and probably at home, too. But with me, she had always given up her power to let me be in charge. I now realized that it was an honour to be given that so-called power. I needed to handle it better than just being a brute. I needed to respect her comfort level. I needed to ease her slowly into new things.

I got out of bed, and met her halfway between the bathroom door and the bed we would be sharing. With one hand carrying her now empty glass of wine, MJ put her other hand up to stop me.

"Can I get a refill?" she asked.

That was a surprise! It took me a moment for her words to register before I leapt to the ice bucket near the window. I refilled both our glasses. As I sipped my wine, MJ sat at the foot of the bed and gulped most of hers before putting her glass on the bureau. I remained standing.

She came face to face with me. She rested her hands against my few chest curls, and kissed me oh so softly on the lips. I took that opportunity to wrap my arms around her back, and just held her there. MJ responded by resting her forehead on mine. We stood there for a while, feeling each other's heartbeats. All seemed forgiven. We could move on.

When MJ finally pulled back, she looked at me and kissed me again. I kissed her tenderly, figuring this was my best approach. Quickly, her lips became more demanding and urgent. But I kept my cool, and kept kissing her softly. My hand rested on the middle of her back. She undid the knot of her robe. As it fell open, her entire body was at my disposal. I wanted to ravish it, but again chose to keep my cool. I was trying to be tender, but my cock started to stir.

When she started undoing my robe, I finally got the hint that this was heading the right way. Tonight, I chose to make love to her. I took my time disrobing her, letting the sleeves slide slowly off her shoulders. MJ put her hands down, and the entire garment fell to the ground. It left her naked body to be seen and loved.

Nothing I wanted more than to pick her up and carry her to the bed. Too challenging. I took her by the hand, instead, and walked her to the bed. I pulled the bedding to the side.

I kissed her naked body as much as her lips. She seemed to be anxious, but I chose to ignore those signals. I continued kissing her. I continued feeling her skin on me. MJ opened her legs, and I entered her. All this time, I was looking into her eyes. I knew that was what she wanted. I came minutes later, and pulled away from her.

I went into the bathroom to rinse myself off. When I returned, I came back to a puzzled MJ. She was leaning on her side. She patted my side of the bed.

"I told you earlier I don't know what I want from this," she said, "but I do know that I don't want this tenderness from you. I want you to love me hard. I need to find the naughtiness in me. And you are going to make me discover that part of me. I don't want boring sex. Okay?"

My eyes grew wider, darker. My ears were barely believing what they were hearing. Her words were ringing in my head. I leaned in to kiss her hard. She laughed in my mouth, ravenous for more. I couldn't supply what she wanted. I was depleted for the time being.

"Give me a couple of hours, and I will give you exactly what you are looking for," I promised her. "Hungry?"

"Any fruit?"

"No, I didn't buy any fruit. But I do believe there's some at the front desk. Do you want me to go get you some?"

"It's okay. I'll eat what's here," she answered.

"I'll be right back," I said. I hopped into my pants and put my shirt on. I headed to the lobby and picked up an orange, a banana and a couple of apples. Who knew what my lady desired. I decided to cover all my bases.

CHAPTER 21

♂

"I want you to share a part of yourself with me," MJ said softly as she peeled her orange. "Tell me about you."

"I don't share that," I quickly answered, closing the door of my past.

"That's not fair," she protested.

"You don't understand," I replied. "I don't share that with anybody."

"I'd like you to make me the exception," she whispered. "For me?"

"Careful what you wish for," I sighed. "I'm one of four children my blue-collar parents had. Three girls and me. My father died in a car accident when I was five." I saw MJ cover her mouth, but I continued. If I was going to spill my guts, it was going to be a one-time-only story telling. "I unwillingly became the man of the house. It's not something my mother wanted me to be. I just assumed the role.

"My sister Irma and I took care of the younger two while our mother went to work on evenings and weekends, just trying to make ends meet. My mom also tried to give us a father figure. But with such a large family, she had slim pickings. She ended up being hurt almost every time. Most of the time, the abuse was verbal. But we did hear Mom get slapped around in the kitchen a few times. Me and Irma hid Denise and Rachel behind a bed. We'd cover their ears. We tried to protect them."

MJ leaned over to me, and hugged me. Her tenderness was distracting, so I walked over to the window. I finished off the rum sample, and then brought the wine bottle back with me. I needed that kind of support.

"Irma married straight out of high school to a supportive but older man. Ben welcomed the rest of us to live with them. I felt lost. I was fourteen, and I felt much older that I should have. I felt like I was being replaced. Tempers flared. Toes were stepped on. One night, I just packed my bags and headed to my father's parents' house, out in the country.

"They greeted me with open arms. Grandpa and Grandma had a large farm, and they had the mindset that if you lived there, you had to put your time into the farm. At first, I loved it. It was all so new to me. I followed my Grandpa into the barn and would milk the cows at 4 a.m. I gathered the eggs under the hens. I picked berries in the field, and I weeded the massive vegetable garden in the front of the house for Grandma.

"Come August, I had to cut and bail the hay. I always wanted to ride the tractor, but Grandpa assigned me to throw the bails onto the wagon instead. I soon built up muscles. I was no longer scrawny."

"That sounds like a better arrangement for you. No?" MJ asked as she scooted closer to me.

"Everything was honky dory living with them all summer. Grandma was a wonderful cook. She was an even better baker. Her pies were to die for. It's why I would pick berries every day," I smiled. "After the milking and egg gathering chores were done, Sundays were free time. After church, of course. So after lunch, I would change into shorts and t-shirt, and bike to the wharf down the road. I met up with my new friends, boys and girls, and spent the afternoons jumping off the wharf."

MJ settled herself against the headboard, and patted the space next to her. I sat next to her, bringing the wine bottle with me for company. I appreciated that she spoke little.

"I lost my virginity that summer to one of those girls."

"At fourteen?" MJ asked, shocked.

"Cathy laughed at all my antics. She saw my body muscle up over the summer. And she was in awe of my eyes."

"I guess I'm not the only one," MJ teased.

"Cathy was sixteen. On Labour Day weekend, school was right around the corner. Wharf jumping days were coming to an end. The boys and I gathered beach wood scattered across the shoreline, and we spread the word that we would be having a bonfire on Sunday night near the wharf. My grandparents were concerned that I was too young to hang out at night with these high school kids. But they let me go, anyways.

These guys had been my buddies all summer. And no matter how late I came home, I was still expected to do my morning chores, tired or not."

"They loved you," MJ said as she laced her legs around mine. I let her.

"I gulped my supper down. After gathering the dirty dishes for Grandma to wash, I put away the many jars going back into the fridge. Then I kissed my grandmother goodnight, and headed back to the beach to finish gathering pieces of wood with my friends.

"I caught Cathy looking at me on several occasions over the summer, but paid no attention to it. I was fourteen years old. My interests, up until moving to the farm, had been sports. Playing them and watching them. As my body developed over the summer, my hormones kicked in. I was waking up with sticky sheets. I had no real friends, so I craved somebody. Anybody. I had no one to talk to. My dad was dead. Grandpa was a man of few words. And I was way too embarrassed to talk to Grandma about the changes I was going through."

"Well, you certainly got to learn them," MJ teased again as she cupped my balls in one of her hands. I took a swig from the bottle, and continued.

"Cathy came from a well-known family, but was super shy and had a hard time talking to people. She'd hang out at the wharf with us. Never swam, though she'd wear a bikini. She stayed dry and simply hung out on top of the wharf.

That night at sundown, the fire got lit. Huge fire, I remember..." I paused, having said enough.

"Well, don't stop now!" MJ exclaimed.

"I think I've said enough," I replied, exhausted by recalling all those memories.

"You have to tell me about how you did it with her. How was it?"

I smiled. "You're turning naughty," I smirked as I shook my finger at her. "Open your legs. I want to sit between them." MJ did as told.

"Cathy was sitting quietly with the other girls, pretending to listen to their gossip. But the whole time, she kept looking at me. Despite my promise to my grandparents, I tasted alcohol for the very first time that evening. I only had two bottles of beer, but it was enough to tip me over. Feeling good, I finally clued in to the glances Cathy had been giving me. Cathy blushed every time I caught her looking. She already had curves at the right places, and long blond hair. Her sundress was ruffling in the wind, showing her bare skin in a way I really hadn't noticed before.

"Fuelled by the beer, I went and talked to her. One of the other girls noticed me coming, but brushed me off as just a kid. So she turned her attention back to the gossip they were sharing. Cathy didn't. She noticed everything I did.

"Hi," I said. I was looking down at her as she sat on a log, taking a peek at her boobs. "I'm Danny. And you are?"

"Cathy," she breathed out as she stood up, fluffing out her dress as she stood in front of me. "Nice to meet you, Danny."

"Want to go for a walk?" I asked. She accepted, and off we went on the moonlit beach. My friends chuckled. The other girls, they barely noticed Cathy had left their sides. When we were far from the bonfire flames, I tried to take her hand. She pulled away, but then put it back into my palm. I closed my fingers around her small-boned hand, and looked up at her face.

"When we sat on the dry sand, she gathered the skirt part of her dress behind her bum, held it against the back of her legs, and sat down like the lady she had been taught to be. Kinda like you."

MJ squeezed my shoulders as I rubbed her thigh.

"I remember the smell of her hair as it flew across my face. It stirred my groin. I grew up to wash my entire body with a bar of soap. Head to toe. And that night, I smelled like the ocean I had swum in, earlier in the day. But not Cathy. Her hair had a magical smell. It smelled like raspberry jam.

"She was sitting too far from me to smell her bare shoulders. When I tried moving my body closer, Cathy turned towards me and kissed my lower lip.

Even though it felt good, Cathy looked away, embarrassed. I, however, was not. I studied her face. This super shy, older girl found the courage to kiss me. I was kissable. I was likeable. I was desirable. Before she could ruin the moment by apologizing, I kissed her smack on her soft lips. I even tasted the skin around them. The urgency. I was forgetting to breathe. I grabbed a hold of her head, and kissed every part of her face. Her eyes. Her forehead. Her cheeks. Her nose. Her chin. But mostly, her lips."

"You were very sensual," MJ interrupted me. "You were a lover boy back then, too."

"To Cathy, maybe I wasn't fourteen. Maybe I was a man. Her mouth was the sweetest thing I had ever tasted. Her skin smelled like a bouquet of flowers. Her tongue tasted minty. This making-out session wasn't scaring Cathy like it was scaring me, but...I wasn't going to back out if she wasn't.

"We kissed some more, tenderly I remember."

Then Cathy stood up abruptly.

"Why?" MJ asked. "What happened?"

"This is too dangerous," Cathy said. "We're getting ahead of ourselves, and there's too many people around."

"I brought Cathy into my lap. Noses touching, I resumed my exploration of her face. Her legs wrapped around my hips and crisscrossed behind my back.

"Once we were both seated comfortably,my cock bounced to life. Its hardness rubbed against her. Ready or not, we were going for the home run.

"I got my t-shirt off. She kissed my chest. I lay Cathy on my shirt. I took her hand and put it on my hard on. Alcohol was no longer fuelling my actions. Adrenaline was. She pulled back, afraid of how far this had gotten. But I put her hand back where I wanted it. I kissed her on her lips, and it calmed Cathy down.

"I pulled down her sundress, down to her hips. And with that swift move, I tasted every inch of her boobs. With both our eyes wide open, understanding what was about to happen, neither one of us spoke.

"I unzipped my shorts and pulled my cock out of my undies. I fell to my knees between her soft shaved legs, and pulled her panties onto one side. I took a feel of her pussy, and found the hole I was looking for. I pushed my cock in, and fucked her."

"And then?" MJ asked, curious.

"Three pumps later, I came."

"Why do you have to use such crass language?" MJ expressed.

"Ah, MJ, we both know you like that about me," I answered as I got up to pee. When I returned back to the room, I grabbed my clothes and got dressed.

"Where are you going?" she asked, exasperated.

"I need a smoke," I answered dryly. I needed a whisky, too. I had never shared this part of me with anyone, before. Not even Tina. It was hard talking about it. But for some reason, I felt I could share it with MJ. Like she was my best friend, or something.

CHAPTER

22

♀

was concerned at first, about Danny leaving abruptly to go smoke a cigarette. But I had to let him be. He just needed space, and I was going to give him all the space he needed. And a shoulder, if he ever chose to tell me more.

In the meantime, I had to examine my own soul. Danny made me hungry for more. I wanted to be bossed around, told what to do, where to stand. I never knew what to expect, and I loved it. I knew he meant well when he laid me down and loved me. But I hungered for more. I wanted to be loved hard. I wanted to be fucked! I can't believe I just said that to myself! My mother would've fainted. What an awful word to explain my entire new me. In no terms was I looking to be hurt physically, mistreated, or humiliated. And certainly no third person involved. Ever.

I put my robe back on, walked over to the snow-encrusted window and looked out at the blizzard swirling outside. I could barely see the

Mayne River across the street. I felt a chill and I pulled up the collar of my white robe around my neck. I was pleased to be tucked away in this room for the night. Nicole and Marcel were old enough to spend a night without me. This would be good for us all, to learn to be more independent among ourselves. I needed to let go of the ropes, so to speak.

I also questioned my sanity. Here I was, basically honeymooning with a man I had no business being with. I was married. He was taken. We were in business together. I was walking on needles the whole time we were here together. What if one of my colleagues saw him come in or out of my room? What if we made too much noise? There was no way I'd be relaxing while we holed up in this room. The whole situation made me nervous.

I tucked away my fears when I heard the click of the door as Danny came back in. I walked over to greet him and gave him a small peck on the cheek, my own peace offering. It wasn't his fault I felt so conflicted.

I walked to the window to close the curtains while Danny took his clothes off. He was drenched from the few minutes he had been outside smoking. He wrapped himself into his own robe.

"I want you to teach me things," I said as sexily as I could muster. "I want to turn you on. As much as you do me."

"Oh Baby," he cut me off, "you have no idea how fucking hot you are. The fact that you don't know that is sexy in itself. Believe me." He grabbed me by my buttock cheeks, and held me against his chest, our faces inches apart. "If I could fuck you right now, I would!"

He then kissed me with a level of passion I had never experienced in my life. As nasty as it was, I loved the taste of liquor and nicotine in his mouth. It was the taste of Danny. When we pulled away, he and I were breathless, saliva on both our faces. Our robes were untied, and my hair was a mess again. I hungered for his ways. But his body wasn't ready. I was anxious. I wanted to be released from this edginess my own body was going through. Life wasn't fair, sometimes.

"I want to see you rub yourself," Danny urged. That cooled me instantly. He must've seen it in the expression on my face, or my body language, because he piped in some more instructions.

"No no no! You don't get to shy away every time I say something that makes you uncomfortable. You want me to push your buttons, to be more adventurous, then it starts now! I want to watch you make yourself come. If you're not comfortable with the idea, you talk to me about it. You do not get to shut down. Understand?"

I nodded like the good little girl my parents had raised.

"Okay, then. Let's try this again."

He brought me to the leather sofa next to the bureau, and made me sit down. He sat on the other end of it, his leg propped up, exposing his private parts. I was feeling warmth on my face, and a strong pulse below.

"And when I say I'd love to see you rub yourself, I'm not talking right this moment. Although, you're more than welcome to," Danny grinned. He waited a moment for me to react. I didn't. So he continued on. "I'm saying it's a fantasy of mine. Not all fantasies need to come true. I'm just opening my heart to you. Okay?"

"Okay," I managed to say, feeling a lot more comfortable in where this conversation was heading.

"I also fantasize about seeing you make out with another woman."

"Not happening!" I snapped.

"That's fine," Danny answered back. "You are definitely clear on that one. And I respect that. This is the kind of talk I've wanted to have with you. And we can continue having talks like this as the need occurs."

"Anything else in your repertoire?" I asked in jest, trying to lighten the heavy mood I was responsible for.

"As a matter of fact, yes," Danny answered with his head cocked. "If ever you want to try out being fucked in the ass, let me be the one to break that for you."

I knew I had turned several shades of red at that moment, never imagining such a request. He was definitely pushing the envelope, and it was testing my limits.

"I've heard you," I cautiously answered, "and I will mull it over. But for now, I just want to go slow. Ejaculating in my mouth, that was something absolutely new for me. Even you using your fingers to arouse me, the other day. I had never had that done to me, before. Do you understand? These actions, and your words, it's all new to me. You're going to have to be patient. Please."

Danny looked at me like I was from another planet.

"You may be the oldest virgin I've ever met," he smirked. "Not literally, of course. But you have so much to learn. I'll gladly be your teacher if you'll give me the honours. I promise I'll be gentle."

"Speaking of which, you need to be gentle with me at all times. I want nothing to do with pain. Or being restrained. Or fear. Understood?"

"Not even a smack on your ass, once in a while?" he laughed. My cross face answered him.

We turned on the tv. Our heads were tired, and we settled on a game show for half an hour.

CHAPTER 23

♂

I snapped the tv off. I still had a few hours to explore this woman lying next to me before we would have to call it a night. MJ and I had been teasing each other for eight months. We were just starting our journey. The more time I spent with her, the more I wanted.

"Are you comfortable?" I asked. "Do you need more heat in the room?"

"No," MJ answered. "This blanket will be fine."

"No blanket!" I answered quickly, surprising her. "I am going to lick every inch of your body. And I mean it." Her eyes widened, getting the scope of what my intentions were.

"May I at least cover part of it when you're not near it?" MJ asked, warming up to my idea.

"I'll decide that," I smiled as I guided her robe off. Her flesh was at my disposal. I made her get off her sitting position in the bed, and instead lay down like a starfish. I untucked the sheet. I wrapped her shoulders with it, giving her some level of warmth. MJ reached up, and started covering her front.

"No, no, no," I teased, wagging my index finger at her. "Your tits are not to be covered until I say so. I want your nipples to pucker as hard as pencil erasers."

MJ giggled as she pulled the sheet back up to her shoulders, leaving the rest of her body fully exposed to my view. She was okay with me continuing.

I went about my feast for the evening. Every giggle she made that night, my cock waved. I was ready to adjust as many times as I needed to. I wasn't going to fuck her, just yet. She needed to be worshipped. Can't believe this woman had never been fingered before. How fucked up was that?!?

My wet finger gently pried her pussy lips apart. When I reached her butt hole, I rimmed it with that same finger. I watched her facial expression as I teased it a bit. MJ tensed, but otherwise seemed okay. Slowly, I inserted it into her ass. She opened her eyes. MJ stared me down, remaining silent. This proved to my perverted mind that I would, one day, be able to fuck her ass, after all. I still had plenty of work to do before that day came, though. Shit, I'd never fucked an ass, before. I'd have to learn, too.

I pulled my middle finger out, and leaned up to kiss the inside of her leg. That made MJ relax. I moved my own body around, making myself comfortable between those two long legs of hers. I stopped and examined the inside of one of her folds, holding it open with my fingers. Her hands came onto mine. I was making her lose her patience, which was my goal. I wanted MJ to be impatient with my torture. At the same time, I wanted to enjoy every moment I spent in the beauty of her deprived body.

I finally moved up, giving her engorged pussy a small tap goodbye. My cock was starting to hurt. It had been hard for some time, now. It needed release soon. I knew I had to get her release first. So from her left armpit, my tongue went into gear and traced the warm moist skin under her tits, slowly going up until I was licking my prize: her tight puckered nipples. I sucked the first one hard, hard enough to keep a grip on it as I pulled away from her, bringing her tit up with me. My knee felt her pussy twitch. And I knew if I took a feel, I'd feel her juices coming down. I let go that nipple and did the same thing with the other one. I watched MJ mess her hair up with frantic hands as she was reaching a point of no return.

I moved up to her throat, licking her from ear to ear. MJ squirmed and giggled, but my hands kept her pinned down. She wasn't able to stop me from tasting her creamy skin. Honestly, I don't think she wanted me to stop. I nibbled briefly at her chin before finally stopping at her awaiting mouth. MJ kissed me hard. She was in desperate need of her release. I twisted my legs around to sit on the bed, and guided MJ to her knees.

"Close your eyes," I commanded.

"It's time for you to come," I breathed out, and she let out a gutteral moan. MJ was beyond ready. "I want you to touch yourself. You can either play with your tits while I finish you off, or you can help me finger you. Your choice."

MJ removed her fingers off of my shoulders, and lifted both her tits in unison. I went to work and stuck three of my fingers inside of her, and her hips bucked towards me. I took the rest of my hand and squeezed her mound, swirling my fingers in and out of her while her hips swayed with my hand.

"Squeeze your tits, Baby," I whispered. "Use your hands as if they were mine."

MJ moaned and did as told, her thumbs pinching her nipples. I was going to keep this in mind, next time around. She liked having her tits played with. I managed to reach up and lick one of her nipples as they were sticking out between her fingers. She let go of her boobs to hug the top of my shiny head.

I started fingering her hard while she bucked and moaned. Then she came. She moaned hysterically. Her knees were barely keeping her up. Her entire body crumbled onto my arm, with her head falling on my shoulder.

I gently pushed her to a horizontal position. MJ laid spent on the bed, but I had yet to come. I looked at her wide-open pussy, and my cock would've gotten lost in it. I wanted her ass, but not like this. MJ was still catching her breath, so I wasn't about to go down her throat. So I started pumping myself. Within a minute, I came on her bush.

CHAPTER 24

♀

woke up around eleven to the sound of my phone vibrating against the night table next to my head. It was a text from Rick, asking how I was doing. Oh yes, my husband! With this make-believe honeymoon I had been having with Mr Russell, I had become oblivious that I was still married to Mr Taylor. Rick knew New Brunswick was under siege with a major blizzard. He was missing it completely. He chose to remain in Mississauga, Ontario, until further notice.

I answered, saying that I was safe and sound in Edwardsville, and our children were safe in Holliston. I was planning to head back home in the morning, weather permitting. Our communication was brief, and to the point. I wished my husband a good night's sleep, and safe travels. Then I shut my phone off completely for the night, preserving the battery until I could charge it in the car on my way home.

The curtains hid the storm. But I could hear the whistling wind doing its damage. I turned to face my partner for the night. Danny was grunting as he slept, not quite a snore.

I wanted to feel guilty being happy, but the guilt never surfaced. I was having an affair. I, Marie-Josée Noël Taylor, respected daughter of Dr and Mrs Louis Noël, City Manager of my beloved hometown of Holliston, volunteer at church, and former volunteer at my children's schools, was having an affair. Yet, this felt absolutely natural to me. I think it was the first time in my entire life that I did something just for me. Me, myself, and I.

Yet, what had Danny and I gotten ourselves into? I didn't blame him. And I will never regret meeting him. Or being his lover. Everything I had experienced with this man, from the moment I first laid eyes on him, I respected every one of my choices. I was going to have to stop seeing myself as faultless, and be the adult. I needed to enjoy my time with Danny and go with the flow. Until I could figure things out.

I brought my chilled naked self to Danny's side of the bed. He mumbled a bit as he became aware of my presence. His arms automatically reached out to me. I didn't question if he thought it was me he was embracing, or Tina. I just appreciated the welcoming set of arms that reached over. And we fell into a deep slumber for hours to come.

The morning greeted me with the sound of Danny in the washroom. I went straight to the window to look at the road below. To say I was disappointed would've been an understatement. This Nor'Easter remained enraged.

I turned on the television set to the weather channel Their forecast announced the strength of the storm to remain the same, as if it had stalled over New Brunswick. I was calling downstairs when Danny emerged from the bathroom. He was scratching his buttocks as he approached the bed. Our bed.

The front desk informed me that the City of Edwardsville remained shut down. That the RCMP urged people to stay off the roads across the southern part of the province until further notice. Danny and I were stuck in town for possibly the day. I looked at him in disbelief. He chose to take it in stride.

"I have had worse news than this," Danny smiled. "So we stay here and watch tv and talk. And play. There's a restaurant downstairs, and we have food here. Let's make the best of it with what we've got."

He saw the good. He always did. I saw the bad. I had colleagues in this building, so I couldn't be seen with Danny. I was trapped. And my children were away from home.

This was going to be my opportunity to change my way of thinking, and be more like Danny. I called the front desk again, and ordered room service for breakfast. Danny smiled. I was turning around in my way of thinking. I was learning from his bright side of life.

I finally spoke to him. "I welcome being stuck here with you, but a few things have to be upheld."

"Such as?" He sounded amused.

"Well, for one thing, no one can know you're in here with me. No one!"

"Reasonable," he answered.

"I may be called downstairs to attend meetings. Or even required to have a meal with these people. You may be alone here for parts of the day."

"That's okay," Danny said.

"I ordered a huge breakfast for us to share. But I won't be able to order big meals, every time. It would look suspicious."

"Okay," he nodded. "Worse comes to worse, we tap out the vending machines." He had a solution for everything.

As I powered my phone back on, the room phone rang. It was the front desk informing me that all meetings were cancelled because of the storm. Our hosts from Edwardsville were stranded at their individual homes, and would not be able to make it to the hotel.

"While I have you on the line," I said, "could you possibly supply me a charger for my Iphone?"

"Yes, ma'am," the young man on the other end of the line replied. "I can charge one to your account."

"Could it be sent up with my breakfast?"

"I'll have that taken care of."

In the meantime, both Nicole and Marcel had texted me. And Rick. School remained closed. They were both being spoiled by their hosts. I would need to send fruit baskets to both these families. Rick's text was letting me know that he was en route back home, keeping a diligent eye on the storm's progress. He added I should simply enjoy being stuck in a hotel room by myself. If Rick only knew.

Annie texted me as well.

> *Quick note to tell you City Hall is closed, today. So don't fret about work. I tried booking you a spa treatment at your hotel, but they're not opening today. Their staff is stranded at home. Imagine that! Lol*
> *Just sit back, relax, and enjoy your company. Wink wink.*

Oh my goodness! What did she mean by that? Did she know? Should I ask? Should I be alarmed? No. I know Annie. She's as discreet as I am. And whatever she was pertaining to, she would bring it to her grave.

There was a knock on the door, and panic shot through my body until I remembered about room service. I waved for Danny to hide in the bathroom before I opened the room door. A tray covered with white linen was rolled into the room along with a bag of supplies. I tipped the young man who brought our food in, and sent him away. The old MJ would've been fully dressed before even thinking of opening a hotel door like that. But this new MJ, she let this stranger in. And all the while I was dressed in the hotel-supplied robe.

I wanted to spend my entire day with Danny. I was going to hole up for the day with this man, and learn more about him.

CHAPTER 25

♂

"Our breakfast is here. Come and eat," MJ said across the bathroom door.

"I'd rather eat you," I said, making her blush.

Leaving the window curtain open, MJ took her robe off and joined me in bed. She kept her bra and panties on. She was still proper and bashful with me, even after our few encounters. I had to get that way of thinking out of her. There was no better time than today. We had, after all, hours to kill in this room. We had nothing worthwhile to watch on television. We had nowhere to go.

I sat back on the mountain of pillows with my legs spread eagle. MJ sat next to me. I pointed for her to sit in front of me, but she shook her head. Not sure if she felt embarrassed, or scared, but this was going to be my first challenge of the day. Taking her by the elbows, I softly led MJ to walk on her knees to face me. She reluctantly did so. I leaned in, propping myself with my hands to get into position, and I kissed her as tenderly as I knew how. MJ closed her eyes in response, and I saw her tense shoulders ease up.

"I promise I will never do anything to you that you don't want," I spoke softly. "Whatever we choose to experience together, we choose together. Understand?"

MJ nodded, not speaking a word.

"I want you to be comfortable with me," I continued. "You are the most beautiful woman I've ever been with, and I don't want to fuck this up. So anything you are completely against, then say so. Okay?"

MJ nodded again. Her hands interlaced together on her lap. Was she getting nervous again?

"I want you to be open with me, so please tell me what you're nervous about."

"Nothing," was her answer.

"That's not true," I said. "You're tensing up, and I don't want you to feel that way. So please be honest with me. I shared something very difficult with you, yesterday. I trusted you with my secret. I'd love for you to do the same."

With hesitation, MJ finally spoke.

"I feel like I'm too inexperienced for you," she answered. "I'm very naive in this openness with lovemaking. You're going to be disappointed with me."

"You've got it all wrong," I cut in, shaking my head. I grabbed a hold of her shoulders, and brought her down to my chest. The two of us fell on the mountain of pillows behind me. I cradled her head as I continued talking.

"You could never be a disappointment. You're quite the opposite. The fact that you are inexperienced is quite the turn on for me. I get to teach you and mould you into the vixen you don't know you are."

I felt her head tilt up, looking at me in surprise. I let her believe whatever she felt like believing. MJ was going to get to know me today. She would get to know how I see her vs how she sees herself.

I kissed her again. This time more urgently. I flipped her onto her back under me, pulled her panties off her hips, and had my way with her. No fuss, no muss.

Once I finished my deed, I let MJ get up and clean herself up in the bathroom while I peeled the parchment paper off a muffin I wanted to eat. I was famished. She came back with her hair brushed. She wore a towel around her waist, and sat in the bed with me.

"Did you enjoy that?"

"Yes," MJ answered.

"You're lying," I chuckled. "You never came."

Choosing her words carefully, MJ looked at me with love in her eyes. "I don't need to come every time."

"That doesn't work for me," I answered, putting her back in front of me as I lounged against the many pillows. "If we're going to be lovers, if we're going to risk everything we have for this, it has to be spectacular. I don't want ho-hum sex with you. I want out of this world sex. Otherwise, why bother. Don't you agree?!"

MJ was starting to blush, again.

"I'll take that as *Yes.*"

"I do want to be adventurous with you..." MJ finally found her voice. "I feel like I've missed out. I just don't know what exactly I've missed out on."

"Well there's your challenge, Mrs Taylor. You need to find out what turns you on. And when you are intrigued by something you've seen or heard, let me know. I can try to make it happen for you."

Her head bowed down in embarrassment. I could see the tip of her ears turning pink.

"And I promise you," I continued, "that as you get comfortable with your own body, you won't be turning red as much as you are. When you're ready to hear my fantasies, I'll share them with you. There's nobody else I'd rather explore them with."

"You have fantasies about me?" MJ asked. She was losing her shyness. She was genuinely intrigued.

"From the day I met you," I answered as I pushed down one of her bra straps. I wasn't ready to perform, yet. But I wanted her to want me. We could be playing all day. Have a three-hour foreplay, for all I care. I was game.

MJ examined the fallen strap hugging her left bicep, but did nothing to bring it back up onto her shoulder. Instead, her mouth turned into a smile, and waited for my next move.

"Tell me, Mr Russell. What are some of your fantasies?" she asked provocatively. Her index finger traced my thigh from the knee up. I liked that she was warming up to my idea, but she was definitely not ready to hear my fantasies.

"Not now," I answered. "I'm hungry."

And with that, I reached over to the breakfast tray and handed her a plate. That's how you keep teasing.

CHAPTER 26

♂

MJ wanted to straighten the room a bit. She went out the hall when she heard the hotel cleaning staff talking and got us some clean towels. Other than that, why bother making the bed if we were just gonna play in it all day? I gave up on tv after surfing through all the channels. Between female talk shows and news report after news report of nothing but bad news, I shut it off. I took a seat at the window while MJ finished her task.

"Have you called home at all?"

"I did a couple of times from the bathroom."

"Oh, is that what you're doing in there?" MJ smiled. "Thought you might have a bladder issue or something."

"Nope," I smirked. "My pipes are just fine."

"How is your family faring without you?" she asked. She really cared.

"They have power, food and the internet. Tina and the kids are fine."

"Tell me about them," she breathed out as she joined me at the window. She sat knee to knee with me and reached out to hold my hands.

"Don't you want to know more about Cathy?" I wasn't ready to bring Tina into the picture.

"Oh?" she asked. "There's more?"

"There's more. Get comfy," I said. "It's another monologue."

MJ brought her feet up to her seat, and crossed her legs. She held her knees against her chest.

"The next day, when Grandpa and Grandma woke up at their usual 4 a.m., Grandma chose to let me sleep in and did my chores for the first two hours. They must've heard me come home in the middle of the night.

"I finally woke up to the sound of my grandfather riding the tractor near my window. I jumped out of bed, and instantly felt the headache that had been brewing during my sleep. I sat on the bed to regain my posture, and there was a glass half full of water and two aspirins next to it. Grandma was beyond a sweetheart, and I never wanted them to be disappointed in me for what I had done just a few hours before. I was, in many ways, my dad reincarnated for them.

"The lingering headache stuck around all day. And my appetite was non-existent. I was in bed by dusk. The next morning, I went down and did my chores. Then I kissed Grandma good morning, and headed for the bus stop.

"I walked around with a grin on my face, one moment; and fear in my eyes, the next. Having fucked a warm body like Cathy's was way more fun than jerking myself off. What bothered me was that I knew I had committed a sin in the eyes of the church. I had let alcohol and my hormones speak for me, that night."

"How is this different?" MJ asked as she waved her hand across the room, reminding me that I was now sinning with her.

"That was decades ago," I frowned. "I got over that. I left the house with breakfast in my belly. My wet hair was slicked back like Fonzy. I was wearing new clothes Grandma had bought me. I walked down the gravel driveway we had, and joined the neighbours' kids down the road. And as we all waited for the bus to arrive, only then did I realize I'd be seeing Cathy again. What we had done was real, not a dream. And I'd be facing her that morning for the first time, since.

"The bus arrived, and I was the last one to get on. For those who didn't know there was a new kid in town, they got their first look at me, then and there. Some of them stopped talking when they saw me, but were soon back into their conversations. Those who had had the chance of meeting me over the summer at the wharf, church, or ball field, those kids nodded a hello. Or waved.

"Cathy...Cathy ignored me. Neither one of us were trusting our guts. We had lost our virginity to each other, and we were now acting as strangers. I chose to sit with Cathy, but with my back at her in order to face my friends in the seat next to us. She was probably fuming at me, but said nothing."

"I would've been!" MJ declared, her eyebrows frowning.

"I. Was. Fourteen," I answered as a robot. MJ nodded.

"Anyways, she probably wanted to have a conversation with me, to break the tension. But the school bus was the last place to have any privacy. That conversation didn't happen until the following Sunday, after church. I saw her looking at me. It was a gorgeous day, so I invited her to walk home with me. Cathy refused, pointing at her shoes. They were pretty. They weren't made for walking. She suggested, instead, a bike ride after lunch.

"I pedalled up her parents' driveway, noticing the different landscape. All of my grandparents gardens produced food. Her parents had flower gardens. We grew up in different statuses. Before I was able to get off my bike, Cathy's mother swung open the screen door. She offered me a tall glass of lemonade. She had heard that the Russells down the road had taken their grandson in. She apparently had never paid attention to me in church. Cathy's mother basically wanted to know my intentions and my age. When she saw that I was only a boy, her worries flew out the window. If she only knew," I laughed awkwardly. MJ grinned.

"This woman greeted me like the child I should've been. I felt awkward with her, knowing what I had done to her daughter, a week before. I didn't have the social skills to deal with my guilt, yet. I gulped down that lemonade, just to avoid looking at her. Until Cathy appeared with her bike. Unlike mine, Cathy was riding a shiny red ten- speed bike. I had whatever my grandparents had in the barn. It had probably been my dad's, at one point.

"The country road we lived on was pretty quiet, especially after the cottage people had packed up and left for the season. Cathy and I were able to bike next to each other instead of behind one another. Cathy let me know she wasn't very happy. She had given up her virginity to me, and I acted like nothing had happened. The first dirt road leading to the beach came up, and Cathy veered down that lane. I followed her. At the beachfront, she stopped at a white and red cottage. Cathy reached under the veranda, and found the key she was looking for. She unlocked the front door, and entered the cottage. She put the key on the kitchen table that wore about eight layers of paint, and finally spoke.

"This is my uncle's place," she said matter-of-factly. "They live in Cassidy during the year, and they always lock up Labour Day weekend. This is a safe place for us to talk...and whatever."

"My eyes widened. And *whatever*? Was she suggesting we do it again? Cathy played coy, but her body shook from trembling. She brought up her hand to her bare shoulder, and motioned with her finger for me to follow her into the first bedroom. On the mattress was a pile of folded patchwork quilts that had seen better days. I learned that Cathy was the only girl on her father's side. And in the summer, her aunt Mary, who owned this cottage, was showing Cathy how to sew. Mary would assemble the quilt covers during the off seasons, and she and Cathy would finish them during the summer. They had a special bond.

"The first quilt on top of the pile was the very first one Cathy worked on. It was made of denim in all different shades. Cathy splayed her hand over it a few times before unfolding the quilt. She laid it on top of the stained mattress, and positioned her body over it. I quickly took off my brand new sneakers. I removed my jeans and tighty whities, and jumped onto the bed. I was inches away from her. She yelped. Maybe Cathy was surprised by my move. Or maybe she feared what was about to happen. Maybe she was happy that I still wanted her."

"Did you ask?" MJ asked, cutting off my trance.

"I. Was. Fourteen."

"Fine, but did you want her? Or just wanted sex?" MJ asked.

I looked at her with a grin. "Sex!" I stated. "I was fourteen."

MJ laughed. "Continue, please."

"Unlike the last time, our bodies were exposed to daylight. It made us feel a lot more vulnerable. The daylight showed every blemish, every curve, every hair. I welcomed the view. Whereas Cathy was much more self-conscious of the size of her nipples, and the few stretch marks she already had on her ass.

"I liked what I saw as I peeled off her tight t-shirt and capri pants. I felt like I was in a candy shop. I wasn't quite sure where to start. I saw Cathy shake off a shiver. So I unfolded another quilt from the pile, and covered her with it. She reached out to bring my face to hers. It was a bold move on her part. I learned quickly that she had read several romance novels, and she was trying to piece together her favourite scenarios she had read. She was probably picturing me as her muscular, tanned and damaged pirate or cowboy, or something."

MJ laughed out loud at the thought. She leaned in, and kissed me lightly on the cheek. "Please continue," she whispered.

"Honestly, I didn't care. I was just happy seeing a naked female body in front of me. Cathy closed her eyes and kissed me with an open mouth. I kissed her back, cupping one of her tiny tits.

"Her tongue snaked itself into my mouth. I copied her moves, and tongued her mouth. But I was quickly losing interest. I wanted to find her other set of lips.

Without a word, Cathy slid from under my body, and knelt up on the mattress. She motioned for me to have my turn lying down on my back. And I obeyed.

"Pushing her ponytail behind her head, she lowered her moist lips towards my hard on. She barely got down my shaft when my salty cum sprayed inside her mouth. Cathy pulled back immediately.

"Are you serious?" Cathy cried, disappointed once again by her expectations of me. She wanted more. I get it. Her needs had not yet been met. Her body was one of a woman, as were her thoughts. But the cocooned life her parents had sheltered her into failed to show Cathy that I was housing a man's body with a boy's mind.

"Leaving me there to recover," I continued, "Cathy picked up her clothes off the floor, and quietly dressed herself in the kitchen. Only when I heard the screen door bang against the cottage did I realize she had left me there alone. I hopped into my pants and untied sneakers, and I ran up to my bike to pedal up to her.

"That's when I understood the depth of my attachment to Cathy. I didn't want to disappoint her. I cared for her. Her happiness mattered to me.

"I caught up to Cathy just before she reached the main road. It took me several seconds before I could catch my breath. I needed to give my brain the chance to mouth the right words, words she would expect from her cowboy. I knew it was my only chance to keep her in my life, as simple as it was."

"So what did you say?" MJ asked, intrigued.

"Please come back. We're not done, yet."

"And that worked?" MJ asked. It wasn't really a question, but more of a statement.

"Those magical words coming out of me, with the right tone of voice. And let's not forget these eyes," I smiled, pointing at them. MJ laughed, her head shaking in agreement. "Those magical words were just enough to stop her in her tracks. Without a word, Cathy turned her bike around, and headed back to the cottage.

"Sorry, MJ, but I need a smoke, again. These memories are hard on my head."

"I'll go out with you," she said. "I'm feeling cooped up in here."

We both got dressed in silence. We left the room in interval, as to not be seen leaving the room together.

What I was about to share next was hard for me, but it needed to be said.

CHAPTER 27

♂

walked back into the lobby first, wet from the blowing snow. I'm not sure why MJ followed me out there. Maybe she wanted to make sure I was okay. I was. Smoking always relieved my tension. I hopped onto the elevator, headed for Room 429 before MJ came through the sliding front doors of the hotel lobby. When MJ did show up, her hands were full.

"I thought this might help," she smiled as I let her in. MJ was carrying a bottle of red wine, tucked under her arm, and two doubles of whisky. She knew my favourites. She didn't judge, even this early in the morning.

"I don't want to do this, anymore," I whined. I wanted to enjoy her company and body.

"You can't leave me guessing," MJ whined back. I'm not sure if she was making fun of me, or not. I relented and quickly finished my story for her.

"Cathy was not a damsel in distress. But in her dreams, she probably pictured herself being saved by me. Like I was gonna sweep her off her feet, or something. She saw me as her hero who was gonna carry her through the threshold of her uncle and aunt's cottage. I was gonna throw her on the bed we had ruffled up a mere fifteen minutes ago, and have my way with her.

"The reality was, I was spent. I knew I liked her presence. I knew she wanted to have sex with me, which I enjoyed. But I didn't know what to do with her. I chased her down that road because I didn't want to lose more opportunities to fuck this girl. And Cathy was more than willing to do that. At fourteen years of age, the last thing on my mind was to have an actual relationship with her. Cathy was pretty and curvaceous. And she was willing to open her legs for me. Anything long term was not on my radar.

"So here we were, back in the cottage, back in that bedroom. We were each waiting for the other one to make the first move. I questioned my eagerness to bring her back in there. What was I thinking, coming back to that cottage with her? What did she want, exactly? Then Cathy lunged towards me, and planted a long kiss on my mouth. My eyes seemed to double in size. Not because of her kiss. But rather because I felt some movement in the crotch of my jeans. Could it be? My cock was about to stir. It was getting ready for a second round. I was certainly willing to find out. So I kissed her back.

"Cathy received the confidence she was looking for. She pushed me onto the mattress. I quickly peeled my clothes off, leaving my sports socks on. I watched with amazement at Cathy's sudden boldness.

"With a cattiness in her eyes, she took off her t-shirt and saw my now hard cock wave back at her. The sight of her bra did that to me. Again, I was fourteen. She removed all her clothes except her bra and panties. In all reality, she was no more or less dressed than when I saw her all summer in her bikinis at the wharf. But it was different. Standing in front of me in her underwear, instead of her colourful bikinis, it felt different. And at that point, she froze. Cathy was no longer ready to expose anymore of her skin to me.

"I, on the other hand, was eager for her to continue. But I was also old enough to see that her lips were trembling. And it had nothing to do with the temperature of the room. I got on my fours on the mattress. I crawled to the foot of the bed where Cathy stood. Her hands were crossed in front of her panties. I kissed her lips with as much tenderness as I knew how to muster. Her shoulders' tension eased up, but her hands remained linked together. I had work to do.

"I took it upon myself to lower her bra straps off her shoulders. I pulled the bra down enough to fully expose her creamy white tits that had never seen the sun, and I traced the tan line on her chest. That move brought shivers to Cathy. Her nipples responded. I cracked a smile, as if I had just discovered a hidden treasure. I gobbled up as much of her right tit into my mouth. It made her moan. She wanted to pee. She wanted to cry. Now she was getting what all these women in her romance novels were experiencing. She unclenched her hands, and they reached behind her back to unhook her bra. The flimsy garment looped itself onto my hard cock that kept poking at her thigh."

MJ and I both started laughing. I leaned over and kissed her hard. Then I sunk down my first glass of whisky, and then continued.

"I promise this is coming to an end," I said.

"It's okay," MJ said. "You're interesting. You've always been interesting."

"Yeah, but I'd rather be playing with you."

"Then finish up!" MJ pleaded jokingly.

"I brought Cathy to the end of the bed. She planted her feet on the green painted plywood floor while the rest of her body laid on the bed. She looked at me as I peeled her pretty little panties off. I positioned myself between her legs, and released my second load, that day. This time, *into* Cathy. Exhausted, I threw my naked body next to hers. I tried to get my energy back. She, on the other hand, got up and started pacing the floor. Cathy was worried about what she was gonna tell her parents of where we'd been. And then she started worrying about the neatness of the room. She worried about which quilt went on top of which one. She was obsessing, and it turned me off completely.

"I broke the silence by saying I needed to go home and finish my homework. Happy with how the room looked, Cathy followed me out. I watched her lock up the cottage then we walked to our perched bikes. We pedalled up the dirt road, and went to our respective homes. The next few weeks, I was nicer to her on the bus and in school. I'd wave Hi, or smile."

"Less of a jerk," MJ said. "And don't blame it on being fourteen. You were a jerk to her."

"I agree," I said as I bent my head down. "Cathy became cold to me over the next few weeks. I would be my friendly self. Yet, she was offended by my gestures. Then one day, she was gone. Not on the bus. Not at school. Not even at church. Some kids never noticed she was missing. She was that much of a wallflower. But I noticed. I didn't want to raise any alarm by bringing up the subject. I was hoping someone else would notice she was missing. Was she sick? Did she move?

"Then the following Sunday, I got the answer. During lunch, Grandma gossiped to Grandpa and me. She heard that the West girl had gotten herself in trouble. Her parents had shipped her to Cassidy, to live with Mr West's brother."

"You got her pregnant?" MJ asked in disbelief. Her eyes widened.

"I asked myself the same thing, trying to understand what my grandmother meant by *being in trouble*. The more she talked about Cathy, the harder it was for Grandma to think Cathy would've gotten herself pregnant. Especially since she was quieter than a mouse. Then Grandma started saying the only person she knew Cathy hung out with was...and her voice trailed off. She realized it might be me. But she said nothing. My grandfather cut her off. He said there was too much gossiping after church service. Grandma gave me the benefit of the doubt. But her intuition, however, made her suspect that her future great grandchild was growing inside Cathy West.

"I was sweating bullets. I wanted to float away from this knowledge, away from this guilt. This is when I realized I had no real friends in the village. I had fun with the other kids my age. But I had no friend to confide into, except Cathy. And she was gone, thanks to me. No one came looking for me, so Cathy must not have told anyone who the father was. I heard her parents were going to make her give up the baby for adoption, and that she was no longer going to school. Her whole future was in shambles.

"One night, next month I think, Grandma was doing the dishes. I was clearing the table. She whispered into my ear that I no longer needed to worry. Cathy had lost the baby. I should've felt shame. Instead, I looked at Grandma in amazement. Grandma would take this secret to her grave."

"Where's Cathy now?" MJ asked. She genuinely wanted to know. "What happened to her?"

"I heard her parents invited her back home after the miscarriage, but Cathy declined. She felt more loved with her aunt and uncle than with her stuffy parents. Last I heard, she had gone to UNB to become a teacher. I never saw her again."

"And you're sure she miscarried?" MJ questioned.

"I presume. Grandma wouldn't lie."

"I'm sorry all this happened to you. It was so early in life," MJ sighed.

"It's life."

"No, Danny. You got a hard going, early in life."

"Life at the farm was what I needed. I had purpose. I had unconditional love from my grandparents. I had freedom. Cathy's pregnancy was a hiccup. Well, enough about that! I have needs to be met now, woman."

MJ squirmed and giggled as my hands approached her legs. It was time to play. Finally!

CHAPTER 28

♂

With this look in her eyes, MJ ran to the bed and took her robe off. She stripped the bed down to the fitted sheet. She wrapped her naked body with the other sheet, toga style. She was up to something, and it wasn't quite noon yet. Trying to ignore the pressure building up in my balls, I climbed into the bed. MJ grabbed the bottle of wine and refilled my glass. Then she refilled her own empty one to the rim and emptied the rest of the bottle into her mouth. Droplets dribbled down her throat. I lunged to suckle the stream that ran between her tits.

Not letting go of her *toga*, MJ handed me her glass and she propped herself up between my legs. She laid her head in the crook of my neck, reclaimed her glass, and sipped some more of that delicious wine. MJ spoke next.

"We need to lay some rules."

"O-kay..."

"I'm serious. We're both hungry to try new things together. If we're going to continue meeting like this, we need to share our concerns."

"And our fantasies," I interrupted. My arm wrapped her from shoulder to shoulder in a bear hug.

I wasn't going to go by her lead. She expected me to challenge her comfort zone, she just didn't know it, yet. She gulped her glass down, as if it was water. MJ had just drunk the equivalence of four glasses of wine in less than five minutes. I was positive that she was not used to that. But I said nothing.

Without a word, MJ put her empty glass on the bed table. She let go of the sheet and turned to face me. Ooh! I was getting the feisty kitten back! And I liked what I saw. She slithered herself toward the foot of the bed, just enough for her head to be at my crotch. Her arms wrapped themselves around my legs, and she went down on me.

I was losing my shit! She was servicing me, at her speed and at her comfort. I struggled to finish my glass before reaching over to the table to put it next to hers. My hands reached out to get lost in her long, wavy hair. I fought the urge to push MJ down on me, as I so craved to throat-fuck her. I learned that she may enjoy being fucked hard by me. But when she was the one in charge, she preferred going at it slow.

For the next few minutes, I held on to my needs, longer than I've held on in a long time. I let her curling tongue and luscious lips play with my cock and balls. When I could no longer hold it in, I grabbed handfuls of her hair, and blew my load into her sweet mouth.

"You taste rather sweet," she smiled as she came up for air. Her hair was strewn across her face. The corner of her mouth was wet with some of my milky residue.

MJ was drunk, naked, and at this moment, I had never seen a more beautiful woman. I grabbed her from under her arms, and lifted her towards me like a limp toy. She immediately put her palms on my shoulders. She knelt in front of me, my legs between hers.

Transferring my hands to her face, I held her head in place and kissed her mouth ferociously. I knew her saliva was laced with my cum, but I didn't care. I wanted to spend hours doing her. Yet, our time was ticking by. She bit softly on my lips. She pressed her barely pink nipples against my chest. I doubted I could come again, but I was certainly going to try. I grabbed her butt cheeks and lifted her up. She landed against my renewed hard on. MJ's hands went down to let my cock in.

Her yelps hid the noise the box spring made as I bounced her on my meat, waiting for my cock to shoot another load into her. When our eyes would meet, I could see how she was letting loose. Today, MJ was not this shy tight-ass I had met a few months ago. She was now my deprived fucking toy who I was going to teach so many new tricks to.

I popped her off of me, and laid her on the bed. I grabbed MJ by the hips. And with her head cocked back, she exposed her long throat for me to suckle. The drippings of wine were still moist. I pounced on her, and licked the entire length of her throat. Her hands came to her rescue as they covered her skin. This is the MJ I was falling in love with. And having that thought in my head scared the daylights out of me. I chose to put this thinking in the back of my head, so as not to ruin the moment.

I grabbed her by the knees, and pulled her towards me. Her butt cheeks rested on my belly. She looked confused. Then she gasped one last time as I braced myself. My two arms locked themselves across her thighs. And then pulling up, I brought her crotch to my face. I devoured her. My tongue licked every inch of her ginger curls. I opened every flap of skin she had down there. I was enjoying the taste, the smell, the feel. But most of all, I enjoyed the sounds MJ made as she tried to keep her composure while I destroyed the lady in her.

I never let up in drinking her in. I'd readjust my hold on her thighs every time I felt her slipping down. I didn't want to ruin her receiving the best oral sex she had ever had. My eyes watched her head turn from side to side as she was approaching her climax. I let one of my hands reach over to her hardened nipples. The first one I felt, I pinched it hard, just as I heard her moan her orgasm out. Man, she was fun!

CHAPTER

29

♀

It took me a while to understand exactly what had happened that
morning.

I had just spent the last four decades building a life my parents
would be proud of. I had been living for them. But not for me. Danny
had left his everyday life at home these past few days in order to focus
on me. I felt appreciated. Special. I was hungry for more.

Danny had such a complicated history compared to mine. But
those struggles made him who he was, and I loved him for it. Yes.
Love. I had to face the fact that I loved Danny. And not just love him.
I was *in* love with him. Scary prospect, maybe, but I was finally being
honest with myself.

I got up from the bed and walked over to the bathroom to freshen
up. I closed the door behind me. I wanted to face the mirror on my
own. I'm not sure what I was expecting, but I knew regret would not
be one of them. Knowing that wouldn't baffle me, either. The fact is, I

didn't regret following my desires. Every tip of my body tingled each and every time I saw Danny. I needed that.

I pressed on the light switch, and the fluorescent fixture above the mirror lit up. I took a good look at the woman staring back. I refused to be critical at the extra flab at my waist, or the stretchmarks from my two pregnancies. I was more interested in studying this individual with a permanent grin on her flushed face. And may I add, dishevelled hair. I liked what I saw. Today, I had unleashed the hidden other half of Marie-Josée Taylor.

In all honesty, I'm quite certain she was always there. The new MJ applauded me, happy that I was coming out of my shell.

I was amazed at what my body was experiencing. Rick and I had never had any complaints over our sex life. We also never explored. Rick and I had tried shower sex, once. And spooning. And we tried having me on top a few times. But mostly, we did the traditional man on top. It seemed to suit Rick the best.

But never in my entire life had I experienced sex like this. I didn't even know such extra pleasures could be had in bed. I'd never had oral sex performed on me. I did spend some time warming Rick up a few times with some of it. I guess I never thought it was something a woman could enjoy, too. Rick never offered. The more time I spent with Danny, the more I discovered how little I knew about sex. Or even my own body.

I am shocked by my reaction, my body's reaction. And the entire time Danny and I made love, I enjoyed every moment of it. I was falling in love with Danny, and I saw no way out. Correction: I wasn't falling in love with Danny. I was already there. What I was doing, now, was getting addicted to him. The more he touched me, the more he controlled my moves, the more I wanted him.

As my heartbeat came down to a regular pulse, and my breathing slowed, my body turned into mush. I was exhausted. Maybe a bit drunk. I just wanted to sleep. I poured myself a bath.

Danny opened the door completely, and knelt in front of me. He fished the facecloth, reached over my chest to the small bar of soap and lathered up the white cloth. First, he concentrated on my neck and back, washing them with loving tenderness. Nothing in his moves showed any sign of wanting more from me.

He kept rubbing my neck, keeping at it until I was totally relaxed. Danny moved down to my shoulders and upper arms. He gave them the same loving care he had just given my back and neck. Once done, he rung out the cloth and put it on the edge of the bathtub. He put the bar of soap on top of it.

Danny got up from his kneeling position, and motioned for me to stand. As usual, I did as told. I got up and accepted his hand in help. He unplugged the bathtub, then he removed one of the four towels folded neatly on the rack over the toilet and patted my skin dry. Even when he was wiping under my breasts, he would lift them up, dab my rib area dry, then release my breasts softly. The more he took care of my body, the more exhausted I felt.

He dropped the towel in the tub, and pulled me into the bedroom. I think Danny would've loved to carry me over. But the best he could offer me was a supportive hold as we walked to the bed he had made. Even the duvets got fluffed. Danny hopped in after me, and offered me the crook of his shoulder for my head to rest on. I accepted it with pleasure. My body suddenly felt like dead weight. I fell asleep within minutes.

I woke up to him sitting in one of the upholstered armchairs. He had a pen and paper in hand. He put them down when he saw that I was awake.

"Hey, Sunshine. You must be hungry."

"I'm starving," I said. My mother would've been shocked at my answer. I was taught that a woman never expressed hunger. She ate the minimal amount in public, as all ladies should. But I wasn't in public. I was in the presence of the person responsible for my deep hunger. "What time is it, anyways?"

"It's almost 2 o'clock," Danny answered matter-of-factly.

I jumped. "Oh my goodness, I need to make contact with my family."

Danny tossed my cell phone on the bed on his way to our mini fridge.

As I called my three family members, Danny microwaved some mini pizzas. I made the conversations brief. I told them that I wanted to conserve the battery life of my phone until I could recharge it in my vehicle.

After I hung up, I joined Danny at the two chairs near the window. He had turned them around so we could view the awful weather continuing outside while we feasted on pepperoni pizza and Coke.

"I'd like to talk more about our fantasies," he said as he wiped tomato sauce from his lips. I reacted nervously, but kept my composure. I let him continue. "I was working on a grandiose list while you slept. But it's definitely way too long. I don't expect you to do half of what I wrote," Danny laughed.

"Should I be worried?" I asked, laughing with him. The more laid back this conversation was, the better it would be for me. God knows what Danny had written.

"Of course not," he assured me. "I've basically written every possible porn scene I've ever watched. What we attempt to do will depend on what you want to try out."

. That last sentence reassured me so much, I leaned over and thanked him with a peck on the cheek.

"Let me finish my lunch, and then I'll read your list. Okay?"

"Okay," Danny answered. "But don't forget: you need to make a list, too."

What a silly thing to say, I thought. How can I possibly make a list of sex acts and positions when I hardly know any other than those we've done.

"I have none," I answered as I put my paper plate in the wastebasket. "I'm just happy being with you. Now let me read your list."

Reluctantly, Danny handed it over. One by one, I reviewed them. I asked questions about some. I flat out refused others. And out of his list of twenty-three possibilities, I accepted nine of them. I blushed through the ones I said *yes* or *maybe* to. I refused even considering having threesomes, male or female. And I was nauseated thinking about being filmed.

"Never say never," he said. "Maybe we'll never get to them. But you just never know how feisty you might become."

"I can assure you," I answered back, "I will never kiss another woman. The thought itself sickens me."

"Okay, okay. I'm good with that. And as we move along into this list, we can both add more adventures as we think of them."

"I won't," I assured him.

"But you have none," Danny exclaimed. "As you warm up to me, and you become more aware of your body's needs, don't be afraid to pipe up. Okay? Do we have a deal?"

CHAPTER 30

♂

could see how vulnerable MJ was feeling. I wanted to hold her. Comfort her. But it was also a turn on to know that I was going to be able to do so many naughty things to her. I felt like a new man around her. I was going to have to pace myself.

My sex life with Tina was enjoyable. We didn't experiment as much as we used to. And that had been okay with both of us. We led busy enough lives between my work, the house, and her kids to drive around. We were parents first, lovers second. We had fun using different positions from time to time. But it was always the same three or four positions. We had purchased toys. We had tried them. But these rubber things had since been collecting dust in the back of my bureau, away from prying children's eyes. Content, we stopped challenging the status quo. If I was away on business trips for more than two days, I'd sometimes find myself looking up porn clips on websites in the privacy of my hotel rooms. I was not addicted. They just gave me relief, and an inkling of what was out there.

Then MJ came along.

All I knew was, I had to go at it slowly with her. But I still had to push the envelope just the same. And most of all, we had to review her likes and dislikes after the deed. Was it worth a repeat? Or straight into garbage?

MJ sat there, puppy-eyed, in desperate need of another good fuck. She was still too polite to ask for it. I knew she wanted me to take control of our times together. But she could still have asked.

"Stand up," I said, almost shouting.

"Wh-what?"

"You heard me, Woman. Stand up."

A huge grin broke out on her face, and she did as commanded. This was going to be fun after all.

"Take your robe off. Now!" MJ did as told. And my cock bounced back to life, hard as could be.

I still had it! Still sitting on that chair, my eyes were level with her nipples. Without touching them with my hands, I nibbled on her right one before deciding to swallow as much of her left tit into my mouth. Her knees shook a bit. A hard moan came out of her from deep within. MJ was way too easy. I was going to have her beg me before I was going to come in her. It would give my cum time to build up. I was surprised I still had some left in there.

I grabbed both her butt cheeks. It was quickly becoming one of my new favourite pastimes. I pushed her towards me. I crushed my face into her chest. I could smell the faint scent of the lemony soap. I looked up to see how MJ was doing, and she had her head tilted back. Her hands reached out for my shoulders to keep her balance.

"Look at me," I said softly. She didn't react. "Look at me," I repeated louder. MJ shook her head, as if I had snapped her out of a daze.

"I'm sorry," she answered as she looked down at me. "My heart is beating so loud, I couldn't hear you."

I was falling in love with this woman, and that was getting scary. But for now, I was going to ignore my human thoughts, and go with my animal instincts.

"Sit on me," I rumbled. MJ looked a little confused. I moved my hands onto her hips, her baseball-sized tits dangling in front of me. I licked the tip of the closest one to my mouth as I made her straddle herself over my legs. MJ giggled at the sensation of my tongue curling over her pinkish tips. I gently lowered her hips down. And as my cock slowly pushed those folds apart, MJ's eyes grew wide. She relaxed as I got my full rod inside her. I brought those cheeks a few inches up then pushed her back down to fully receive my cock up that warm tunnel.

MJ warmed up to the action quickly, getting the gist of things. She then put her hands on my shoulders, and started doing the movement on her own, without my guidance. That freed my hands to go explore wherever they felt like.

Watching MJ go up and down on my lap was an amazing treat. And as she started speeding up, I figured she was on her way to an orgasm. I had to decide if I was going to let her have it that easily, or if she had to work harder. Her moans increased with the speed of her hips. It was such a sight to see. I chose to lean back, and watch her bounce.

I was still in build up mode for my own orgasm to come, when her moans turned into a cry of pleasure. MJ threw her head back. I made sure not to lose my grip. I watched her get the release she so desperately wanted. There's definitely an inner contentment in oneself when you see your sex partner come in front of you. When MJ was done, she came back into the real world we were in, blizzard and all. She leaned towards me and looked into my eyes in embarrassment.

"That was the hottest thing I've ever seen," I reassured her. She smiled, astonished. "I want you to come that hard, every time."

"Really?"

Without speaking, I led us to the bed. MJ laid on it. Her legs dangled over the edge. I knelt down in front of her, and started sucking her dry. I wasn't trying to make her cum again. I just wanted to dry it off a bit so that my cock would not get lost in there. I wanted my rod to feel her lips peel open for me. I felt MJ's hands greet the top of my head. She seemed to approve the sensation my mouth was giving her. And at the sound of her first moan, I pulled away. I wanted to do everything to this woman, but I knew I had to restrain myself. I had to pace every adventure, one at a time.

I settled on lifting both her legs up, with her heels resting on my shoulders. The V her legs made, and with her pussy waiting to greet my hard cock, it was all I could do not to cum at that moment. I grabbed a hold of her thighs to keep her in position, and I let my rod go find its tunnel. MJ sighed as I made my way into her. I came, but didn't erupt with great force. I had barely built up any. But the release still felt amazing. And MJ looked content. One day, I would like to see us come at the same time. Watching her come on my lap, that could've been an amazing moment to come together. But my build up hadn't reached its peak, yet.

I pulled away. My cock was limp. I helped MJ stand up, as her legs were still a little wobbly. It amused me to see her so expressive with her body. Before I could walk away to clean myself off, she took a hold of my face. She kissed me hard. And she thanked me.

"Thank me?" I asked. "For what?"

"For today," MJ answered. "For being so patient with me. For... for...for making me have orgasms."

"You will feel a whole lot less vulnerable once you learn to talk dirty. You didn't make love to me and had an orgasm. We fucked hard, and you came all over my cock. Say it!"

She shook her head, pulling away.

"It's okay," I replied. "You don't have to do it tonight. But you will learn to talk dirty with me. I promise you. You'll like it."

I left her behind while I peed and rinsed myself off. We crossed paths as I came out of the bathroom, and she went in. I settled into the crumpled bed.

MJ came back into the room. She was shy again. She tiptoed over to the other side of the bed. She settled herself sideways, her back at me. She was facing the window. I rolled over to her, and rolled her body into mine. I just held her silently while she dealt with her thoughts.

It took close to half hour before MJ sighed. I felt her shoulders go limp. Her head rested against my chest. It wasn't even 8 p.m., yet, but MJ was done for the night. I turned on the tv. I settled on an NHL game, the volume low. Tomorrow would be a new day.

CHAPTER

31

♀

S itting in one of the armchairs by the window, I sat with my knees crossed, my feet on the seat. I had one of the duvets wrapped around my shoulders and sipped my tea while watching Danny sleep in. How had I gotten to this point? Here I was, a man's wife, waking up next to another woman's man. Without any shame, may I add.

I watched Danny stir. I knew my time alone was coming to an end. The storm had finally subsided overnight and the RCMP were no longer warning people to stay off the highways, but to still drive with caution. I was secretly hoping for one more romp before we left, even though I was still raw down there.

Our previous night had been amazing. We had bonded. Fuelled by one glass too many, I had found myself expressing desires I didn't know I had. It wasn't that I wanted to back out of them, or hold Danny to his. But fantasies were just that: fantasies. They were not set in stone. We could explore their possibilities without promises of coming true.

Swallowing the last gulp of herbal tea, I was greeted by a gorgeous smile. Danny had propped himself up on his left arm, crooked so that his head could rest in his palm. His baby blue eyes were examining me from head to toe, spending extra seconds on my nether region.

"Still a little red down there, I see. Maybe we can bathe you, and make you better."

"Maybe," I responded as I shifted the duvet to cover me more.

"I was thinking more of a tongue bath," Danny said as he sat on the edge of the bed.

To say I was embarrassed would've been an understatement. My manners kept coming out, despite all I'd been through these last couple of days with him. I still had some of the juices from the previous night inside me. The thought of him tasting that...

"Oh, Danny, I can't. It feels too dirty for me," I protested.

Getting up, Danny walked silently to the washroom. I heard him urinate, followed by water running. He came back into the bedroom with a steaming hand towel.

"Come here," he demanded. He pointed at the pillows next to him. I put my head at the edge of the left pillow. My body splayed in the middle of the bed. He pushed my knees apart and caressed my mound with his towel-covered right hand. I welcomed the soothing heat of it.

For the next few minutes, Danny delicately bathed my folds, his movements soothing me to the point I was ready to go to sleep again. Once done he slowly took a long lick with his tongue.

It startled me, and my head jerked up. Danny shushed me. His left hand pressed against my rib cage. He motioned for me to lay down again. I obeyed.

I wanted to stay in oblivion. My eyes stayed closed the entire time. I never even thought of reciprocating. I was being a selfish lover.

After what seemed like a lifetime, I started writhing. I started panting and moaning, like an animal in heat. I reached out to hold his head in place. I could feel the end coming. Danny pushed the duvet aside, and sucked the closest breast he could find. I screamed unrecognizable syllables, and before my body was done riding the wave, he drove his member deep, coming quickly as usual.

. I freshened up in the bathroom, doing my best to rearrange my hair before returning to the bedroom. I opened the bathroom door, only to find a fully dressed Danny waiting for me. I was startled.

"Are you okay?" he asked, his eyes showing concern.

"Yes," I answered. "I was just cleaning up."

I smiled at him. This pudgy, bald, short man in front of me was somehow the person I needed to introduce myself to the other me. I'm glad, in a way, that he showed concern, that he had a soft side.

"Thank you," I continued, "but I'm surprisingly fine. The MJ that arrived here a few days ago is not the MJ you see now. And I'm okay with that."

I don't think he was comfortable with my answer. He nodded as he put his coat on.

"So now what?" I asked, slowing his pace towards the room door.

"I think a couple of days to reflect should be in order," he answered.

CHAPTER 32

♂

I came home from this trip with panic in my head. Could Tina smell MJ on me? Could Tina read it in my eyes? Had I washed my hands enough?

I had a two-hour ride from the hotel. I had two hours to fabricate a believable story of how my stay went. Yet Tina wouldn't ask any details of my trip. She never did. She trusted me. It was my conscience that was making me go mad with the what-ifs.

How could I do this to her? Of all the men she'd gone through in her life, I was finally the security Tina sought for her and her children. I was her knight in shining armour.

I was two blocks away from our house, and my heart thumped hard. I no longer trusted my ability to face Tina. I turned around and headed to the nearest bar for a quick couple of glasses to calm myself.

"Hi Honey," Tina said from the kitchen when I came in an hour later. She was glad I was safely home, but she never left her post in the kitchen. "I'm making cherry pie," she shouted as I stomped my boots.

"Hi Babe," I said, sounding as casual as I could muster.

"How was the drive home?"

Just like that, the conversation continued between the two of us, as if I'd simply gone to the corner store for milk... Panic left my body. But guilt wrapped itself around my heart. I leapt into the kitchen, came up behind Tina and wrapped my arms around her svelte waist. I kissed her neck. She shooed me away like the pest that I was.

"I missed you," I said. My hands cupped her breasts over her sweater and apron.

"Stop it," Tina laughed as she brushed my hands off her body. "The kids are downstairs, and I need to make supper. We'll take this up later, when we go to bed. Now go take a nap or something. You must be tired."

I was. MJ had wiped me out. In the shower, I let the steam wash away the edge my body had been under while navigating the messy roads. Fatigue hit me like a brick as I stepped away from the shower stall. I towelled myself off, and wrapped myself in my robe. I then headed for the comfort of our master bedroom. I slipped into my flannel pyjama pants, and fell asleep almost immediately once my head hit the pillow. Forty-five minutes later, Alex knocked at my door to wake me up for dinner. Life as I had known it continued.

CHAPTER 33

♀

Hi MJ. Could we meet sometimes today?

That's the text I received from Danny on my way to work the following week. I had started my day rather calmly, still in a daydreaming mood, planning to head home after a workday filled with deadlines. I would have the house to myself, settle in front of the television and watch one of my favourite love stories, a bowl of popcorn for supper. Nicole and her friend Angela were going out for pizza and Marcel was going to the movies with his vast group of classmates. Rick would only return tomorrow afternoon. The evening would be mine. Danny's text changed all that.

Was I going to give up my evening to see him, or stick to my original plan of watching my tearjerker movie? It was a no-brainer. I wanted to see Danny.

Good day! I am available any time after 4.

Ten minutes passed and there was no immediate response, so I gathered my belongings and headed to my office. Annie was waiting for the elevator when I walked into the building. We rode up together.

"I've been meaning to ask you and Aaron over for dinner, sometimes," I said as the elevator door closed in front of us.

"How kind of you," Annie said. "I'll have to check with Aaron, of course. But that would be nice."

"I'll have to check with Rick, also. He's out of town so much," I smiled. I tried to hide the tone in my voice, but it still came off harder than I wanted to. Or expected. I knew his absence was a major factor in my vulnerability, my need for attention.

"If it doesn't work out," Annie said, "you and I can just go out together. Girls' night."

"We can do that, too," I answered. "We shall talk."

I had yet to address the text she sent last week, the one hinting that she knew I might have had company in my hotel room. That conversation would have to wait at a more appropriate time..

I sat in my cushy office chair, and as I powered up my laptop I took another look at my cell phone for any response from Danny. There were none, and I would hear nothing from him all morning. What was he up to? I didn't want to sound like a nag, so I patiently waited for him to answer back.

At 2 p.m., Danny finally replied.

> *After work, can you pick me up at the corner store near my office building?*

First the text at 7:50 a.m., then this unusual request to pick him up. What was wrong with his car?

> *I can, but only after 4,* I answered.

> *Might be better after 5. When it's dark.*

5 p.m. Corner store. Two buildings over, I answered back.

Okay, thanks.

And that was the end of our messaging for the day.

I finished work. And I didn't want to drive home, only to come back downtown an hour later to meet Danny ten blocks away from my own office. I had no errands to run. No great little store to explore, only to kill an hour. I pictured us going parking like teenagers, and it excited me. I wanted to feel myself up. Yet, the proper side of my upbringing banned me from those thoughts immediately. I thought of him doing that to me last week, and my loving it...

At the end, I drove to the corner store and fed the parking meter for an hour. I watched the traffic go by while I tried to concentrate on writing in a journal I kept in my handbag. It was mostly a jumble of notes and little grocery lists. But I occasionally fed it some thoughts. I wasn't having much luck today. I wanted to see Danny. Feel him. Smell him. Taste him.

I gave up on writing a meaningful entry, opened my black leather bag and put the book in a zippered pocket. When I straightened up, Danny was looking in the passenger door window. I smiled and unlocked the door for him. My smile weakened when I saw his expression. His eyes seemed drained of any blue, which meant Danny wasn't in a good mood. I hoped it was just a bad day at work for him. But deep inside, I knew this visit was not going to be what I had hoped for.

"Everything okay?" I asked. I'm not sure I wanted to hear his answer.

Danny turned to face me.

"I don't think I can do this, anymore."

He sounded like a little boy. It's like he didn't want to say it, but had to. I hardly heard anything after that. My heart was too busy breaking into a million pieces. I struggled to look Danny in the eyes.

"Okay," was all my voice could muster.

"Let's go for a ride," Danny suggested. And like the good girl that I am, I did as told. I started driving towards the country, distracted by the words coming out of his mouth.

"It's not you, it's me," he started. "It really is. I'm having panic attacks. I'm not sure I can handle this...this complication. I like you, MJ. I really do! But I'm not sure my heart can handle the palpitations."

I let him talk his brains out while I drove. I pulled into a side road off the country lane we were on, drove all the way to where the dirt road ended, and shut the car off. Then I fell apart. I sobbed loudly, unable to contain myself. More than anything, it stopped Danny from talking.

He unbuckled his seat belt, and moved closer to take me in his arms. I don't think he understood the irony in what he was doing. But I let him embrace me just the same.

Danny's hug soothed me. I let my guard down, and I snuggled into the pit of his neck. I watched the tears running down his shirt, and I pulled back to wipe them with the inside of my hand. Instead, Danny took my movement as a sign that I wanted a different kind of comfort, and proceeded to guide my mouth to his. Crazy as it may sound, brokenhearted or not, I lost myself in his kisses.

He didn't have sex with me like other times. He made love to me. I was a blubbering fool after that. I watched him smoke outside in the cool evening air while I shivered.

I drove Danny back to that corner store, and watched him walk away from my life. He walked out the door without even a goodbye. I went into the store, and bought junk food. I knew those chips and Dr Pepper and chocolate bars would haunt me all night, but I was no longer myself. I paid for my purchase and drove home. Once in my flannel jammies. I flipped through the vast collection of romantic movies Nicole and I had accumulated over the last few years, and found the most tear-provoking one. I bawled through the entire film while I guzzled two bottles of cherry cola before calling it a night. The chips were opened, but I barely touched them.

I went upstairs, made the mistake of looking at myself in the bedroom mirror, and had another fit of tears. I had to compose myself before the children came home.

Marcel arrived first, and simply spoke from the other side of my door.

"Good night, Mom," he said.

"G'night, Marcel," I managed to say.

"You okay Mom? You sound a little croaky," he asked. The word croaky made me chuckle, and that worked in my favour.

"I'll be fine, Marcel. Good night, sweet boy."

About an hour later, I heard Nicole come in through the front door. I had had time to compose myself, knowing I couldn't fake my way out of her attention like I could to my seventeen-year-old son. As per our established routine, Nicole came to my door, knocked slightly before opening it. Then she would tell me her adventures of the evening. But she stopped dead in her tracks when she saw me. I guess I hadn't quite cleaned up well enough.

"Mom?" Nicole asked with concern. "You look like crap."

"Love you, too, Baby Girl." I feigned a laugh.

"Can I bring you something? Fever meds?"

"Maybe some antihistamines," I answered back, knowing I'd have a terrible time falling asleep that night.

The night came and went. I barely slept an hour. I cried and relived the last twenty-four hours. And then I relived the moments I'd had with Danny. And then the time we met. I was torturing myself. I had no distraction to change my path of thinking. Had Rick been here, I could've at least cuddled to him for comfort.

I got up to pee around 5:30. I took a look in the mirror: I was a mess. And as I headed back to my bedroom, I met Nicole in the hallway. She had heard my shuffling. She looked at me with her arms crossed. "You are calling in sick, young lady," she stated. "You are in no shape to do anything today except sleep. Take care of you."

I smiled and saluted her. Nicole was always caring, observant. I needed to take her advice and not go to work that day. I looked awful.

I felt awful. And I would be of no use, at all. So two hours later, when the switchboard was staffed for the day, I called in sick.

I let myself mourn for a few more hours. Then I got up in the late morning. The house was quiet. I had it to myself until my family returned home for supper. It was a rare occurrence these days that we would all be together for dinner. I busied myself into whipping up a fantastic meal. Rick, Nicole and Marcel deserved to have my full attention again.

By the time Rick showed up, I was feeling much better. I tackled him at the door, and we showered together before our children came home from high school. Rick was surprised by my feistiness, and took it in stride. If only he knew.

Nicole was equally surprised to see how well I had recovered in just one day. She related her observances to the male members of our family. She explained how red-eyed and stuffed up I had been. Whatever flu I had caught, I was obviously winning the fight. I'm glad she saw it the way she did. One day, when her heart would get crushed like mine did, maybe then she'll figure out.

"You know what you need," Rick said. "What you need is to step away from your desk for a few days. You need a break from work. You should hop on the truck with me. Road trip. You and I."

I tried to look amused, wanting desperately to step away from work, from my day to day life, since it included non stop thoughts of Mr Russell. However, hopping on a transport truck and driving awful hours in the night, that was not the answer.

"I have a better idea," Nicole, our forever outspoken daughter, piped in. "We should go on a family trip. Pretty soon, Marcel and I will be working. And then we'll be gone. This might be our last opportunity as a family to create such memories."

"Good pitch," I laughed as I saw the bills ring up in front of my eyes.

"I agree with Nicky," Rick said. "We should look into going away for Easter."

Both Nicole and Marcel straightened up at the dinner table,

seeing this suggestion as an actual possibility. They linked their hands together, hoping that their parents would come up with a real plan. Ever since Rick had changed career paths, our family trips had basically disappeared.

Needing a boost to my morale, I chose to look into the idea that my little family of four needed to create a few more memories before Nicole and Marcel moved away.

"I'll look into it," I answered. I was feeling a lot more lighthearted.

By the end of the following week, once Rick confirmed his availability, I booked a week in Key West. Our children were old enough to appreciate the non theme park part of Florida. We would be basking in the hot sun within a few weeks. Away from work. Away from school. Away.

Our first flight brought us to Miami, and our connector one to Key West was scheduled two hours later. It gave us just enough time to refresh, and maybe grab a small meal at the many eateries in the International Miami Airport. Nicole and I headed for the nearest women's washroom, while the men of our family grabbed a few burgers for the four of us.

Out of habit, I powered up my cell phone. And that's when I saw it. A text from Danny. Just when I felt my heart was repairing itself, just when I could survive without thinking of him every hour of every day, just when I thought life without him could be a possibility, Danny had to make contact with me.

Can we meet? We need to talk.

CHAPTER 34

♂

She refused to see me at our preferred room, #429 at our hotel off the highway. So I had to settle on meeting MJ at the same spot we had seen each other last, on the dirt road up by a future subdivision just outside city limits. Prompt as usual, MJ was there before me. She was sitting in her car, showing zero expression.

"I am truly sorry for hurting you," I said as I got into her vehicle.

"It's my issue, not yours," MJ said, cold as ice. "If I get hurt, it's for me to deal with it. Not you."

You could cut the crispness in the air, her voice was so frigid. I had some major repairing to do if I wanted to keep her in my life. I leaned in to kiss her. But MJ pushed me back with both hands on my chest. I tried again. And once again, she pushed me away.

"You hurt me," she screamed. Tears of fury welled in her eyes at the sight of me. It took her breath away. It took mine too.

"I know I did," I spoke gently.

"I don't think you understand how painful this has been for me," MJ continued. Her eyes were brimming, ready to spill over. My heart sank. "Losing my mother was nothing compared to losing you. Especially right after Edwardsville. I kept questioning what I had done wrong..." Her big brown eyes glistened. They were looking straight into mine.

"I'm a coward, MJ," I sighed. "I got scared. I don't want to lose what I have at home. I'm comfortable. You, you're exciting to be with. I can't seem to have enough of you. I always want more. And that scared me. It still does. But I can't imagine living without you, right now. Do you know what I mean?"

"If you *ever* do this to me again, it will be the last time. You will never see me again. And I mean it," MJ said as she bit her lower lip, trying to stop the quiver. Her nostrils flared. Her eyebrows frowned. Her voice croaked. She was struggling not to cry. Her index finger poked my ribs. "My heart broke into a million fucking pieces!"

I looked at her. I had destroyed the best thing in my life.

"You have the right to do what you want," she bravely recovered, "but I will never let you play with my feelings again." MJ whispered to herself...but I heard it.

"I know, Babe," I said, surprised at the words coming out of my mouth. Babe? I couldn't deny my feelings for her. "I promise never to do that again."

"If you need to break this off, so be it," MJ said, her tone turning defensive. "But this is the last time I will ever take you back. This arrangement is hard enough as it is. Don't add heartbreaks on top of it. I am giving you one chance. That's it."

I patted her lap, trying to show remorse, empathy. She responded by leaning into me. Her hand pulled my neck towards her. Our lips hungrily found themselves, and my hands quickly got busy. She was ready for me, once again. I opened my eyes to look at her. There was a pained but happy look on her face. My fingers lingered on her scalp as I tasted her spent tears on her cheeks.

Then she smiled, her pearly teeth glistening. I never thought I'd see that smile, again. I rubbed my tongue against them, and MJ squealed. I knew that sound. It meant she was hungry for me. Reaching second base wasn't gonna do it, today. I had to fuck her, then and there.

Nothing would've been more satisfying than to rip her blouse open. I wanted to do so much to her. With her. And to think I had broken this off. Yes, it was complicated. In a big way. And I may have been playing with fire. But watching MJ experience sex with me like this, it had become my personal aphrodisiac. I wanted to try everything with her.

I started to undo the first few buttons of her blouse. But then MJ took over and popped her entire top open. Her heaving chest was begging to be manhandled. I looked around, even though I knew there would be nobody nearby for miles to come. My hands got busy. She tasted warm and salty. And the sigh coming out of MJ only made it taste that much better. I thought all this time that I was the horny one. We were both equally hungry for each other, and I was going to enjoy the ride.

"Come sit on me," I said as I lowered my seat down. I tapped on my lap, inviting her to join me on my side of the car. MJ, in turn, looked around, as well. There were no humans around to see or hear us. She took off her shoes before climbing onto her seat. She studied the best way to move onto my side with the least amount of effort. All the while keeping her dignity. I watched her struggle. She was trying to decide where her right foot should go. I helped her along by grabbing the contour of her ass, and guided her onto me.

"You feel that?" I whispered. " I hope you're ready."

MJ moaned. Her hands were unsure where to land. I still had her semi-suspended.

With all we had gone through in Edwardsville, MJ was a newbie, all over again. I was hoping it would go away quickly. I wanted to concentrate on exploring new things with her, not revisit the progress we had gone through so far.

Watching her over me with her hands busy keeping herself up, I had the perfect opportunity to take advantage of feeling her up any way I wanted.

"Kiss me," I commanded. MJ leaned in on me to do just that. It was a tender kiss. Not needy. She was no longer upset at me. The touch of her lips on mine proved that. "Do it again."

She smiled as she followed my wishes. MJ leaned in again to kiss me. She pulled back from our kissing, and looked down at her skirt. She was wanting more.

"I no longer want to see you in any underwear. I want immediate access, whenever I please." MJ's eyes rolled in heat. "And I mean it. I don't care how pretty or lacy or frilly these bras and panties of yours are. I'm not interested in them. I'm only interested in what they're hiding."

"I need you," she moaned. She wasn't going to be able to handle this foreplay much longer.

I, myself, was being tortured by everything she did, touched, felt. Her tongue was licking her lips while her eyes stayed closed. Her throat was fully stretched as her head leaned back.

MJ was definitely in her prime, and I had the privilege of exploring her new awakenings. I was responsible for teaching this woman anything I desired.

With no mercy, I rammed in her hard. I had control of her emotions, of her body, of her every want. I lifted her hips slightly, and rammed them back down. I could feel my end coming, and I wanted her to come, as well. My only way to insure she would come hard was to tilt her body back, towards the windshield.

I remained laying down. I pushed her body back towards my knees. I pushed down both my belly and her small flap of skin under her belly button. My eyes didn't want to miss a thing. And as I let my middle finger rub her sacred clit, I finally got to feel MJ pulsing. She came hard. I came too. She was also sobbing in the process.

"Are you okay?" I managed to breathe out. I was still waiting for my own heart to slow down.

"I'm not ready to let you go," MJ panted as her tears zigzagged down her face. Her arms wrapped themselves tightly around my neck.

"Neither am I," I answered back. "Let's just enjoy the ride. We'll take this one day at a time."

And from that moment on, I never saw MJ wear underwear in my presence. And I never broke up with her, ever again.

CHAPTER 35

♀

As we got into a routine of meeting weekly at the cheap hotel up the road from my home, I started relaxing more. I was very particular of all things I did concerning him. I needed to make sure that if this affair was to work for us both, I needed to keep it hush hush. I deleted all communications as they got received. I wouldn't wear perfume on the day we'd meet. I didn't want Tina to suspect anything. I fretted less about Danny's musky and tobacco scents on me.

I needed Danny in my life. He knew which of my buttons to touch, buttons I never knew I had until he pressed them. But he also became my best friend, something else I never had. I confided in him, as he did with me. We started relying on each other, and looking forward to our time together. Then one day, Danny brought up the unspoken subject. What were our goals in this affair? How far were we ready to go with this? And then what?

"Honestly, I don't know," I answered. "I miss you when you leave. And I'm so grateful when I have you back with me."

I didn't want to spook him by mentioning the unmentionable. Maybe one day, we would be one. One day. But it was just a dream of mine.

"I don't know, either," Danny said. "I enjoy every moment I have with you. You are like an addiction to me. The more I see you, the more I want. I'm just not sure what to do about it."

"I'm at that crossroad, also," I said as I pulled away from his embrace. I leaned my head into the crook of my arm. I wanted to be able to see his face, especially his amazing eyes. Most people have body language to dissect. Danny had the colour of his eyes to speak his truth. "I want you in my life, but I don't want to hurt my family."

"I feel the same way," Danny added. He mirrored my position, facing me as we spoke. "But I want to wake up with you, again. And share meals with you. And create memories."

I think Danny saw the fear forming in my eyes. He reached over and rubbed the ball of my exposed shoulder. He tried to comfort me over his own anxiety.

"We don't have to make any decisions about this," he whispered as he pulled me in. He feathered my hair away from my forehead, then planted a strong, comforting kiss on my hairline "This is just a conversation. Nothing more."

"I know," I breathed out, "but it's one we can't ignore forever. We need to know what's next for us."

"No, we don't," Danny said firmly as he yanked my hair back so we could see each other. "I know what I want. I'm just not sure how to get there. And if I never get there, it's not the end of the world."

Danny sat on his knees. The bed shook as he positioned himself comfortably. "I want you in my life. I want to have you in my bed. I want to have access to this goddess in front of me. Right now. At all times."

That made me laugh aloud.

"I mean it," Danny continued. "You are goddamn sexy, and I want a piece of you whenever I feel the need."

"Oh please," I waved my hand. "I am far from a goddess."

"Get up!" he said. He got up himself from his own sitting position.

"What? Why?" I asked, confused again.

"Get up!" he repeated. This time, he extended his hand for me to take. He walked me up to the full length mirror facing the make-shift closet. "Now look at what I see." I was embarrassed to be standing with him in front of such a revealing mirror. I kept looking away, so Danny turned on the overhead light. It gave off shadows that were far from complementary.

"Please, no," I begged.

"No," Danny stood firmly. There was a lesson he wanted to teach me. "I want you to see what I see. I see this beautiful soul living in a great body with soft creamy skin."

I giggled, but he continued feeling my body parts as he described them.

"Look at those long, lean legs," Danny continued, bending down to my ankles. He was feeling my legs on the outside as he slowly stood up. "These legs are athletic, yet tender to the touch. And they wrap around my body so well."

This time, I burst out laughing. Danny ignored me.

"And then we have these hips!"

He spoke those words slowly, purposely. And with his deepest voice possible. It made me lick my lips.

"Yeah, Baby," Danny whispered in my ear. "You lick those soft lips of yours. I know my words are getting to you."

My knees trembled. I was getting cold, so I joined my hands together to try to keep myself warm. Danny kindly turned around, grabbed his jacket off the closet rod, and put it on my shoulders to keep me warm.

"As I was saying," he continued with both his hands back on my hips. "Those hips I've held. I've kissed. I've seen them gyrate as you come. Those hide the sweetest pussy I've ever had the pleasure to drink."

I know I moaned, but I was more concerned in seeing my knees buckling again.

"Can we sit down?" I asked. I was no longer trusting my legs to support me.

"Actually, I need to go," Danny answered, cutting our time together short. "I need to see you again. Before next week. I want to finish this conversation."

"I can make it happen," was all I was able to say. I was relieved from the wonderful torture my body was enduring as he dissected my body parts in front of that mirror. I was also disappointed that our afternoon got cut short. But that's the life of being the other woman.

"You have plans tonight?" he asked, as if the idea had just popped into his head. I thought quickly. After feeding the kids, they'd be gone again. It left me with a few hours to myself.

"I'm free after 5:30," I smiled, hoping for the best. Danny nodded in approval. His eyes brimmed grey, and switched to piercing blue, right in front of me. He was happy. I just wanted to fall in his arms and make love to him, again.

"Okay," he said, talking fast as he gathered his things together. "I have to go home, now. But I can meet you back here after 6. I'll just tell Tina I'm meeting friends for a round of pool. Here's the key. Get here first. I expect you naked."

CHAPTER 36

♀

Summer was approaching quickly. Hotels would be raising their prices for the tourist season. The road traffic would increase, as well. Walking across the parking lot of our hotel, I started thinking that Danny and I needed to find another spot for our rendezvous.

I went straight to the elevator. On the fourth floor, I started walking towards our usual room. There was Danny, leaning against the door frame. He made me smile. I sped up my pace and opened my arms wide to embrace him. And he, in return, grabbed my buttocks, lifting me up. After crossing the threshold, Danny put me down so he could close the door behind us. Once the latch over the door was in place, our escapade began.

Unlike what I had known with Rick, Danny was not the type of lover who would meet me in the bed and then start touching me. Danny always started as soon as he had me in sight. With both of us still fully dressed, he started licking my exposed collarbone. He went up my throat, settling his tongue inside my ear. I dropped my handbag, and stepped out of my heels. Every breath I drew was heavy. My throat was releasing sounds only Danny could make me do. I wanted out of my clothes. But the heat of his breathing inside my ear canal paralyzed me in place. I let him do whatever foreplay he chose to do. I was always game for anything.

Without losing a beat, I felt his right hand get under my skirt. I was without underwear, as requested. I had my silky piece tucked into my handbag, waiting to be put back on before I'd leave. But for now, I was at his mercy while his fingers explored.

Danny's tongue stopped flicking my ear so that his teeth could nibble my earlobe. I wanted to crumble, I was so desperate for his loving. Danny tortured me with his lingering touches. As he pulled on my lobe, I felt my entire basin put its weight onto his hand. I wanted out. I wanted my release. I wanted him to stop. I wanted him to never stop. What a mess I was in his presence.

I heard him snicker in my ear as he continued to nibble. His fingers below rubbed my private area. He was lubing me up for what was yet to come.

"Come with me," Danny growled as he led me to the bed.

I walked crookedly to the bedside and waited for Danny's hands to release me before I could sit down. His eyes were staring me down. I was losing my reality. I wanted to exchange heat. Or bodily fluids. Or kisses. Anything else but this nerve-racking glare in silence.

Without letting go, Danny dropped to his knees. My body crumbled across the bed. Piece by piece, slowly, methodically, Danny removed my clothing. And as every item came off, his finger traced my exposed skin. The urge to urinate was instant. My nerves were spent by the time he had me completely naked.

My blazer and blouse were thrown behind me. My skirt was slumped at my feet. The Cheshire Cat smile Danny wore said it all. He knew he owned me when I was in his presence. I was his puppet.

He could do as he pleased with me. He quickly stripped himself of his own clothing, standing completely naked in front of me.

All he wore was his Bulova watch, his socks and the most aggressive pair of human eyes I had ever seen. His blue irises were dark like a brand new pair of jeans. His mouth was curling like a lion before pouncing on its prey. I was mesmerized by Danny's fierceness, and was unable to look away.

CHAPTER 37

♂

The other women I've had relationships with, and not just sexually...I'm talking about people like my mom and my sisters... they've always wanted something from me. Needed something from me. I rescued them. I protected them. This made me feel wanted. Valued.

But MJ is unlike any other woman I've known. Though she's educated and independent, respected at her work, I, Daniel Charles Russell, have something that MJ needs.

Yet, here she was changing me as well. I was becoming more sensitive to her way of living. To be truthful to my own feelings. Call it a mid life crisis, maybe. But I was heading down that tunnel, faster and faster. I was just glad to have MJ tag along with me.

I have never been known as a man of many words when it comes to expressing my feelings. No true man is. I say what I want. I say what I need. I say it as it is. But when it comes to the matters of the heart, I have never been comfortable sharing how I felt. I tell my woman of the moment that I like how they look, or which one of their body parts attracts me. But select few have heard me say the word Love as a verb. It's just my nature. Maybe because I saw my mother seek it so desperately, I prefer not showing my feelings to a woman. Any woman. Cathy. Ellen. Tina. A few in between them. I always seem to keep a distance between us, just so I'll have the upper hand if it doesn't work out.

But maybe I should rethink this coolness with Tina. We have survived this long. I should be softer for her. But then again, I'm sleeping around with another woman behind her back. I can be such a jerk, sometimes.

I know deep inside I have fallen for MJ. But if I keep it buried inside, it won't be real. This charade might go on forever. Right?

We'd been going through our lists and MJ's list was coming to an end, since hers was so short. In her defence, she didn't know what was out there. I knew she'd never seen porn. But I was also pretty sure she'd never seen a naked woman. The fact that I was the only other man she'd seen naked besides her husband, that said a lot. Unlike MJ's list, mine kept growing as I saw her get over her shyness. MJ was warming up to my dirty language. I kept pushing my luck every week. She let me.

Tina, bless her heart, did not suspect a thing. It made running around with MJ easier. I know I should have felt more guilt than I did, some remorse. But I hadn't reached that point, yet. Me feeling sorry for Tina, that was more like it. Anybody deserves to be respected by a faithful mate. Tina was no different.

But like I said, MJ sparked a flame in me I didn't know I had. And her sense of wonderment was super fucking sexy to me. I couldn't let her go. I tried once, but I ended up feeling empty and miserable without her. So I continued seeing MJ despite all the dangers of being caught. The dangers of losing what I'd created with Tina over the years.

On this particular Wednesday, now greeting the front desk staff by their given names, I headed for our room. They knew what we were doing. They knew who MJ was. But they kept our privacy safe, greeting us by nods only. I came in with a can of whipped cream and a bottle of maraschino cherries. I'm not 100% certain what I was planning to do with them. But one plopped inside MJ's belly button came to mind, as well as spraying her entire chest with the whipped cream. Of course, I would have to suck it all clean, and hear her giggle. How I loved her giggling. It took years off of me to listen to this woman genuinely laugh at my gestures and bad jokes.

MJ arrived a half hour late. And as I opened the door to let her in, she flew into the room a bit kerfuffled, out of breath.

"I'm so sorry for being late," she explained. "I was on my way out of the office, and I got a phone call I had to deal with before I could come here. I made it as fast as I could. Please don't be upset!"

"Relax, MJ. It's all good."

"I was upset that this happened," she continued. "I was upset that nobody else could actually deal with the issue in hand. I swear I tried my best to come quicker."

"I'm not upset," I smiled as I took her coat off of her.

"I didn't want you to be angry at me," she pleaded.

"How could I be angry at you? I love you too much."

And there it was. As the words escaped my mouth, my world crashed into slow motion. How could I have said those words to her? I had forgotten to filter them out. I had said the *L* word to her. And I knew how crucial women took this. I became instantly quiet. I was trying to recover, trying to see if she had actually heard me. I finished hanging her coat in the closet, and looked at her for any signs of the word love penetrating her heart. MJ continued undressing as if I'd said nothing at all. Maybe she hadn't heard me.

"I also had to make a few wardrobe changes before coming here," MJ smiled as she lifted the side of her skirt to reveal a naked bum. She had listened to me, and always showed up without panties or a bra on. Yes, it was easy access for me. But it was so much more than that. I was subject to seeing her level of excitement develop by how stiff her nipples were as they poked through her clothes. And it also excited her, despite MJ not wanting to. She would get herself into the predicament of being without a bra as she drove. Or she'd leave whatever gas station she'd stop at to remove those pieces. And with her loose boobs pulling at the buttons of her blouse, MJ was quickly starting to enjoy the physical challenge of it. But even more, the mental fun of being a little naughty.

I've learned with her that attraction is what gets two people together. But to sustain an attraction, a desire for that person you're with, you had to fuck their minds. Not their body. The body was the vessel you use to have sex with. But it was the soul that kept one coming back for more. That was the difference between having sex and making love. She and I were making love, but in my hard way. MJ taught me that lesson, and it had been a long ways coming.

Don't get me wrong. MJ is a gorgeous middle-aged woman. She has wavy brown hair with some red in it. She calls it auburn. Her dark brown eyes are sparkly whenever I see them. Her hourglass figure is fantastic when she covers it with a dress or skirt. It really pops out those curves of hers. I want to slap her ass every time I see her. And those tits! I could bury myself in her cleavage, and have her suffocate me with them. I want to play with them. Fuck them. Suck them. Nibble them. Lick them from top to bottom. Next time we have an overnighter, I want to suckle them for an hour while she tries talking to her family. I want to see her struggle. Yes, I'm that depraved.

I'm amused by MJ's appearance. She walks around in these conservative clothes she wears, carries herself like a lady. Yet, she has this eager beaver hiding under. I don't see the little flab of skin over her tummy like she does. MJ frets too much. I mean, I see it, obviously. But it's never been an issue for me. Every woman I've bedded down in my adult life has not had a Barbie figure. Heck! I'm no Ken. But MJ, she has the best shaped body I've ever had the pleasure to play with.

But what's attracted me the most about Marie-Josée Taylor is her unrelenting smile. She has these two rows of perfectly aligned white pearly teeth. And she smiles like she breathes: effortless. It comes so naturally to her, she doesn't even know she's smiling. To be that happy. To feel that happy all the time. What a gift she has. And I want some of that.

Even after all this time, MJ has remained fun and new to explore. As if she was a brand new toy to play with. In many ways, she is. I made it my goal to push her envelope as much as I thought she could handle. And in return, I've searched for a different part of her body to explore with my lips. That afternoon would be no different.

I dove into the bed, startling MJ. Yet, she didn't move. She was finally comfortable with my antics. That meant I could attempt something new that day. MJ's body was warm and soft. She greeted me with her legs open, ready to receive me. She was either sex deprived, or falling for me. Or both. Either way, I took advantage of her vulnerability. As I knelt in front of her, I brought her legs up to me.

"Look at me," I commanded. MJ looked straight into my eyes. Her mouth was barely open. I could hear that her heartbeat affected her breathing. She knew we were in for a ride, that afternoon.

I explored her contour, focusing on her divine hips. And I made myself a mental note that I would one day fuck her ass. It had been asking for it. It had been provoking me. The way MJ was moving her hips as I touched her back, her ass was begging to be loved, too. Just not today. I needed a condom for that. And MJ wasn't ready, anyways.

However, I did the second best thing. I knelt back a bit on the bed, and opened her legs wider. MJ was panting, she was so ready to be fucked. I plunged right into the warm embrace of her body.

I waited for her to be done before releasing my own load. MJ got up and used the washroom while I waited for my heart to slow down. MJ came back with a wet washcloth, and tended to my parts. She held them tenderly as she wiped me clean.

"Do you feel as stuck as I am in all this?" she asked. "Because I'm finding myself stuck. I don't know where we're going with this... this affair. And it's making me batty."

"Come here," I said as I opened my arms. MJ sat in between my legs while we faced each other. I put my arms around her. "I'm as lost as you are," I started. "But I do know I don't want to lose you. You're my best friend. Heck, you're my only friend."

"You're *my* best friend, also," she said. "I hate being apart from you. I feel so alone when I'm not with you." Her words were starting to scare me, so I pulled away from the embrace.

"Listen," I said, my voice firmer. "I grew up in a broken home. I don't want my step kids to go through that. They're like my own. And I am committed to be there for them."

"So what are you saying?" MJ asked.

"I'm saying, I want to be with you. Let's face it: nobody fucks me like you do. And I'm sure you can say the same thing about me." MJ lowered her head and smiled. "But I will not abandon these kids until they're adults. It's up to you if you want to wait for me."

MJ remained quiet. I left her in the bed to ponder while I used the washroom. She hadn't moved when I came back out. I didn't want to push it. I walked to my clothes and started getting dressed. That's when MJ strode over and pulled me back into the bed, and pushed my underwear down my legs.

"I wanna play some more," she smiled as she knelt in front of me.

"Oh, Baby," I started protesting. "I am all about playing with you. But I don't come that easily. I haven't been able to do that since high school." No matter what I said, MJ refused to listen. She gave me a relentless blowjob until I came again, no matter how long it took.

"I'm ready to wait for you," she said as she wiped me off her mouth.

CHAPTER 38

♀

"Can you talk?" Danny asked.

"Yes," I answered. "Annie's away from her desk at the moment. And I see no one else. What's up?"

"Tina is at bingo, tonight. You wanna share a bite?"

Hearing her name, even though she had done nothing to me, still felt like salt stinging my eyes. It just rubbed me wrong. My own two children were gone for the evening. And of course, Rick was out of town. So nothing kept me from accepting Danny's invitation. Except, I didn't want to be seen publicly with him on a social outing. It was just not prudent.

"What do you suggest?" I asked. Even I couldn't believe the words coming out of my mouth.

"Take out," Danny answered casually. "We'll eat it at my office. Nobody else is there. What do you want to eat?"

"Sushi?" I suggested, knowing darn right he'd refuse. It made me laugh out loud.

"I'll pick up some Chinese," he decided. "Anything special you like?"

I wasn't a fan of Chinese. But I went along, for his sake.

"As long as there's beef & broccoli, I'm good," I answered him.

I got to his building, and Danny was already inside. I walked up to the back entrance, as he'd instructed. And Danny opened it before I had the time to knock.

"I heard your van pull up," he smiled as he let me in. He grabbed my derrière as I walked by him. His child play amused me.

Danny had set up an eating arrangement in the staff room, taking up a corner of the table where we could sit knee to knee. He had bought fried rice, sweet & sour chicken balls, beef & broccoli, and pork chow mein. I watched as he devoured his food, forking it in.

"Let me feed you," I suggested. His head tilted in question. "Please," I continued.

Danny put his fork down, and let me feed him his supper with the help of chop sticks. I wanted to slow down his consumption. I wanted him to taste every morsel. Instead, it turned into a romantic moment between the two of us. I continued giving him his dinner while he fed me with his fork. Halfway through our plates, I had had enough, and told him so. However, I continued feeding him. Danny took the opportunity to grab both my breasts that were being crushed on the table. I smiled, and let him.

My intention had worked. Danny got full without eating all the food he had purchased. His intention had worked also, as my body warmed up to his touches. Now we both wanted more.

"Let me pack this up for you," I offered. "You can have the rest, another day."

Danny took me by the wrists, and led me down the hall to the copy room. Unlike the staff room, this one had no windows.

I turned around to kiss him, knowing where this was heading. My eyes closed while his hands squeezed my chest.

"Fuck me."

He looked at me in awe.

"You said the word *Fuck*," Danny frowned. "You've never said that before."

"There's a first for everything," I smiled. "Now fuck me."

CHAPTER 39

♂

Once the deed was done, I pulled up my pants while she straightened her clothes. I glanced momentarily her way, and saw the calmness in her face. The affection she had for me was real. It was mutual. I adored this woman. She made me want to be a better man. She made me like myself again. And my feelings for her were growing in leaps and bounds.

"I bought you a gift," I said, breaking the silence.

"Oh?"

"The last time I had some of these, I'd fished it out of your bra."

MJ laughed out loud as she caught the box of chocolate-covered almonds in midair.

"Anything else I should know about you?" she asked as she snuggled under my arm, the two of us sitting on the floor of the copy room.

"I finished school living with my grandparents. Then I enrolled at New Brunswick Community College. I was planning to become a plumber. I was actually doing real good. I had completed two of my blocks before more tragedy happened at my mother's house."

"What happened at home?" MJ asked as she sat up straight.

"Actually, I no longer called it home. It hadn't been home since moving in with my dad's parents. Once my mother's new husband came into the picture, I probably never called it home, again.

"Pete died suddenly-"

"Happy ending?" MJ said, hoping for one.

"Not a story I'm ready to share. But with Pete's income gone, and my mom unable to work for a while, my sisters turned to me for help. And out of loyalty, I left college and went to work for a plumbing company as an apprentice."

"What a good son, you were," MJ's sad face was turning to a smile. "You're such a good person, Danny Russell." She kissed me hard on the cheek before I continued.

"I spent the next five years living with Mom and my sisters until they all married off. Rachel is the one who had Mom move in with her and her family. It left me, at twenty-eight-years-old, alone. I had to start my life all over again.

"I hadn't lost my dream of becoming somebody. I looked into going back to college. Continue my education. Instead, my employer offered to teach me the business part of his company. He wanted me to handle the books. I welcomed the opportunity and dove right into the challenge. I took evening classes in finances to hone in my new learned skills.

"As the business grew under my management, the need to hire an assistant of some sort came up. I asked to have a girl to book appointments, answer the phone, do some filing. She could even do some of the bookkeeping. That's when I met Ellen, my future wife."

"Wait, what!? You're married?"

"*Was* married," I answered.

"I never knew you were ever married, Danny," MJ exclaimed as she pulled away from me. "Why did you never tell me this, before?"

"Old history," was my answer.

"Old history?"

"Anyways," I continued, trying to ignore her shock. "Ellen was shy. But she took an immediate liking to me. She liked my outgoing personality. My skill to take lead in everything I did. Ellen liked the twinkle in my eyes. At first, I didn't notice her sneaking glances at me. But eventually, I could no longer ignore them. I'd catch her looking at me. It was flattering, but she wasn't my type.

"Ellen was a kind person, but not a catch for a date. But I still ended up asking her out. And then I asked her out for another date. And another one. Next thing you know, we were engaged. But once we got married, we both became antsy. We couldn't figure out why. So we decided to pack up and move out west.

"I got a job at the CBC in Edmonton in the administration office. Ellen became part of a secretary pool at the University of Alberta. A year later, still not feeling happy, Ellen packed up and moved back to Holliston. I was going to join her a month later once a work project I was working on would be completed.

"The day came for me to rent a U-Haul and drive across the country to join my wife. Instead of rushing myself and making the trip in three days, I did it in six days. I enjoyed my time alone. As I reflected on my last month in Alberta, I realized I hadn't been alone with my thoughts in ages. I enjoyed the peace and quiet.

"Ellen was staying with her parents while waiting for me to come back. By the time I got there, Ellen had decided that she wanted out of our marriage. I gladly gave her her freedom. But then I found myself alone. Again. Ellen quickly found herself an old boyfriend and married him."

"Wow!" MJ sighed.

"Anyways, I needed to find a job ASAP, and one that would keep me busy. That's when I got hired by Juno Electronics. At first, I was a phone rep. I answered phone calls and scheduled repair appointments. Within six months, I climbed the corporate ladder. Eventually, I became the Regional Sales Manager. I now have eight reps under me.

"I was still recovering from my break-up with Ellen. I was not looking at all for anyone, but I did befriend this waitress at the local breakfast diner. I soon learned of her struggles of being a single mom. I started staying longer whenever I ate there, and I asked Tina a bit more about herself." MJ nodded, understanding.

"Tina was pretty with straight black hair. She wore her t-shirts snug around her chest. She's much younger than me. But I don't care. I just got a liking to her. And I wanted to be her hero. So I asked her out. She accepted. And by our third date, I had moved in with her and her two young children. Four months later, Tina and I bought a house. And we're still there, today."

"You were married..."

"Enough of that," I said as we both got up off the floor. "So...I believe we've done everything on your sex list."

"I'm not sure I need to learn anything else," MJ said. She was sucking in her bottom lip.

"Oh, Baby, was that a challenge?" I laughed. She seemed lost in her thoughts.

"Okay, MJ. What's going on?"

"With great hesitation, I'm offering to check a few more off of your list," she said.

"Wow!" I exclaimed. "What changed your mind?"

"I'm afraid you'll tire of me once these lists are completed," MJ answered as she looked away.

I waited. I knew that every word coming out of my mouth needed to be perfect.

"MJ, when we run out, we'll just make new lists."

Her head swung towards me, making the tears that had welled in her eyes swirl down her cheeks. My message had come through clearly. MJ was not going to lose me that easily.

CHAPTER

40

♀

As I had predicted, those following summer months were not a good time to meet at Room 429. Danny and I had to be creative in where to get together. We needed to find an alternative establishment that wasn't far. And also, I needed to be unknown to the locals.

Danny came up with a motel in rural Nova Scotia. It was less than an hour's drive for us both. Nobody would know me. And if they knew Danny, it was through his business. So they wouldn't know his personal family members.

I played hooky from work once again, off for the afternoon. Danny had taken the entire day off, and I found out he had once gone fishing up the river behind the motel. That's how he had discovered the place. We met at a gas station a hop skip away from this inn. I climbed into his car, leaving mine unattended in the gas station parking lot for the few hours we'd be gone. I'm not sure why I was surprised by what

I saw in his car. Empty wrappers were strewn all over the backseat. Empty pop cans littered the floor behind me. Maybe I was too clean, but I was certain this was the other extreme. Even more surprising was the cigarette butts ready to overflow in the ashtray. I didn't even know they still made ashtrays in vehicles.

"I knew you smoked," I said as Danny put the car in gear, "but I guess I didn't know to what extent."

"Tina and I both do," he exhaled. "Last time, I cleaned the car up for your sake."

Until then, Tina was just a name to me. But I now saw myself sitting in her seat. And it was her lips that touched some of those cigarettes. It made her real for the first time, and I felt uncomfortable. I needed to shake off my guilt before Danny and I stepped out of the car. Their car. I was no longer certain I wanted to be doing this.

Danny shut off the car and put the key in his pocket as he stepped into the warm breeze that welcomed us to the motel. He saw my long face, but chose to ignore it. The motel key was attached to this massive wooden key chain with the room number hand-carved and painted in black.

"Okay, MJ. What's bothering you?"

"Seeing her stuff in the car made her real," I answered.

"Tina?"

I nodded.

"Well that's the last time we take my car," he laughed, wanting to end the conversation.

"You're not disturbed by that?"

Danny wrapped his arms around me.

"Listen," he started, choosing every word carefully. "You and I are living the same parallel. We are both in this together. We're both attached to someone else. Yet, we keep showing up for these get-togethers, week after week. That means we both benefit from it. Don't worry about Tina. She's my business. Just like your husband is your business."

"His name is Rick," I mumbled.

"I don't care," Danny said as he rubbed my buttocks. "All I care about, right now, is to get you naked and breathless."

As I pulled my blue polka dot dress over my head, I smelled the cigarette smoke.

"Oh no," I cried out. "I can't go home smelling like this."

"Can you wash it in the tub?" Danny suggested.

"And then what? Wear a wet dress back home?"

"If you want," he smiled. "Or we can wait here until it dries. Give me your car key. I'll bring mine to the gas station, and return with yours and drape your dress on your seat to dry in the sun."

I looked at him as if he'd just grown an extra head. "Have you done this before?" I had to ask.

"No," he answered, offended. "But doesn't it make sense?"

"Perfect sense," I breathed out.

I kissed him on the cheek and he drove off. In the meantime, I opened the small bar of soap supplied in the compact bathroom, and filled the bathtub with lukewarm water. I lathered my dress while kneeling on the floor. As I was unplugging the tub, and rinsing off my dress under the running water, Danny came into the bathroom, having returned from the gas station.

"One day, I'm going to fuck that ass of yours," he proclaimed as both his hands grabbed a hold of my derrière. He brought me closer to him, turned me around and kissed me tenderly on the lips.

I wrung the dress dry to the best of my abilities, then gave it to him to go spread it over my dashboard to dry. It gave me time to hop under the sheets. Danny quickly came back into the room and locked all locks on the door behind him. He then drew the curtains closed and stripped naked.

"Now where were we?" he joked as he jumped into the bed with me.

CHAPTER 41

♀

anny brought my dress back in. It was still a bit damp. At least, it was warm. I put it on, and struggled to pull it down my thighs as the wet material clung to my skin. He watched me with amusement. Danny was enjoying the show.

"This will always be my favourite dress on you," his voice rumbled as he took a hold of my buttocks. "The way it clings on you. The colour against your flushed skin. The colour against your hair. And with no bra, your nipples are creating extra polka dots."

His right hand came up and pinched my left one, twisting it slightly. Despite having had an amazing afternoon of playing with him, my knees still wanted to crumble at his touch. I managed instead to lean in and kiss him.

We hopped into my vehicle to drop off the gigantic room key. But once inside the motel office, I changed my mind, and kept the key with me. After all, it was ours until eleven the next morning. I just didn't tell Danny. I drove him back to the gas station and watched him speed off towards home. Then I drove back to our rented room. I locked myself in, and peeled off the moist navy dress. I turned on the television set for white noise, and hopped back into the bed. I could smell him on the bed sheets, and I snuggled myself into them. I fell asleep watching a nameless soap opera.

I woke up to a dark room with flickering light coming from the television set. Good gracious! I had slept hours, and it was now dark. I scrambled to find my cell phone. I saw that both Nicole and Marcel had texted and called me several times.

"Mom! Where are you?" were the first words coming out of my firstborn's mouth when she answered my call.

"I'm so sorry, Honey. I lost track of time, window shopping. I'll be home within the hour."

"Mom, you need to come home," Nicole's voice croaked. "Grand-Père is in the hospital. They think he had a stroke."

My heart dropped. My father was invincible in my eyes. He couldn't be ill. He always had my back, and here I was, gallivanting for an entire afternoon. I wasn't there for him when he needed me.

"I'm on my way straight to the hospital."

"Marcel and I are already here," she whimpered. "Please hurry."

"Does Dad know?" I asked as I gathered my clothes together.

"He's not answering, either," Nicole said.

"Okay. I'll be there as soon as possible."

I hung up, and put on the now fully dry dress. I bee-lined for the hospital, trying to drive calmly. I tried to think of anything to keep my mind from wandering towards the worst. I tried to make sense of my last few hours. Why did I return? Why did I find comfort in a motel room with the television on? What was happening to me? And the more I tried to understand, the more confused and edgy I became. So I settled on the radio, zoning out until I got to the hospital parking lot.

I was heading to the ER to find my family when I saw Marcel in the lobby.

"Mom," he said as bravely as he could. "I'm glad you're here. Follow me."

Quickly, silently, we sprinted to the ICU on our right. I found my father covered in a jungle of tubes and wires. By his side was Nicole. My face dropped at the sight of him. I took his hand into mine, feeling how chilly it was. Just then, the nurse assigned to him came into his room. She looked at us, and slowly shook her head. There was not much more they could do, except keep him comfortable, she said. I spoke tenderly to the first man I ever loved.

"Allô Papa," I said as calmly as my voice would let me. "It's times like this that I wish I would've learned French more. To be one with you. You have been the best Papa a girl could've asked for. I will forever be thankful for that."

My children watched me with their eyes wide.

"You have been very brave. You stayed awake until I came. I'm here now. It's time to let go. It's time for you to be with Mom. It's time. Je t'aime." I kissed him goodbye on his forehead, and my children followed suit. "Bonne nuit, Papa," I said as I squeezed his hand.

He died a few hours later, the three of us watching him pass. Embracing Nicole on my left, and Marcel on my right, we walked out together. We drove home as a family.

Once home, I whipped up a batch of brownies, despite the hour, and the three of us ate that for a late supper, laughing and crying while reminiscing about my Papa, their Grand-Père, before calling it a night.

Sometimes before four in the morning, I woke up, and remembered what had happened just a few hours previously. I was now an orphan. Checking my cell, Rick had yet to make contact. Where was he?

I went downstairs to quench my thirst. In my darkest moments... heck, in our family's darkest moment, the man of our house was nowhere to be found. These last several years, without really paying attention to it, I had become a single parent. I ran the house, raised the children, and coordinated repairmen. Had we grown apart? Had we fallen out of love with each other? Is that what this was all about?

Nicole found me on the family room love seat with my feet tucked underneath my legs and a cup of lukewarm tea nestled in between my palms. I was staring blankly at the horizon as the sky changed its colours.

"You okay, Mom?" she asked as I moved over to make room for her on the velvet love seat. I tapped the empty cushion next to me.

"I'm surprisingly quite okay," I nodded. "Can I get you something?"

"No. I'm just worried about you."

I put my cup down, and stretched out to hug my firstborn. "I'm fine, Honey. Honest, I am."

Nicole looked at me. She hesitated before speaking again.

"Did you start smoking, Mom?"

Before I could answer she cut in again.

"It's okay," Nicole continued. "I mean, I don't want you to smoke. But if you do, it's okay."

"No," I said firmly. "I do not smoke. Never did, never will. Why would you ask that?"

"Your hair reeks of cigarette smoke."

Oh darn it! I had to think quick for an answer, so I blurted out the first smoker I could think of.

"I went to a meeting with the mayor, late yesterday, and I hopped in with him. He didn't smoke in my presence, but his car smelled like it. I'll go shower immediately."

The next few days were a blur. Between the funeral planning, and such, I was not ready to return to work. I called the mayor, and told him I'd be absent the next two weeks to get my father's affairs in order. I had a funeral to plan, outfits for the entire family to purchase. And the death certificate, bank issues, life insurance policies, my father's will...

Rick finally showed up the day of the wake. He called me to say he'd just received the texts we had sent him. Something was up with him. But I wasn't willing to go there, yet. Not this week. Even the children were not impressed by his lack of remorse for not being contactable.

CHAPTER

42

♀

The week following my Papa's funeral, I found myself sitting on the dining room floor amongst a sea of sympathy cards. I held a position that made me known throughout the province. Marcel and Nicole were popular and my father was a well known physician, one who had been generous with his time and money. There were hundreds of cards. I chose to take the time to address each and every one, as that is what my Papa would have expected from me. Also, it took my mind off the mess of my life.

Rick had returned to work almost immediately, leaving me to comfort our children and myself on my own. He returned the following weekend, coming through the door when we were all snuggled in the family room under separate throws, watching a sappy movie.

"Do I get a hello?" he joked.

"Hi," I managed to say, not even looking away from the flat screen.

"You guys are a bunch of killjoys," Rick dared to say. He probably regretted it the moment it came out of his mouth. All three of us looked at him.

"There's some food left in the fridge if you're hungry," I offered. "Would you like me to make you a plate?"

"I can fend for myself," Rick answered.

"Let me help you," I said as I got up from my cross-legged position.

"I'm fine."

I opened the fridge door while he took out a plate for himself. Silently, we worked together, side by side, barely touching one another. There was no tension between us. But also no heat.

"I'd like you to come to Papa's house with me, tomorrow," I suggested. "I could use your help. Even just for the morning."

"I was hoping to go have breakfast with-"

"Please reschedule," I cut in. "This is important."

Rick looked at me. He knew I was serious.

"Okay," he breathed out. "I will."

The next day, an hour after I'd arrived at my father's house, Rick showed up. He found me sitting at the formal dining room, rummaging through our wedding photos my mother had kept. The frown developing between his two thickening eyebrows showed that he knew this was going to be a serious talk.

"What happened to us?" I asked, feeling sorry for who we had become. I didn't want to fight; I wanted to remain on speaking terms for our children's sake.

Without saying a word, Rick pulled up the chair next to mine and put his arm around my shoulder as we looked at the photos sealed in the white velvet album.

"We both have changed," he started. "I've changed. I'm no longer the same person. I don't like being MJ Taylor's husband. I never did."

"What?"

"I don't mean you, my wife. I mean you, the City Manager. You, the Big Shot."

"So..."

"I...I...I haven't liked it in a very long time. And instead of talking about it, I just changed jobs. Went places where nobody knew you. Where I was simply me, and not your husband."

"That's very small of you." I snapped the album closed. I could feel anger flushing my face.

"Maybe," Rick answered. "But that's how I feel."

We stayed quiet for a long time. Rick made us a pot of tea. We sipped it, sitting on the back porch swing. We watched the birds flutter around, and listened to children play nearby.

I finally broke the silence. "So now what? You want me to quit my job?"

"I think we're beyond that," Rick answered as he stopped the swing. "I need to tell you something."

I looked sideways to catch his eyes.

"I've met someone in Ontario. And I want to be with her."

With all his absences these last few months, it didn't surprise me. But I was still sad, just the same. How could he just come out and say it? How could he end any possibility of reconciliation between the two of us?

"Who is she?" I asked, not really caring for the answer.

"Don't be angry," Rick begged. "She's a waitress at a truck stop. Her name is Kaylee."

"Kaylee?" I asked in disbelief, pronouncing both syllables of her name slowly. "How old is she?"

Rick looked down at his shoes before answering. "Old enough to be carrying my child."

Even if I'd been having an affair behind his back during all this time... Even if in my own truth, I knew I was no longer in love with Rick... Even if I hadn't needed him in my life these past few years... Hearing that another woman was carrying his baby, that our children were going to have another sibling, it still cut right through my heart. I gasped. My hand immediately covered my mouth in shock. My eyes teared up.

"I never meant to hurt you. We just grew apart, MJ. You know that."

I knew he was right, but I didn't want him to know that. I wanted Rick to suffer. I wanted to mourn our couple a bit longer. I lost my last parent. I was now losing my husband to a woman-child who was pregnant with his latest baby. Rick was moving on. I had to let him go with the least amount of discord.

"So you're leaving us?" I asked. I wasn't really questioning. I knew.

"I need to be happy," Rick answered. "Neither you, nor I, have been very happy these last few years. You know that."

"What about Nicole and Marcel? You have to tell them, not me. It's part of being a responsible parent." I wanted to be angry with him for making our break up official, for him leaving, instead of me. But I had to let it go. "I can be there with you when you tell them, if you'd like. But it is your responsibility to tell them."

Rick got up from the swing. He extended his hands to help me, as well. Once standing, he wrapped his arms around me in a bear hug, and held me prisoner in his embrace. Our heads rested against each other.

"I never meant to hurt you," he said. "We've had great times, and I couldn't ask for a better mother for Marcel and Nicole. But... we grew apart. We need to move on."

I bobbed my head under his, and he finally let me go as I struggled to look up to him from his hold.

"Rick," I said, my hands grabbing onto his arms. "This couldn't come at a worse time in my life."

"I'm so sorry about that."

"But I agree with you," I continued. "We have grown apart. And children deserve happy parents."

We locked up my Papa's house, and took our separate vehicles back to our house. We waited for Nicole and Marcel to come home from their Saturday activities. Then Rick broke the news to them.

CHAPTER 43

♂

MJ and I met up at the hotel off the highway. Our original 429. MJ showed up wearing a denim mini skirt and a floral-print halter top. Knowing her the way I do, I knew neither item would have been hanging around in her closet. These were not Marie-Josée Taylor regular wardrobe material. She had purchased these for my eyes only. My cock twitched at the thought. MJ was becoming good at judging my reactions.

This particular outfit allowed me to feel up every one of her curves without ever taking her clothes off. It made me drool.

I waited for MJ to put the security latch over the door before lunging at her. My mouth went directly at her left earlobe. It was the nearest skin I could touch. I suckled at it as if I was trying to make her come. My tongue dipped into her ear, back and forth, whispering nasty porn shit for her to hear. I wanted to go down on her, and get a taste. But I wanted MJ to be desperate for me. I wanted her to beg for me. I wanted her to come a few times before I actually pulled my cock out of my tented shorts.

My God, that woman made me bat shit crazy. But in a good way. I wanted to try everything with her. I wanted to taste every inch of her. She didn't seem to mind. In fact, her moaning told me she was quite okay with my moves, that afternoon.

"Don't move," I exhaled in her ear. My voice barely came through, it was so low. I also felt MJ shake. Her knees were buckling on her, again. One day, MJ was going to have to explain that reaction to me. All I've been told by her is that I was the only one to have that effect on her, ever. I wore that title with pride.

We ended up going missionary. It was never my position of choice because I had to physically support myself. And second, my beer belly made it tricky to penetrate properly. After a few pumps, I leaned sideways and spooned MJ instead. Our legs intertwined like scissor blades. It gave her control of the pumping. One of my arms supported her head, leaving the other arm free to roam.

"I love you," she breathed out, and I swear my cock went soft for a moment. Panic stricken, I pretended not to hear her, and resumed our fucking.

Minutes later, both of us satisfied, I got up to clean myself in the bathroom while MJ stayed in bed. I returned to the room with MJ still laying in bed, naked. Her head was propped up by all the bed pillows stacked together, leaving me none. She patted them, asking me to join her. I hesitated. I figured this was what people called pillow talk, and I wasn't sure I wanted to venture there after hearing her mention the L word a few moments ago.

MJ patted them again. Her face had lost the giddiness she had minutes ago. She could see in my face that I was off, as well. I chose to please her, and got back in bed with her. I was going to tough out whatever she had to say.

"I need to tell you something," MJ started.

"O...kay," I answered slowly and deliberately.

"Rick left me."

I was blown away. I'm sure all her people - her friends, her neighbours, her co-workers - must have been, too. But I was also surprised at how calm she was, and how matter-of-fact she was about this. "What happened?"

"He got a girl pregnant in Ontario, and he's going to move in with her."

My mouth dropped open. The dynamic MJ and I shared, the dynamic we were both playing with...well, that was no longer. She was single. MJ would want to see me more.

I tried not to move in bed, wanting to be the cool person I wanted her to believe I was. But the entire time MJ continued with the details of their separation, my heartbeat increased tenfold. I could barely hear what she was saying. The only part of me that showed any sign of life were my eyes. And I guess they showed plenty.

I didn't want to be alarmed, but it was hard not to. It was one thing to be playing this dangerous game with MJ. But it became a very different game now. MJ was no longer committed to anyone, and she became a danger to my future. She said she wasn't. She said she didn't leave Rick to be with me. And until now, I never considered the possibility that either one of us would actually leave our mates. Daydreamed it, maybe. But never thought MJ nor I would actually go through with it. Yet, MJ did. And our playing field had just done a 1-80.

CHAPTER 44

♀

"Those eyes of yours," I said as my hand felt the contour of his face. "They have been the downfall of me. But they have also been the downfall of you."

Danny looked at me, puzzled.

"You have the most gorgeous eyes I have ever seen. They make me weak at the knees. Literally! They are also the entrance to your soul. You are afraid of me no longer being married. Am I wrong?"

"No," Danny mustered.

"Let me assure you," I spoke as I sat on my knees on the bed, towering over him as he remained laying there. "I will never pursue you. I will never show up at your house looking for you. I don't ever expect anything different than what we have been doing, you and I. Is that clear enough for you?"

Danny sprung up from the bed. His member flopped from thigh to thigh. It made me smile. This was also the first time I ever saw embarrassment from him. Obviously, he felt vulnerable at the moment, and I wasn't expressing myself well enough.

"I said I loved you, a while ago."

"Yes," he said firmly. "I heard that. Cut that shit out."

"I will not," I said as I crawled across the bed to him, taking his penis into my mouth without any help from my hands.

I may have been doing something naughty, but I knew I would get his full attention. It would calm him down. And I was right. He sat on the edge of the bed, again. And my mouth followed his genitalia to where it would lay. I kissed it gently. I invited his head to go on the pile of pillows I had put together, earlier. Danny accepted the invitation.

"You're not playing fair," he protested as he created comfort for his entire body in the bed. I laid on my stomach while waiting for him to settle in. My knees were bent, and my feet dangled in the air. Once Danny was settled, I crawled under the sheets, brought them up to my shoulders to keep me warm, and I rested between his legs.

"I want you to truly listen to me," I said after licking his entire length. Danny managed to nod.

"Loving you is one of the most wonderful things I've ever experienced. It brings me happiness and comfort. And I would hope that one day, you will feel the same way. Loving you doesn't mean I want to marry you, or even live with you. It just means I want the best for you. I want you to be happy. Healthy. Be comfortable in your own skin. Understand?"

Again, Danny nodded.

"I love you. And maybe one day, I would like to see us being more. But my life, as I've known it, is no longer. It has changed. And it's going to change so much more before the dust settles. I don't need you by my side. I need you to be supportive. Someone to talk to, from time to time. And to play with, of course," I grinned.

I felt Danny's hands grab my hair. He directed me towards his leaning face. Danny and I kissed passionately, our hands going everywhere. I let him have his way for a minute or two, and enjoyed the more relaxed version of him. But then it was time to take control again. I backed out of his grip, settling once again between his legs.

"Let me love you," I whispered as I went down on him. After what seemed like forever, I finally got to drink him in.

I crawled over his belly and settled into the pit of his left arm. I stared at the ceiling with him. He spent the next few minutes smoothing out my tussled hair.

Danny broke the silence. "I'm sorry for not coming to your father's funeral. I figured it would be inappropriate and awkward."

"Thank you for the flowers," I whispered back, my fingers twirling among his eight chest hairs.

"I don't want my stepchildren to grow up in a broken home," he said. His breath came out broken as if he was running.

I didn't respond.

"I grew up with my mother sharing her bed with a string of different men over the years, trying to find comfort. Or peace. Or security. I don't want that for these kids."

"No one is asking," I started, but he cut me off.

Danny tilted my face towards his. Our eyes locked. "I want Emma and Alex to have a stable home until they can be on their own. If you can wait for me... I know it's a lot to ask for...but if you want to wait for me, I will be yours forever."

He then kissed me with a level of tenderness I had yet to experience from him. I didn't know what to say. I could never be with another man. Danny was my absolute true love. But at the same time, we were talking several years.

"I will wait," I answered, "but let's just take it one step at a time. Okay?"

"If I told you I loved you, would that make a difference?" he asked.

"Not under duress," I answered. I wasn't pleased with his tactic. "If you want to express your love to me, do it under different circumstances than this. Do it under a romantic setting, not an entrapment."

And with that, I got up and dressed. It was a quick thing to do since I was barely wearing anything to start with.

I gave Danny a quick peck on the cheek goodbye and left him behind in the room, myself heading back to a husband-less home.

CHAPTER

45

♀

Over the next several months, I stepped away from the office indefinitely to settle my father's affairs. At the same time, I started to examine my own life, and where it had gone wrong. How did I end up being a middle-aged orphan, about to be a divorcee? The more I thought about it, the more I was convinced this situation wasn't a bad one.

My Papa dying was a bitter pill to swallow, but his health had started to deteriorate. He was elderly, and remained married to his career, even at his advanced age. I had a much better relationship with him than with my mother, especially in my adult years. But it was still not ideal. His priority remained his practice, not me. Not even his only two grandchildren. It was admirable to see him enjoying his chosen career, so late in life. He continued working into his eighties. But sitting in his private office off the master bedroom, filtering through his filing cabinet full of personal papers, all I saw was how much money he had accumulated that he never got to enjoy. Instead of relishing his senior years, and finding some sort of happiness in his retirement, my Papa spent it working. Maybe in his own world, this was his enjoyment. It wasn't going to be mine.

I made a life decision, then and there. Life was too short, and I needed to make changes in mine, as well. I was no longer sure I wanted to spend the next twenty years working where I was. I liked working at City Hall. I enjoyed holding the position of City Manager. But if I was going to make any changes in my career, the opportune time to do it was now, while I was off. The question was: did I want to? And if so, what was next? Having all of these thoughts swirling in my head, I needed to clear my mind. I needed to step away from my life for a few days.

"Hi Annie," I said cheerfully as soon as she answered. "I miss seeing you."

"Oh my gosh, MJ! How have you been?"

"I'm doing okay," I answered. "I'm holding my head up. And I have amazing children who keep me grounded. How are you keeping the fort down?"

"We have a great team in here. We're keeping afloat without you. But your promptness and organizational skills, those are missing," Annie laughed. "We're doing the best we can. But we're not you. So what's going on?"

"You're my go-to person, Annie. I can't seem to function without you," I said gingerly. "I need to get away. Suggest something, please. I can't think straight, anymore."

Annie understood my plea. She always did. When she finally stopped laughing, she came up with an answer.

"Give me an hour," she said. "I'll figure something out."

As soon as she finished her sentence, my shoulders slumped down to where they should have been resting. Annie had taken a burden off of me, once again. I stepped away from my father's life in paper, and went for a walk around the neighbourhood, the same neighbourhood I had grown up in. Neighbours had changed. Trees had grown. But otherwise, it remained familiar to me. Yet, my heart had left here decades ago, once I graduated. It had no longer been home for some time.

I came back to my father's house, just in time to hear my cell phone ring. I hadn't realized I had left it behind until I heard it ring on the catch-all table across from the front door.

"Well, that was quick," I answered.

"You should know me better than that, by now," Annie chuckled. "So? Do you want to know what you're doing next week?"

"Next week?!?" I answered. I got all excited at the prospect of walking away from these four walls so quickly. "Tell me!"

"I'm sending you on a four-day cruise on the Caribbean Sea. Every day, you will start with a surprise spa treatment. You will have breakfast brought to you on your private balcony. And you will be sleeping in a king-sized bed, just in case you want company."

"Company?" I asked, confused. Was she referring to Nicole and Marcel?

Annie's voice lowered, so as not to be heard. "In case Mr Russell was to join you."

"What?" I asked, shocked. Was that who she meant when I had gone to Edwardsville? How did she know? I had thought we had been super discreet all this time. I had to feign ignorance to save face.

"It's okay, MJ. Nobody else knows," she said. "I can't book his spot on the boat if I don't have his information. But there is room for him if you choose to invite him."

"How? How do you know?"

"It doesn't matter," Annie continued. "Now do you want to know the rest of your vacation?"

"There's more?"

"I am sending Nicole and Marcel to Ontario to visit their father," Annie hesitated. "I think they should make peace with him. They need to go see where he's moved to. And on your way back home from Tampa, I've booked you to land in Toronto, so you can go meet Rick's new woman. You need to make peace with them, as well."

"Annie," my voice trembled. "I don't think I'm ready for that."

"You never will," she answered, "which is why I did it. It's one night in Toronto. You don't have to go see them if you don't want to. But your flight is booked. You need to go find closure in this chapter of your life, before you move on. You know that."

"Yes, I know. I just find it's too early," I answered. I was still angry at Rick.

"Then if you're not up to it at the time, you don't go. It'll be your choice. But you'd be a great example to your children if you did. They're about to have a new sibling in their lives, and that baby doesn't need to grow up in turmoil."

I sighed. I puffed. And I puffed some more.

I'll think about it," I finally answered.

"That's all I expect from you. Now, I don't want to call Mr Russell. It would be awkward for us both. So would you please have him call me? I have to know by the end of the day, today."

"He won't be coming," I replied, 100% certain of my answer. "I need to be invisible for a few days. And sleep. And cry. And read. Zone out."

"That has been a long time coming," Annie said, her voice so soothing. "I agree with you. You need to be by yourself for a few days. And you'll have a huge bed to roll around in. Take care of yourself, MJ. And come visit us after that. If you're up for it."

Minutes later, I received our travel packages by email.

CHAPTER

46

♀

My week away from home was exactly what the so-called doctor had ordered. I lived off tea and fruit in the morning, and treated myself to margaritas and light dinners in the evenings. I declined having the customary dinner with the captain of the ship. I didn't accept going on this cruise to impress anyone. I followed my heart, and pretty much stayed in my room the entire four days I was there.

I vacated the room for two hours every morning to be surprised by whatever spa treatment Annie had booked for me. It also gave the staff a chance to straighten up my room. I really just needed fresh towels to replace those I'd used the previous day. But it was always nice to return to a sparkling clean room.

Every day, I received massotherapy. I also got treated to a manicure and a pedicure. Three days of massage therapy may have sounded excessive, but Annie knew what she was doing by booking me these treatments. Tension had built up on me. Between my father's sudden death, and Rick leaving us, Juan's hands loosened up my muscles every single day. I couldn't have asked for a better ending. But sweet Annie had given me one more treat, a refreshing facial to remove all that the sun had damaged those last few days when I would spend my afternoons reading on my balcony. I felt renewed, rejuvenated, and ready to confront Rick and his new family-to-be.

I was one of the first to come off the boat that evening, catching one of the first taxis parked along the dockyard. The ride was quiet, so I called both my kids' cell phones to see how their vacation with their father was going. Both Nicole and Marcel sounded fine, which pleased me. My life with Rick was over, but they would always have a connection with him. I didn't want their relationship with their dad to be damaged just because our marriage was over. And Rick moving two provinces away complicated things, but it didn't have to end their contacts together.

By the time I spoke to both, my driver was pulling up to my hotel's driveway. I handed him money that would more than cover his fare and grabbed my carry-on. I checked in, and called it a night. I had an early morning flight to Pearson. I needed to be well rested to meet my children's future stepmother. I had to make peace with Rick.

CHAPTER 47

♀

I came back from my vacation with new purpose in my heart. I needed to become fully independent. I couldn't depend on anybody but myself to do what I needed done. Emotionally. Physically. Financially. I needed to figure my next chapter in life, and I needed to figure it out on my own.

I had given Rick and Kaylee my full consent on a quick divorce, giving them a chance to marry before their baby girl would be born. I wished them well. Not sure I meant it. I was upset that he had cheated on me, that he ended our marriage. Even though that made me an immense hypocrite. Nobody knew I had been cheating all this time. But I knew. All they knew was that I was a graceful loser. I also chose to give them the profit of our house after it sold as a divorce settlement. Rick knew I was probably going to inherit a fair amount from my father's estate. But he was still content in taking our house profit, thinking he was the one at fault for our marriage's failure. In reality, we both were. Weren't we? I couldn't punish Rick for something we both were guilty of. He was, after all, the father of my children. The difference between his affair and mine was, he confessed. Maybe he couldn't hide it much longer, having gotten themselves pregnant. But he was remorseful for his part in our marriage crumbling, and was truthful when the time came to tell me.

I couldn't say the same about myself.

I knew the potential amount I was going to get from my father's estate. I would no longer need to work if I chose to. The question was: did I want to?

I had taken a leave of absence from work for three months, letting the Assistant City Manager take over my tasks. I knew settling my father's estate would be a full time job. And even though I had hired an accountant and a lawyer to help me manoeuvre the business side of death, I still needed to be accessible to these people while they paved the road ahead for me.

Those three months off were quickly coming to an end. I dreaded the prospect of going back. It's not that I disliked my job. Life was too short to dedicate all my energy to a paycheck. I wanted more in life. I wanted more freedom.

Resigning wouldn't be easy. The job suited me so well. I had worked for the City ever since I had graduated from university. It was the only employer I'd ever known. And it was a good one. But my life had changed so much. And so much more was coming now that I had an empty nest at home. Nicole was now studying journalism at Carleton University in Ottawa. And Marcel was following his father's footsteps, training to become a long-haul truck driver.

Then I discovered my father had mortgaged his house. At eighty-six years old, Papa owed money. Following his bank account statements, I discovered he gambled...a lot. He was a regular at the casino, playing the tables. He played enough to mortgage his house. Enough to never retire.

All this time, I had thought I was sitting on a fortune, between his life insurance policies, stocks he had invested into and the worth of the house. With these devastating discoveries, I now knew I would have to return to work.

Ready or not, I had no choice but to return to work and look for a new place to live. I sold my parents' house to pay off Papa's debts. Then I bought myself a condo downtown. I was single now. No husband. No children. No inheritance money to live on. I had to fend for myself. I wish I wouldn't have settled so quickly with Rick. He was faring better than me. Angry tears spilled on my pillow that night.

CHAPTER 48

♀

had found out during my cruise that my passport would be
expiring within the next twelve months. I knew the Holliston
branch of Service Canada could easily have dealt with my renewal
application. But I thought I'd take a day trip to Edwardsville, and get
it processed there.

It was a gorgeous September day, and leaves were colouring our
surroundings. I wanted to take the Old Edwardsville Road, for old
times sake. I grew up with my parents bringing me every autumn to
this quaint city, taking that exact same road. They tried to make it fun
for me, stopping at vegetable stands along the way. We'd buy corn on
the cob, freshly picked apples, and recently-harvested pumpkins and
gourds to decorate our front step. I intended to do the same purchases
on this trip, except I'd be trekking alone.

On that day, I pulled up at any farmers' stand I encountered. I
made sure to feel each and every tomato I purchased. I looked for any

blemish on the cucumbers I carried to the till. In total, I stopped at four different vegetable stands. I bought vegetables to pickle and apples to snack on. I purchased pumpkins to decorate with. And finally, I found some red potted chrysanthemums to put on my new patio.

I lunched all by myself. A new Allan Hudson book kept me company. After finishing a hearty vegetable soup I'd ordered at a local bakery, I headed off to downtown Edwardsville. I leisurely walked up Queen St after parking nearby. Walking into the suite, I pulled out a numbered stub, and waited to be triaged. Once my number lit up, I went over to the counter I'd been called to. On the other side of the counter was a polished young male employee, whose eyes stopped me dead in my tracks. I threw him off by gasping.

"I apologize," I answered, grasping the counter to sit myself across from him. "Your eyes remind me of someone."

"How can I help you?" he asked politely.

"Passport renewal," I answered. I felt defeated.

I handed him the form I had filled out at home, as well as the two copies of my photo taken yesterday. As he examined my papers, I pulled out my phone. I was looking for a clear photo of Danny's face.

"Ma'am, no," he protested as he put his hand up. "Follow me to the payment counter, please." I put my cell phone away and followed him.

Once outside, I noticed a photo shop nearby. I walked over, and asked for their assistance. The two gentlemen were very helpful in extracting an older, but clear shot of Danny.

When I returned the passport office had closed for the day. I pleaded for them to let me in for just one moment, to no avail. I pulled a pen out of my handbag, wrote my name and phone number on the yellow envelope holding the 8x10 print of Danny's face. I slid the envelope between the door and its rubber casing. In front, I had written: *To the blond, blue-eyed employee who served me today.* I was hoping he'd receive it, hoping he'd see what I saw. Two days later, he called me during his lunch hour.

"Ms Noël?"

"Yes."

"My name is Luke. I served you at the Passport office the other day..."

"Yes!" I said it louder than I wished, startling Annie briefly. I dropped everything I was doing to speak with him.

"I'm not quite sure what to ask, Ms Noël."

"MJ," I replied. "Please call me MJ." I swung my desk chair around to face the window.

"I may be fishing for something that doesn't exist. But those eyes of yours, they match the ones my boyfriend has. You saw the resemblance on that photo, didn't you?" I pushed back the thought of calling Danny my boyfriend, for the moment. I'd deal with my chosen words later.

"I have," Luke said hesitantly.

"Honestly, I just wanted you to see what I saw. I thought maybe you'd be related, in some sort. A nephew, or something. I didn't mean to poke into your personal business."

"Who is he?" Luke asked.

"His name is Danny Russell. He lives in Holliston. You share a strong resemblance," I sighed. "I thought you might know each other."

Luke remained silent.

"Thank you for calling me, Luke. You've rested my thoughts. You have a great day." As I was about to push *end*, Luke piped up.

"I was adopted."

My face blanched. I swung back around to face my desk. I needed to support my elbows as they held my head up. "Do you know who your birth parents are?" My mind was racing.

"All I know is that the people who raised me went through a private adoption. My birth mother is now my cousin. Our mothers are sisters."

"May I ask your cousin's name?" I asked. I almost answered it in my head at the same time he spoke her name.

"Cathy."

"Oh my!" I sighed.

"As for the seed who created me," Luke continued, his words

coming out like venom, "he's dead to me. If this photo is of him, so be it. I have no intention of ever meeting him."

"Luke," I interrupted, trying to lighten the air a bit.

"Ms Noël," he spit my name out, "you may love this man, but he's a deadbeat to me." Luke then hung up on me.

CHAPTER

49

♀

Telling Danny about Luke would only cause a ruckus. And I had no real proof, yet. All I knew of Cathy was that she had moved to Cassidy when she became pregnant, and that she was two years older than Danny. That would make her forty-seven, and Luke in his early thirties. I didn't even know which village Danny's grandparents had lived in, except it was near a beach. Holliston was surrounded by beach country. And I remember Danny mentioning Cathy's last name, once. But my memory didn't retain it.

I asked Annie to join me for lunch at a bistro near the university one day. We ordered different items from the menu, and then I started speaking.

"I do need to ask you how you know about Danny."

Annie simply smiled, and took a forkful of her colourful salad.

"I'm serious. How did you find out?"

"Oh, MJ. You may be older than me, but your naivety betrays

you," she grinned. "Your glances. Your body language whenever he was around. The fact Mr Russell still came around months after our business with him was long done. And then there's this one time, you left your leather gloves in your hotel room. Their staff called the office to tell you they'd found them but you were in a meeting, so I picked them up myself. So you wouldn't be embarrassed. That's when I knew for sure."

"I'm so sorry to put you in that position," I said. I was feeling rather embarrassed, after all.

"It was my choice. And no judgment on my part, by the way. Understand? What you do on your own time, it's none of my business. And I have nothing to offer but respect. You're a grown woman. But you ogling him during his presentation, it was almost comical. I'll never forget that," Annie laughed.

I blushed as many shades as my skin would turn. This entire time, I always thought my secret was protected.

"Who else knows?" I asked.

"I don't believe anybody else does. I just happen to know you like the back of my hand. I've seen your marriage suffer the moment Rick changed careers. Your stress level went sky high. Your support went down. And with growing children and aging parents, you were due for a good distraction. Mr Russell walked in at the opportune time, that's all."

"Thank you for understanding," I said as I squeezed her hand. "You should consider becoming a therapist. You have a great head on your shoulders, and you give really great advice."

Annie laughed harder. "Thanks, but I'll stick to my job, for now. A whole lot less stressful."

"On one bill, please," I said as the waiter gathered our plates. "You've been a great friend, Annie. How are the wedding plans going?"

Annie went into tremendous details about her upcoming nuptials. I let her take over the conversation for the rest of our lunch date.

CHAPTER

♀

Since meeting Danny, I had been sneaking out most Wednesday afternoons with him. I felt I was betraying the Council's trust in me, even if they didn't know it. I replaced those hours by staying later all the other evenings. But I still felt like I was cheating my fellow colleagues of my presence during business hours. And since my father's death, since taking a leave of absence, I knew I had a lot of catching up to do on my work, but I also wanted to manage living my life more fully.

Nicole was now pursuing her education at Carleton University in Ottawa. Marcel had followed his father's footsteps, and was now a long-haul truck driver. Both of my children presently lived in Ontario, near their father and his growing family, while I stayed behind, picking up the crumbs of my once crazy, busy life.

I loved Danny. But he was not truly mine. Until his relationship with Tina ended, if it ever did, I could never call him mine. I was his mistress. I had gotten into this relationship with him knowing we were both side pieces to one another. Our affair remained a secret, with the exception of Annie.

I booked myself a flight to Ottawa to visit Nicole for the weekend. I needed to spend time with my daughter. I hadn't realized how much I missed her. I thought we'd catch up and bond, when in fact I ended up cleaning her apartment and freezing her meals while she went out with friends. I also went out daily and explored our nation's Capital. I took advantage of the many tours given around Parliament Hill. Not quite the mother-daughter weekend I had imagined. But I made the best of it.

The following long weekend, I flew to Toronto to visit with Marcel. I found out he had already made plans to fly to Montreal with friends for a hockey game, so I was left alone in his abode. He did leave me the keys to his car, at least. I wasn't spending another visit cleaning and cooking. I did what I should've done months ago.

"You seem well," Rick said as we embraced. "You remember Kaylee."

"So glad to see you again," she exclaimed with her arms wide open. Kaylee wore a genuine smile on her pretty young face. She was also with child, again. Kaylee did not seem threatened by my presence, nor should she have. Her protruding stomach hadn't disturbed her level of energy as she bounced around the kitchen making us dinner.

"Please spend the night with us. You've never had the chance to meet Abigail. I swear she looks like Nicole."

I'm not sure if I was ready to spend so much time with Rick and his new family, but these people were now part of my children's family. And so, my heart quickly warmed up to the idea, awkward as it may have seemed.

I woke up shortly after eight, the next morning. This trip, so far, had been such a whirlwind. Here I was, in my ex-husband's new home, and I felt contentment. I believe I had finally found peace within myself in being in a happy divorce. There was no awkwardness between Rick and myself. Or with Kaylee, for that matter.

Today, I was going to be spending a day with Rick and his bride

Kaylee. I was also going to meet their daughter. Abigail was as adorable as they said. And she did resemble Nicole a lot.

Kaylee made us a beautiful lunch for us to feast on. I insisted on doing the dishes with her. I wanted to hate that woman. I was supposed to be angry with her for breaking up my marriage. But I knew better than to blame this lovely young lady for the failure of my union with Rick. Maybe nobody knew of my affair with Danny. But I did. Breaking my vows to Rick was as much to blame as his breaking his to me. I had stopped trying. I had stopped working on my marriage long before Danny came into the picture. I had stopped caring, until it became too late to change the course Rick and I were tumbling through. Finding comfort and excitement in my time with Danny had dulled the pain of feeling alone and abandoned at home. And I bet Rick had probably felt the same.

He found his own comfort and excitement in someone like Kaylee. Chances are, Rick had probably started looking before even meeting her. No matter, this was now in the past. They both looked happy together. I had to let bygones be bygones.

We walked to a nearby park. Kaylee and I sat on a bench while Rick followed Abigail around to all the playground equipment she chose to test out.

"I can see why Rick is so happy with you," I said as my hand brushed hers. "You bring out the best in him."

"That means the world to me," Kaylee smiled.

"I mean it," I continued, turning to look her straight in the eyes. "Rick and I did have a wonderful relationship. We connected from the very beginning. We were full of adventures, and he taught me so much about life. I had been so sheltered. Then we became real adults. We were no longer students. We had real jobs. And a mortgage. And children. And responsibilities. I see now, he wasn't quite ready for that, just yet. I see now that he was miserable. He needed to step away from it all. But at the time, I needed him to keep appearances with me. That was my need, not his. Rick was so much ahead of me in this middle-aged life. You, Kaylee. You are what he's needed for some time."

"I'm so sorry you got hurt in all this," Kaylee replied. "And the children..."

"But look at them now."

We walked back to their recently purchased mini van, and headed for the nearest supermarket. Kaylee and I purchased items for dinner, while Rick bought beer to drink for tonight's hockey game on tv.

"I enjoy your company. It's nice to have a woman to talk to for a change."

"Thank you for your hospitality," I repeated. "You are a gracious hostess."

"I tell you what," Kaylee suggested. "Let me bathe Abigail, and put her to bed. Then you and I can meet in the master bedroom and watch our own program. Say, in an hour?"

"I might just go take a bath, myself," I said.

"Yes!" she answered, excitedly. "You do that, and I'll finish up with Abigail. Then you and I can watch a movie while Rick watches his game."

And that's exactly what we did. Kaylee and I settled into the master bed, enveloped by pillows and blankets and duvets. We watched a sappy romance movie. We criticized scenes from time to time. Wiped tears at other times.

Kaylee and I woke up the next morning, next to each other. We had fallen into a deep slumber, and Rick had let us be.

During these crazy months, between settling my father's affairs, readjusting to my job again, and spending some weekends in Ontario, time alone with Danny became sparse. I continued being in contact with Danny. Mostly through texting. It sustained us for the time being. I missed him terribly. I missed his voice. I missed his touches. Danny had become my only source of release, and my body missed the contact. He remained my best friend, but he was no longer my only friend. Oddly enough, my ex-husband's new wife was now part of that pool. Through Kaylee, I had learned to relax. Be less judgmental. I could go home, and attempt making new friends with what I had learned from her, if I so chose to.

CHAPTER 51

♀

I asked to go on Danny's next road trip with him. I needed to see him. I needed to spend time with him. I wanted to spend a night with him. He hesitated to have me along.

He had recently gotten a new company car. It was a high-sided vehicle with much better leg room. It had more trunk space and heated leather seats. Danny picked me up at a Tim Horton's restaurant just outside city limits. I walked up to his car as he pulled up next to mine. I was leaving the building, carrying two coffee cups and a bag of bagels.

"Where are we heading to?" I asked with the biggest smile I could produce. I saw the beginning of a frown. Suspicion was forming on his forehead. It went away as he brusquely took the cups from my hands and placed them in the cup holders. It liberated my arms as I struggled to get myself seated and buckled. I ignored his missing manners.

"Prince Edward Island," he answered abruptly. Not once did he look at me.

"I missed you," I said casually, rubbing the right side of his lap with my empty left hand as we drove off. Danny didn't respond or react. There was definitely tension in the air.

We ate our bagels in silence, each trying to read the other person's mood. I attempted to start another topic of conversation.

"I like your new set of wheels. It's a lot more spacious. And I just love the smell of a new car."

Once again, I was met with tension-filled silence. I waited until we had both drunk our coffees completely before speaking again.

"So in which direction are we going?"

Silence remained. Enough is enough. I waited until we had crossed the Confederation Bridge before talking again.

"You know you're gonna have to talk to me eventually."

Danny pulled over at the first gas station we saw. He put his Nissan on park, and twisted to look at me. His words came out deliberately and slow.

"Why are you here?"

His eyes were charcoal in colour. He was upset. Or as Danny would say: pissed. I had learned years and years ago, back in university time, that anger was a way to express the real feeling hiding behind. Danny was afraid. I knew he was just venting. He didn't want to hear what I had to say. He didn't care. No matter what I would've said, he wouldn't have listened. Whatever I would've said wouldn't have mattered. He would've taken my words, sliced them up, twist them around, and spit them back at me. At the moment, he was just letting me know that he was upset. That he was hurt. That he felt abandoned.

"To be with you..."

Danny frowned. He shook his head and drove off towards his first destination. He dropped me off at the Canadian Tire thirty kilometres away from the bridge, and I spent the rest of my morning walking up and down every single aisle of the store. He found me about an hour and a half later. I was reading the ingredients to a bottle of floor cleaner. I caught him smiling at me.

"You hungry?" he asked.

"Starving," I answered with a smile. I put the bottle back where it belonged, then followed him outside.

There was a seafood restaurant on the waterfront where one could watch sailboats dance before one's eyes. These beauties made the sea glitter as the noon-hour sun shone on the waves they'd make. It wasn't a fancy establishment, but we were mainly looking for nourishment. Danny ordered fish'n'chips, while I ordered a tuna melt.

His next appointment was also in in the same town, so I walked to the mall nearby. I waved him goodbye as he drove off. When Danny returned two hours later, his mood was much improved.

"I booked us a treat for tonight," Danny chirped as I slid into the passenger seat.

"Where are we going?" I asked eagerly.

"It's a surprise!"

My eyes took in every building we drove by, whether a house or a small business. They were all tucked in between recently harvested fields. After some time of silent driving, I felt his hand reach over to mine. Danny gave it a small squeeze.

I smiled. How I loved this man. I continued surveying the properties as we whizzed by, all the time holding hands with him. My thumb mindlessly massaged the knuckles of his right hand. We got off the highway and followed a more coastal route, eventually pulling in at a motel with a lighthouse attached to it.

"We're staying here," Danny exclaimed. "Isn't this great?"

I'm not sure how many stars this place was rated, but it was certainly below what I was accustomed to. I managed to smile enthusiastically.

"This should be fun!"

Danny bought it, thankfully.

We walked side by side, but never touching. We never showed affection publicly. Just in case. Danny did open the door for me, like the gentleman he always was. I was pleasantly surprised by the charm of the building. Memories to be made, I thought. There were only two rooms to be rented in the lighthouse, and Danny had reserved one.

We went up to our room and sat on the bed for a mere minute before our lips went searching for each other.

CHAPTER 52

♂

MJ was flying to Ontario too often for my liking. I figured she was gonna move. I figured she wanted out. I was afraid. I was gonna miss that woman. I wanted her to suffer for it, like I was. But staying mad at her only made it worse for me. The angrier I got, the more I drank. And the more I drank, the more I smoked. And the more I did these, the more Tina became suspicious.

I had a lot of pent up energy to burn. I soon regretted coming to the quiet Lighthouse Inn. The walls were too thin for my liking. I knew MJ. She'd be noisy, that night.

MJ and I locked lips seconds after bolting the door closed. My hands went fishing up her bra within seconds, and I crushed her left tit against her ribs. We were desperate to feel each other. Taste each other. I now knew I'd booked the wrong room. This was not a place to fuck, but more a place to make love.

Yes, I loved MJ. I knew I loved her. There was no more denying my feelings. I just didn't want her to make life plans with me just because I'd professed my love for her. She seemed torn between being with me and being with her son and daughter.

MJ pulled her t-shirt over her head, exposing the massaged tit I'd uncupped from her yellow bra.

"Yes, I wore undergarments today, against your wishes," she said as she put her hands behind her back to unclasp the velvety contraption.

"Wait," I said with great hesitation. MJ looked at me confused. "I haven't fucked you in over three months. I can promise you that when I do, I will be fucking you hard. This may not be the place to do it."

"I can be quiet," she pleaded, obviously disappointed by my answer.

"I don't want you to be quiet," my voice lowered. "I want you to come hard. And I wanna hear you scream my name when you do."

"Let's have an early supper," I suggested after we woke up from a nap. "Then we can go for a drive. There's a lot of private roads on the island. We can do it in the car."

I had one of the best fisherman's platters I'd ever tasted at a restaurant nearby. MJ had their seafood chowder. She did, however, order a piece of blueberry pie. A la mode, no less. I helped her eat it.

We followed the shore, watching the sun go down for the evening. And as the night sky turned different shades of grey, I pulled into the first dirt road available. It led us to a patch of cottages boarded up for the upcoming winter. I parked my new vehicle away from any possible view from prying eyes. I shut off the engine, and pounced.

MJ squealed and couldn't get to the backseat fast enough. She'd left her new sandals in the front, and had dressed to my liking. She wore a halter dress with zero underwear. No bra. No panties. Let's go!

Unlike MJ, I couldn't hop between the two front bucket seats. I had to use the doors to get out of my driver's seat in order to get into the backseat. No big deal. Except when I opened the door, it lit us up like fireworks on an abandoned beach road. I quickly closed the door behind myself and locked us in, hoping the interior light would shut off faster.

MJ helped me take my pants down to my ankles as I sat there, panting like a dog.

"Get your ass over here," I commanded as I guided her hips onto my cock.

Her head brushed against the roof of my car, messing her hair up as a fucked woman should look like. Switching positions, I sat on the edge while she positioned herself along the width of the backseat. Her dress rode up enough to reveal the length of her legs. I took the opportunity to take a feel. She took a deep breath before laying her head down on my shoulder.

I knelt between her two legs, and brought them up over my shoulders. Her head and shoulders were the only part of her body touching the seat. I grabbed her across the stomach as my arm held her in place from hip to hip. It gave my other hand full access to play with her. No softness today. No gentle touches. My three longest fingers went in while my thumb pressed on top of her clit. I dove those fingers in and out.

"You're so mine," I said loudly, trying to be heard above her moaning. "You know no one else can fuck you like I do."

MJ nodded yes. Her hands moved from her mound to my chest to her dishevelled hair. She was getting frantic.

"What's it gonna take for you to come. You know what I'm gonna do once you're done? I"m gonna flip you over, and ride you like you've never experienced. I'm gonna fill you up..."

And bam! She came. I couldn't let it stain my new company car. I lapped it up for her to watch. I then flipped her over like a rag doll, and she made the right noises. I knew she enjoyed being handled rough. I positioned myself to enter her hard. I put my other hand over her backside, and rammed her deep half a dozen times until I spewed my own pent up cum inside her.

We disembarked, and she stepped outside in a scramble. I didn't want to stain the upholstery. While MJ readjusted herself in the dark, her fingers flattening out her clothes and her hair, I had a smoke. We then headed back to the Lighthouse Inn.

We climbed the stairs to our room, and I settled into the bed before her. I reached over to the bag of goodies she had bought earlier at the pharmacy. I spilled the stuff onto the handmade quilt covering the bed. Among the bottles of fruit-infused sparkling water, crackers, and expensive chocolate, I found another box.

"What's this?" I asked, holding a box of condoms. MJ grinned, but didn't shy away as she joined me in bed.

"I might be ready for anal whenever you are," she answered. I tried not to react. But inside, I was doing jumping jacks and flips. I was blown away by her purchase. "But now that we're here," she continued, "I don't think this is the place to do it."

"Why not?" I asked. I didn't want her to change her mind when I was this close to getting her ass.

"In case I hurt. Or bleed."

"Come here," I said as I opened my arms to hug her. "I would never make you bleed. Or hurt you. This is for pleasure only. Don't you get that?"

"I still don't think this is the place."

"Oh, I agree with you on that one," I said as I released her from my bear hug. "Can I just hold you?"

MJ smiled. She got up and twisted the wooden mini-blind of our only window shut, then crawled into bed. "Danny Russell wants to cuddle. Now, there's a first!" I ignored the chiding, even though she was right. I let her settle into my arms.

"You warm enough?" I asked as I smelled her hair. I was gonna miss her scent. I was gonna miss the silk of her hair. The smell of her skin. The generous curves of her body.

Then my phone rang, and we both jumped. Tina checking in on me, wishing me a good night's sleep. I spoke sweetly with her, as I always did. I answered all her questions. I even asked a few of my own. When I hung up, MJ was nibbling on crackers. From the body language she was showing, our cuddling was over for the night.

"I'm not upset," she said. "Or jealous, for that part. That phone call is a simple reminder that these road trips of ours are just make believe. Tina's real."

I had no words.

MJ brushed the crumbs off of her hands. She walked to the bathroom to brush her teeth before rejoining me in bed. This time, she faced the ceiling. Her hand reached out and touched my leg.

"How old is her son, now?" she asked. She was getting tired of waiting for Alex to grow up. The thing is, the closer he got to reaching adulthood, the more spooked I became. The reality was hitting me, but I tried not to let on.

"Just have patience," was all I could say.

We shut the lights off. Our room was aglow by the moon on the water. We remained silent, listening to each other breathing.

The next morning, we woke up early since I had a full day ahead. MJ and I both ordered bacon and eggs, and we enjoyed the full bodied coffee they served. I had hoped to walk the beach with MJ during our stay. I had booked a room in this lighthouse to get a romantic setting. I wanted us to have a stroll on the beach after dinner. But our hormones dictated a different outcome. And we had sex in my car, instead. Maybe if there was ever a next time, it could be a more romantic stay for us. Last night, we were too eager to fuck to think of anything else.

We headed for the western part of the island where I had already several existing clients in the many rental properties they managed. I was hoping to introduce them to better technology than they presently worked with. I had seven or eight to check up on. Unlike yesterday, there wasn't much for MJ to do. She opted to sit at a bakery, sip on more coffee, and read a Hudson book for the next few hours while I did my thing.

I ended up hitting the jackpot with most of these businesses. We wrote up orders, then and there. I stayed cool and professional. But inside, I was doing cartwheels. It felt like Christmas. By the time I'd visited them all, I could feel my stomach growling. I looked at my watch, and saw that it was 2:30 in the afternoon. Yikes! I called Tina on my way to pick up MJ. Juggling two women at a time had its own challenges.

"Hi Babe," I started. "How's everything at home?"

Tina proceeded to tell me every detail.

"How about you, Dan?" she asked.

"Well, I'm hitting sales. Left and right," I answered. "And I haven't even reached Monet, yet. Which is why I'm calling. I'd like to set up a meeting with their City Hall, but it's too late for the day, today."

"So you're staying another night?" Tina sighed.

"I think I'd better," I answered.

"Do what you have to do. But hurry home after that."

I could hear the disappointment in her voice. One day soon, I'd have to break the heart of one of these two women.

I hung up with Tina, and then called Monet City Hall to set up a meeting with their Purchasing Department. I was only able to set one up for two weeks from now. I accepted the appointment, just the same. I arrived at the bakery where I had dropped MJ off, hours ago. I just hoped she wasn't too pissed at me. I walked in, and the place was empty.

I approached the counter, and soon a woman came out of the back. "I'm looking for my...girlfriend," I said.

"You must be Danny," the woman, whose name tag said Betty, smiled. "Come see what we've done with MJ."

I followed her into the back of the bakery, and into the kitchen area. I found my woman wearing a hairnet and an apron. MJ was learning to decorate cupcakes.

"Hi, Sweetheart," she smiled as she finished up her last cupcake. "See what happens when you forget about me?"

I was better off not answering. I was surrounded by a bunch of mature ladies. Keeping my mouth shut was my best defence.

MJ used her white apron to wipe the icing sugar off of her hands, and then hugged every worker goodbye before taking her hairnet off. She joined me where I was standing at the swinging doors. She gave me a quick kiss on the cheek. That was the first show of affection we had ever shared in public. I led her to the car with my hand placed on the small of her back. It was nice touching each other like that.

"I'm so sorry for being late. But my sales are going to be fantastic! Have you eaten at all?"

"I had a sandwich," she answered while buckling herself in. "Have you?"

"No."

"Well, let's go back in there, and get you some food."

"No. It's okay," I answered, too tired to think.

"Nonsense!" MJ insisted as she unbuckled herself. "I'll be right back."

A few minutes later, she emerged from the bakery with a ham and cheese on a croissant and a bottle of homemade lemonade.

"I told Tina I had to stay another night," I said after devouring the sandwich. "Can you stay another night with me?"

"I'd love to spend another night with you. I'll just call in sick."

So off to Monet we headed.

CHAPTER 53

♂

We drove up to the first hotel we found in Monet. It was a multi-level establishment on Portage Road. They had a pool, and they served breakfast. Pretty much offered what any other hotel on that road did. MJ sat in my new Rogue while I checked in. The chances of seeing someone we knew in the small metropolis of Monet was minuscule. But until I texted MJ with our room number, she would stay behind in my vehicle.

On the other side of the front desk stood a young lady named Ashley, according to the pin on her vest. As I handed her my Visa, a thought came to mind.

"Excuse me. Before you assign me a room, would you mind checking if room 429 is available? It brings fond memories for us both."

"Yes. Certainly, Mr Russell," Ashley answered. "And you're in luck." She smiled as she punched in information on her keyboard.

"It comes with a king-sized bed instead of two queens. Will that be okay?"

"That's perfect. My lady friend and I will appreciate that."

I rode the elevator up alone to the fourth floor. I walked up to our room and unlocked the door. Oh, the things I wanted to do to MJ that evening. I would have to pace myself.

I called the front desk, and the same pretty young clerk answered the phone.

"Is there a problem with the room, Mr Russell?"

"No, no," I assured her. "I would like you to set some things up for me while we go out to dinner."

"How may I help you?" Ashley asked.

"I would like flowers waiting for my friend when we come back. And beautiful flowers. Not just a supermarket arrangement."

"Consider it done," Ashley answered.

"Also, I'd like breakfast brought up to the room. Omelettes, or Eggs Benedict. Something fancy. With coffee and orange juice, of course."

"One moment, please," I heard her muffled voice say. Ashley probably had another guest standing in front of her. I had to wrap this conversation up quickly. "Will that be all, Mr Russell?"

"Ashley, if you can do these two things for me, I'll make sure you're well compensated."

"It would be my pleasure, Mr Russell. Have a great evening."

I knew MJ was waiting for my text. But I chose to call Tina, not wanting to interrupt the evening again.

I rode the elevator back down, and walked up to the car. MJ was surprised to see me. I had better plans.

"I've decided to take you out to dinner," I said as I climbed back into my car. "We're going to take our chances. Being out of province, we should be okay. If not, if someone sees us, we'll just say we're acquaintances. But first, I'm going to need clean clothes for tomorrow. Wanna hit the mall?"

We entered the Monet Mall together. We went our separate ways once inside. MJ and I chose to meet up an hour later. She wanted a new ensemble, and went to a boutique. I went to Walmart. All I needed were fresh underwear and socks. Once there, I veered towards the pharmacy department. I walked up to the family planning aisle, and picked up a tube of lube. If anal was going to happen, it was going to be that night. And I wanted to be as ready as possible.

Dinner was eaten at a steak house. I love seafood. And there's nothing better than eating seafood while on Prince Edward Island. However, my stomach was growling in protest for red meat and potatoes. MJ would have to make do. She ordered a filet mignon for herself accompanied by a chef's salad. I had a tenderloin as thick as a roast and a twice baked potato with all the trimmings. We shared a bottle of red. I ached to reach out and touch her hand tenderly. It was one thing to be seen together. Showing affection for one another, that would be so much more. And forbidden.

We skipped dessert, and headed to the car. The setting of the restaurant and the effect of the wine was getting to us. MJ felt my right arm up and down. I couldn't seem to get to the hotel fast enough. Within a few blocks from the building, we saw the first of many lightning bolts flash across the heavy skies.

By the time we got to the hotel, it was raining buckets. MJ and I ran and skipped across the parking lot until we found cover under the main door canopy. As a gentleman, I should've dropped MJ off at the door. That way, she could've remained dry. However, I did want to see her get wet in her new sleeveless dress. I wanted to see the fabric stick to her body. I wanted to see it follow every single one of her curves. I saw a few roving eyes in the lobby as we entered. A few men saw what I wanted them to see, that she was not wearing any underwear for me. The fabric stuck to her tits and hips like glue. MJ's arms crossed in defence. She struggled to keep her dignity for the ten seconds it took for the elevator door to open. A few men followed us in. MJ was near tears so I gave her my jacket. I enjoyed the admiration I got from those men. But I also did not want them to see her nakedness, wet fabric or not. Her body was for my eyes only. I held her to make her feel less exposed, more protected. I had to remind myself that she had chosen this dress for me. I had had no part in what she was wearing tonight. I did expect her to be without a bra or panties, though, as per our agreement. Why she kept it up, all these years, I'm not sure. I just liked that she did.

MJ held me by the arm as we walked the hallway to my chosen room. 429. She seemed surprised, and looked down at me with a smile. I unlocked the door with one of the cards Ashley had supplied me with. We entered a room waiting for romance. I don't believe I had ever courted MJ before. Or any woman, for that part. So this was a shocker for us both.

Our room was peppered with battery-operated candles. It smelled of pink and red roses that awaited MJ's touch. A bottle of sparkly was chilling in a bucket. Ashley had outdone herself. MJ's hands were on each side of her chin.

MJ seemed to have forgotten she was still wearing her soaked dress. I went around her, and unzipped the back of it. I pulled it off of her since it was too wet to fall off by itself. I ran over to the bathroom to get a towel. And when I came back, I fell to my knees. Now I knew how MJ felt when she first saw me. My knees buckled at the MJ standing before me. This gorgeous redhead with big sparkling brown eyes, with her face aglow by the candlelight, she brought me to my knees. I took the towel and started drying her legs off. As MJ changed her posture for me to dry the inside of her legs, that's when I lost it. Like a calf looking for his mother's milk, my mouth went searching for MJ's pussy. I suckled hard. All she had for defence were her hands. Her fingers went looking to clamp onto my head for support. Without success, MJ ended up letting out a gut wrenching sound I had never heard come from her, before.

I crawled between her legs, tickling her with my grizzled face before getting up in front of her. MJ took my face between her hands, and kissed me with a deep level of passion. I didn't want to have her stop what she was doing. But there were more parts of her body I wanted to taste and explore.

I undressed super fast, remembering to put the squeeze bottle of lube inside the night table next to the condoms I had put there earlier. MJ didn't seem to notice. She was too busy tucking the sheet and duvet around her neck. Her body heat hadn't returned yet. She was shivering. I lay next to her, and brought her on top of me so my own body heat could warm her up. We kissed like teenagers, fuelled by the wine at the restaurant. And now the sparkly.

We laid side by side, and face to face. I directed her hand to my erection. I waited for her to grab it. All the attention was going to go to her. But a little bit of pumping with her hands was always welcome. I took MJ's chin with my fingers, and brought it up to my lips. I kissed her tenderly, for a change. I wanted to make love to her. Yet I had had anal in my head, all day long. It was going to have to be a build up for us both if we were going to reach ass fucking, that night. But the more tender were my touches, the more MJ fought back with lip biting. The tigress was here, and she wanted to play. I had no problem obliging. I figured the best way to get everything I wanted out of her, that night, was for me to come.

I pushed her shoulders down. MJ was now laying on her back. I came up with my knees on each side of her face, and I pushed my cock into her mouth. MJ accepted it eagerly. She was fully surprised when she tasted my spunk go down her throat. She didn't say anything, but I could see she was disappointed.

"Who said we were done?!" I exclaimed as I watched her have some bubbly, probably to change the acrid taste in her mouth. "We're just getting started here, Missy."

"But you came," she whispered, her eyes lowering.

"I can come again. It'll take me longer, this time. That just means more time spent on you." MJ took in a deep breath, then released it slowly. "Now where were we?" I asked as we settled back into bed.

In reality, deep inside, I felt like I needed to fuck her in every possible way. I had a notion that this may be my last night with her, like she was going to move away from me. I'd waited too long to make a decision. I had made her wait, and she ran out of patience. Her family was in Ontario. It's where she belonged, now. I had to let her go.

But not yet. She was mine for one more night. I had to make the best of it. I started jiggling my own cock to get it hard again while I stood next to the bed. It would take a while. So I pointed with my eyes for her to do the same.

"I wanna watch you feel yourself up."

"You know I don't do that," MJ answered.

"For me. Do it. Close your eyes. Pretend it's my fingers." And she did. MJ opened her eyes and looked at me. I was now beating my own. My cock was now back to its full glory. "Keep your eyes closed," I instructed.

"I can't," MJ said as she stopped. She pulled her fingers away.

"That's okay, Honey. I can take over." And I did. I crawled over her with my hard on, and I laid my palm on her bush. I dipped my finger into where hers had been, barely a minute ago. I kissed her hard on the lips, to the point I wanted to swallow her tongue whole. I wanted to fuck her boobs. But instead I entered her. I held her tits together, as if my hands were her bra. I sucked up one nipple after the other. Back and forth. Over and over. My slurping made the right amount of noise to get her wet. MJ giggled. MJ jiggled. She made me enter her, again and again. However, I did not come. My cock wasn't ready, yet. It was gonna take more than five or six pumps, this time. I knew, from previous occasions, that a second load could take up to an hour to come. Not sure she could take that much of a workout, but I was more than willing to try.

Her face was flushed. Her body was tired. Yet, MJ wanted more. Maybe this was the time to try entering her ass. I flipped MJ over, and I rubbed my pulsating cock across the back of her thighs. I went into her pussy doggy-style, and went at it slowly. It wasn't so much a race to the end. It was more for her body to feel me moving inside her as I went in and out.

I started feeling her butt cheeks. I massaged them, warming them up for things to come. I pulled my cock out, and let it go up and down her backside. I went in her pussy, passing by her butt crack. Eventually, my cock rested in between her cheeks. I stopped at the small of her back, then returned down to her pussy. I did that for a few minutes. MJ never moved. I finally left my cock inside her while my hands separated her ass cheeks. I introduced one of my thumbs, wet from my saliva, into her ass. MJ froze up. I felt her tighten her bum muscles, so I pulled my thumb out.

"Relax," I breathed out, my voice coming out as low as it could. I was barely audible. "Let me try something. But you have to relax."

I leaned over to the night stand and opened the drawer. I pulled out the box of condoms, as well as the lube. MJ turned her head sideways, curious to see what I was doing, always remaining silent. I could also feel her thighs relaxing, no longer squeezing together. She was ready to participate in one of the things I'd always wanted to try with her.

I kept kissing her back, neck and arms. I had to keep the mood going. All this while I struggled to open the sealed box of condoms. I finally put one on. And then I worked up a sweat taking the plastic seal off the mouth of the lube bottle. I could hear MJ giggle, but I ignored it. Once I was ready, I went back to warming her bum up.

I rubbed the cheeks, pulling her glutes up and around in circles, loosening her up. I then inserted a finger. Then two. She needed to get used to the width of what was to come. MJ breathed in with large intakes. Her hands clamped the fitted sheet of our bed. It was her way of relaxing. I finally went in for the kill. I lubed my rod with about a tablespoon's worth of gel, and gently pushed it in. I felt MJ squeeze her butt cheeks, but then let go. Her hands turned into fists while holding on to the sheet.

"Are you okay?" I whispered as I put in the head of my cock into her ass.

"It's uncomfortable," she lied, holding her breath, "but it doesn't hurt."

"You let me know when you can't handle it, anymore," I spoke softly. My excitement was building up, and I wanted to ram myself in her. But I knew better.

"If you don't go fast, I'll let you stay there," MJ smiled as she extended her hand onto the small of her back for me to squeeze briefly as a makeshift hug.

"Does it still hurt?" I asked as I started inserting another inch.

"It burns like walking barefoot on pavement in the summer. It's bearable."

That's all I needed to hear. I pulled her bum towards me, and I leaned onto her. My belly spread across her back.

"I can turn around, if you'd like," she said in between her quick breaths.

"I'm afraid if you do, you won't let me back in."

"This is a one time deal, Danny. We will never do this act, again. So have your fill."

OMG! How I loved this woman at that moment. I helped MJ turn around onto her back, and I got myself sitting on my heels. Not the best position for me with the thick legs of mine, but it did serve its purpose. I pressed her thighs wide open, with her heels on my shoulders. And with more lube spread from one bum cheek to the other, I let my cock penetrate her ass, again. I watched her facial expression, making sure it wasn't too uncomfortable for her. Her hand held my wrist tightly. The harder she squeezed, the more discomfort she felt. Once I was back in, my entire rod having disappeared inside, MJ let go of her grip, and I could resume fucking her ass.

In front of me was the most beautiful woman I had ever seen naked, and she was letting me have my way with her. MJ's trust in me was at 100%, and that didn't go unnoticed. I now knew I wanted to have her for the rest of my days.

My cock was letting me know I needed to wrap this up. My second load was about to come out. I put in most of my hand inside her pussy, making her entire fuck area full of me. MJ moaned loudly with her eyes popping out of her head. MJ cried out my name as she squirted onto my hand. That's all I needed to see to get my load out.

CHAPTER 54

♂

Fully spent, MJ and I crumbled next to each other. Neither one of us moved for a while. I used the bathroom before her. I showered. I didn't hear MJ come into the room. I didn't even hear her pee. So I was startled when the shower curtain opened, and she climbed in with me. There's no way I could perform again, that night. I started to wave her away.

"I just want to shower with you," MJ protested. "I can barely stand up. You've ruined me for a few days," she smiled. "May I simply wash up with you?"

I didn't answer. But I did help her step in next to me. We took turns under the steamy water. MJ held the bar of soap the entire time. She lathered herself up. Then she did the same for me. I had never showered with a woman that didn't include sex at the end. This was new for me. This act wasn't sexual. It was sensual. MJ was changing me, bit by bit, to her side of thinking. I didn't mind.

I towelled off first, leaving MJ to enjoy the hot water pouring onto her exhausted limbs. I don't know about her, but I knew I could use a snack. I wanted to order a pizza. But it just didn't seem like the right thing to do after such an amazing night with her. I walked around the room with a towel barely staying around my waist, and I shut off the candles. I lit the lamps on both sides of the bed, and I poured myself a glass of bubbly. It was the only alcohol in the room.

"Pour me one, too," MJ said as she walked in with a towel wrapped around her wet hair, her body naked. We sat against the headboard, and MJ lit the tv on. She also pulled out a box of crackers, and we snacked on those, then MJ pulled out a large bar of dark chocolate. She snapped a piece off, and let me suck on it. She wouldn't let me chew.

"You're too much in a rush all the time," she smiled. "Some things you just have to take your time and enjoy the moment."

"Like the chocolate?" I asked.

"Yes," MJ laughed. "And me. Tonight, you've accomplished your entire sex list."

"Not quite," I smirked. "There's still the one about a second woman."

"Never. Never. Never."

I laughed. "Okay, then," I said. "I guess it's time to write another list."

CHAPTER 55

♂

We were awakened by a knock at the door. I scrambled to put my pants on. MJ hid her body behind the duvet while a cart of colourful food was rolled in. She smiled from ear to ear at yet another surprise I had scrambled up for her to enjoy.

I tipped the young man, then put the Do Not Disturb sign on our door. I locked us in for a morning of resting bodies and minds. MJ had wrapped herself in the sheet, her new dress pooled nearby on the floor. She checked what was hiding under each lid, and discovered two Eggs Benedict under one, and a large veggie omelette under another one. There were no toasts, but instead an array of mini muffins in a basket. All this was accompanied by a carafe of freshly brewed coffee, and another one of orange juice.

"You did all this," she breathed out. "The flowers. The champagne. This breakfast. If I haven't told you lately: I love you. I know it scares you to hear it, but I am truly in love with you."

I kissed her hard, holding her head in place so she couldn't pull out. "I love you, too," I finally said it. And without hesitation, or fear of the unknown. MJ stepped back to take in the moment.

"I want to live the rest of my days with you, Danny Russell," she said as she wrapped her hand around mine. "And there's no pressure on my side. When you're ready, I'll be waiting."

"What about Ontario?"

"What about Ontario?" she asked back, sounding confused.

"At what point were you going to tell me about Ontario?" I asked, finally brave enough to hear her goodbye.

"Is that what's bothering you?" she asked.

"Kinda. You fly to Ontario every chance you get. I figure you're gonna go move there near your kids. It's only natural..."

"Is that why you were so distant to me yesterday?"

I nodded yes. She scooted her bum to the edge of the bed, our knees intertwining. She wrapped her arms tightly around my neck, our chests against each other, and just held me for what seemed an eternity. When I tried pulling back she tightened her hold. I gave it a few more tugs before finally pushing myself loose of her hug.

"When are you moving?"

"I have no plans to move there." MJ shook her head. "I missed my kids. I went to visit them. That's all. Besides, they were too busy to visit me. I actually spent my last trip visiting Rick and his new family."

"Awkward?"

"Not as much as I thought it would be," MJ answered. "The point is, my life is here. I have my job. I have you. I have my routines. I'll continue to visit my children and hope they do the same. Maybe one day you'll be able to come with me. My life, Danny, is with you. You are my future."

It was music to my ears.

"You going to Ontario scared me," I whispered. It was the only way to stop myself from weeping. "I've made the decision to leave Tina in June. I like her...but I...I no longer love her."

"Are you sure?"

"Alex doesn't graduate until next year, and I've been patiently waiting for him to grow up. I'm tired of waiting. Tired of putting everybody else's needs in front of mine. Alex. Emma. My mother. My sisters. What about me?! When do I get my turn at being happy? Truly happy?"

MJ didn't speak. She simply smiled a knowing smile. I was finally becoming myself. Finding peace within. My eyes welled up. I didn't care.

MJ scooted deeper into the bed, pulling me in with her. She tucked my head onto her shoulder. She hummed a lullaby and rocked me gently until I dozed off for a small nap. I had found my heaven in this woman's arms.

I awoke to my stomach gurgling. MJ was still cuddling me. We were still in an embrace. She released me and started preparing herself a plate while I called the front desk.

"Good morning. This is Danny Russell at 429. I'd like to extend my stay by one more night, please." I saw MJ's eyes show surprise while I waited for the clerk to process my request. I ignored MJ's waving. "Okay, thank you."

"I have to get back to work tomorrow," MJ protested. "I can't keep playing hooky with you. I have work to do!"

"Absolutely. I'm just not ready to let you go, yet. I don't want to check out at eleven. I don't want to rush. Let's enjoy our day, here. Kinda like a mini honeymoon."

"Like we had in Edwardsville a few years ago!" she smiled.

"Edwardsville was different. We were scared...nervous. We barely knew what we were getting into. We barely knew each other."

"I'd love to spend more time with you, Danny," MJ sighed as she wrapped her arms around my neck, pressing our two foreheads together. We breathed deep, simultaneously. I never wanted this moment to end. My stomach protesting ended our embrace.

Once I rolled the empty breakfast cart out into the hallway, I sat in the desk chair that I had pulled up next to the bed, and held MJ's hands into mine. She sat at the edge of the bed, a corner of the duvet covering parts of her front anatomy. It didn't take long for me to strip that off of her.

"I would like to marry you," MJ said as we lay in bed, having dirtied the sheets... again.

"Why?"

"Because I love you?" she breathed out.

"That's not good enough," I said as I glanced at her. "You realize you said the same thing to Rick. Yet, you cheated on him. How's marrying me gonna be different?"

"All I can say is, perhaps all I know is who I am," MJ answered. "I've changed. I'm not the same MJ that you met a few years ago. At first, you became an escape for me. But now, you've become my life. And if you don't ever plan to get married with me, then we need to talk about that. It's important for me to get married."

"For real?"

"How can I possibly love another man, knowing you exist?"

MJ was like no other woman I had ever known. She was bright, educated, independent, full of life. And quite the firecracker in bed. She now *was* part of my life. As a lover and a friend. I wanted to share the rest of my days with her. But married?

I squeezed her thigh. I was good at that. I leaned in to give her a quick peck on the cheek. She leaned in, as well. MJ touched my cheek as our lips met. Her eyes looked straight into mine. It was something she couldn't do the first year we knew each other.

"I will never move in with you without a ring. I'm just saying."

CHAPTER 56

♀

took the opportunity to call Annie while Danny went out to buy us lunch.

"Hi Annie. How are things in the office?"

"Honestly, a little hectic. There's a pile of contracts accumulating on your desk. They need your signature before they can go forward. Festival season is around the corner. And submissions for municipal financing show up daily."

"Well I'll be back after the weekend.. It's too late today to make it on time. First thing on my agenda Monday will go through those submissions."

"MJ...?" she hesitated.

"Yes, Annie."

"I can't cover for you, forever. You need to come do your job. You need to fully return to your position...or let it go."

"Has there been any complaints?" I asked as I sat up straight on the desk chair in the room.

"Complaints, no. Questions, comments, innuendos, eyes rolling... maybe."

"By whom?" I asked abruptly. Before Annie had the time to answer, I cut in. "Never mind. You're right. I need to smarten up."

"I get it," Annie sighed. "I get you want to be with...with him. With Mr Russell. I get you have to sneak around because your being together is not permitted. But you also have to think about your job, MJ. That's important, too."

"Annie," I started, feeling like a heel. "I'm so sorry I put you in this position. You shouldn't have to protect me."

"Enjoy your time together. See you Monday."

And then Annie hung up.

I spent the next hour reflecting. Reflecting on my situation. Reflecting on Danny's. Reflecting on my career. My future. On the spin my life has been on since my Papa died. No, since I met Danny actually. I had to stop coasting, and make decisions.

While waiting for Danny to return, I decided to step outside for a brisk walk. Walking on Portage Rd, where our hotel was situated, was out of the question. Traffic whizzed by at high speed. So I walked the outside perimeter of the hotel parking lot since the grass was still wet from last night's thunderstorm. It wasn't an ideal place to walk, but still better than on the highway.

What was next for me? Danny would be mine within the year. Fully mine, but with no plan to marry. He made that pretty clear. I never thought he wouldn't want to marry me. I just presumed he would. I wasn't hurt, per se. Well, maybe I was. Danny has always been closed up when it comes to sharing his feelings. But we both knew he loved me. We've enjoyed each other's company from the very beginning. We've always loved each other. So what was so wrong about getting married?

This trip had been amazing. In Edwardsville, we got to learn about each other. It was our green button to go ahead with our affair.

PEI became our seal of approval. I had to stop fretting over the what-ifs and the what nots. I was happy in my skin. I wanted this man. He made me feel sexy, sensual. I grew as a person because of him. I will be forever thankful I showed up at his presentation. It feels like so long ago, yet it was just like yesterday that our eyes locked. I had to accept his not wanting to get married. He wasn't rejecting me. Just the legality of it.

I tried not to stress about it. Yet, here I was speed walking around a hotel parking in Monet, PEI. It was helping decrease my anxiety level. I didn't want to ruin one last day with him before returning to our real lives.

CHAPTER 57

♂

I took advantage of my time alone in my SUV to call Tina and to tell her I'd be staying a third night.

"What's going on, Danny?" she asked, peeved. "This isn't like you."

"I'm just meeting with new clients and my PEI rep over drinks. I'd rather not drive home under the influence. There's nothing to worry about."

"I thought you said you were meeting with Monet City Hall people?"

Shit! I'd forgotten about that story. "Yes, Tina. That, too. I'm meeting them within the hour, actually."

"Are you lying to me?" Tina was sounding more and more upset.

"Of course not, Tina. I have no reason to lie," I lied. "I'll be home tomorrow. Now I've gotta go. I don't want to be late for this meeting. Love you. See you tomorrow."

"Love you, too," Tina answered matter-of-factly.

She didn't sound happy. I'd have some repairing to do. At least until June. I don't know how long I can carry on with this make believe. My nerves are frayed. I struggle with anxiety every day. My chest tightens every time I try to make sense of my life. Why does it have to be so hard?

I hoped my afternoon with MJ was worth it. I wanted to play with her. I wanted to discover more about her. I wanted to spend my whole day talking with her.

Struggling to glide my room card into the slot, I heard the deadbolt turn. MJ was opening the door for me. With my hands full of groceries, I welcomed her assistance.

"I had a few errands to run," I panted as MJ bolted the door shut behind me. "I stopped in at the grocery store. I bought us a roasted chicken and some potato salad. I hope it gets your approval."

"It's perfect," MJ replied as she grabbed a bag from my hands.

As we nibbled through our meal, MJ spoke up.

"Would you believe I may actually have a request?" she smiled.

I froze in time. My brain wasn't registering what my ears had heard. "You? MJ Taylor? You have a request?"

"First, I'm MJ Noël now. I'm no longer a Taylor. Second, if you're gonna mock me, I'm not gonna share."

"Ah, come on Babe," I pleaded. I laughed. "I'm sorry. You just blew my mind! What's your request?"

MJ remained quiet. She had closed up. At what point would she *ever* be comfortable with me? I didn't push. I didn't prod. I just hugged her, rubbing her back. The best thing to do was have her come to me instead of me insisting on her talking.

I felt content knowing I knew her well enough to do that. After a few years, you would think we'd know each other like the back of our hands. In some ways we did. But at the same time, our times together had always been limited. Mostly, a couple of hours each Wednesday. I knew every sensitive spot on her body. Every dimple. Every freckle. I'm not sure Rick could say the same thing.

But her sensitive nature, that was endlessly changing, making her grow faster than she was ready to. I had accepted that, letting her heart and mind acquaint themselves with everything I taught her. It made me grow patience.

"You clean up," she ordered me. *That* was a first. And I obeyed! I put the empty containers in the garbage can while MJ laid down in bed on her stomach with her phone in hand. I took the opportunity to go pee while she was searching for something. I figured it had to do with her pending request. At least, I hoped it did.

"Come here," MJ said, barely audible. But I did hear her. I understood the importance of this moment. I stripped down to my undies, matching her own attire, and climbed in bed with her. "Have you ever heard of Kama Sutra?"

"Kinda," I answered. This subject was new to me, too.

"I looked it up," she answered. "but all that came up was porn sites."

I smiled.

"But I forged through," MJ continued. "I wanted to know what it was all about, so I watched a few clips. Wanna see them?"

"Yes!" I answered eagerly. Yes, I wanted to watch porn clips with her. Yes, I wanted to see what she was interested in. Yes. Yes. Yes. What I saw was out of my knowledge, though. It was all new to me, and I felt uncomfortable. I didn't know how to do these things. And I told her so.

She smiled back at me. "Now you know how I've been feeling all this time, Danny."

I responded by giving her a puzzled look.

"Everything. And I mean *everything* I've done with you has been new for me. It's been a very difficult journey wanting to be with you, but scared to do things with you."

I wrapped my arm around her back as we remained on our stomachs looking at her phone screen. I'd been pushing MJ's buttons for years. I found a thrill in it. Now here she was, asking to be vulnerable *with* her. And I was bucking. I was such a coward.

"All I'm asking is that we learn more about it. See if it's something we could try, one day."

Against my diminished level of bravery, I answered her back. "For you my lady, anything."

MJ kissed me hard, her phone discarded onto the floor. She removed my underwear, then hers. For a change, I let her lead this afternoon.

She squatted on top of me, her fingers letting my cock slip into her pussy. Her fingers then splayed, doing magical stuff all over my body. MJ's movements were slow. Warm. Loving.

CHAPTER 58

♀

Now both on our backs, panting from another vigorous workout, I turned to Danny to try to relieve my conscience. I had to tell him about Luke. It was eating away at me. If we were going to start a life together next summer, I couldn't have this loaded secret hanging over me.

"Do you ever wonder how your other women have fared in life?"

"Meaning what?" Danny asked as he wiggled sideways to face me.

"Do you ever hear from Cathy? Or Ellen?"

"Nope," he smiled.

"No. Seriously," I continued as I sat up. "They've marked you. They must've been marked by you, also."

"Where are you going with this?" Danny asked as he frowned. His eyes were turning grey.

I hemmed. I hawed. I took in a deep breath and spilled my secret out. "I met a man who I think might be your son." I grimaced, waiting for some backlash. I don't think my statement registered, for Danny remained stoic. So I continued. "At the Passport Office a few weeks ago. When I drove up to Edwardsville. I was served by a man with the same eyes as you."

"MJ, be reasonable. They're just eyes."

"I spoke to him," I said while on the verge of tears. Letting this out was therapeutic. "He told me he'd been adopted. His birth mother's name is Cathy."

Danny's head jerked straight, finally understanding what I was saying.

"I'm not angry at you," he snapped. "Disappointed, maybe. But I'm not angry. I am fuming at Cathy, though. If this is all true..."

"I was building up the courage to tell you," I cried. My emotions were raw. The tension in my body was letting go. "I'm so sorry for keeping this from you. I just didn't know how to tell you."

"Passport Office, huh? His name?"

I hesitated before answering. "His name is Luke. But I think you need to talk to Cathy, not him."

Danny got up. He paced the bedroom floor. His hands fisted.

"Danny, please calm down," I begged hysterically. He was turning red. "Don't be upset at Cathy. She was a teenager. A teenager who was kicked out by her parents. She probably didn't want to burden you with her situation."

Danny stopped pounding his feet on the floor. He turned and looked at me. His eyebrows furrowed. His nostrils flared. His neck and throat reddened.

"That was three decades ago. Why still keep it a secret? She never even had the guts to tell me she was pregnant in the first place!"

"Honestly," I said, pleading Cathy's case. "You have to talk to Cathy herself. How much you want to know is up to you."

"She shut me out! Completely!" he yelled. His lip trembled while angry tears zigzagged down his inflamed cheeks.

"I need you to calm the fuck down!" I yelled back, using a

vocabulary he'd absorb instantly. "I met a man named Luke with piercing blue eyes. He says he was born to a Cathy, and then privately adopted. These things could *all* be coincidental. I suggest that in the next few weeks, you get in touch with Cathy. Go have a calm adult talk with her. Find out what she's been through. And be nice!" I smiled as I pecked his nose.

Danny stood there stunned. He was speechless. He was numb. I topsy-turvied a part of his life he thought was done with.

"You look tired," I said calmly as I embraced him, my left cheek resting on his forehead. "You wanna go in for a nap? Or just take a shower?"

I wanted him to calm down. I needed him to. I suppose his reaction was normal. But it still scared me. He was shocked. He was hurt. He had to process it all.

"I'm too worked up for that," Danny exhaled in a gruff tone.

He flipped me around. He pushed my torso onto the mattress. My body was now in the form of a V with my derrière sticking up. I tried to protest by getting up on my hands instead of my head and shoulders laying on the bed. I was afraid he'd be too rough. Letting his frustrations of Cathy, he might pound me.

Danny pushed my shoulders back down on the bed. He stripped my pants and underwear off, leaving me naked from the waist down.

"Danny, no," I whined, my words muffled by the duvet. Before I could protest again, I felt his grizzled face on my mound. He was devouring me. His movements were hard and deliberate. But not rough. His actions came with grunting moans, vibrating against my core.

I had no control of my body or its reaction to his actions. I felt heat. I felt wet. I felt my legs tremble. But the entire time Danny slurped and sucked and kissed my nether region, I cried moans of relief. How loud, I couldn't tell. My heartbeat pounding in my ears made me deaf to any other sound.

When Danny finally relented, I wanted nothing more than to crumble on the sheets. I was done. But apparently he wasn't.

"Stay up," he rumbled, lifting my hips back up. "It's my turn, Princess."

I could hear the slamming of our two bodies together. I could feel my body suctioning this man inside me. I grabbed onto the fitted sheet for support, hoping it would keep me grounded. Literally. Until Danny got his release.

And when he finally did, Danny collapsed over me, his body crushing mine on the bed. He pulled out and flipped me around. He wasn't done, yet. We made out like teenagers, our mouths everywhere, our hands exploring every crevice. Danny was insatiable.

He finally gave it a rest after suckling my breasts for what seemed an eternity. They were red. They were hot. They were super sensitive. But Danny made it worthwhile.

"I'm ready," he murmured as he looked up at me, my left nipple between his teeth.

"Ready for what?" I breathed out.

"Ready to leave Tina. I don't want to wait 'til June. I want you... us... now."

CHAPTER 59

♀

The next day, we headed back to New Brunswick. Our real lives were waiting to resume. I always enjoyed crossing the Confederation Bridge. It never got old. Rick and I had even skipped classes on the day before it opened. Runners and walkers alike could walk the thirteen kilometres from start to finish. I remember crossing the strait by ferry for the very last time, then running with Rick by my side. It was a sunny day, but the winds were strong. One of those great memories.

After we passed the Murray Beach exit, I looked at Danny with lust in my eyes. I felt naughty. He was rubbing off on me. I wanted to show my appreciation for these last few days with him. I also wanted to play on his level.

"What...what are you up to? You have that tigress look on your face," he smiled.

Without saying a word, I unbuckled myself and slithered across his console between our two seats. I struggled trying to unbuckle his pants. His belly was in the way.

"Are you crazy? I can't concentrate if you're gonna blow me while I drive."

I ignored his plea and managed to unzip him. Despite his protests, I pulled out his erection from his dress pants. Careful not to get my head stuck, I performed fellatio on him while he drove the mostly deserted road. I felt his right hand splay itself across the back of my head, trying to control my bobbing. It was still not my favourite thing to do with him sexually. But I knew he enjoyed it. And my lips tingled from the workout.

Minutes later, Danny screamed as both his hands gripped the steering wheel. I barely had time to pull my head from his lap when the sound of wheels screeching and metal hitting metal echoed through our heads. Not being buckled, my body flew across the cavity of his vehicle. The airbags deployed. The smell of sulfur was nauseating.

Twenty-three seconds after hitting the other vehicle, we were trunk-first into the ditch. The Equinox we slammed into was stopped across both lanes of the country road, its windshield smashed and the doors on the left side were dented in.

All four men in the Chevrolet SUV escaped from the passenger side. Their injuries seemed minor. Enough to come see how they could help us.

If I was hurt, I didn't know. The pain had yet to surface. Adrenaline took over my nervous system. I was more worried about Danny who moaned in pain. The left side of the engine had trapped him into his seat.

"MJ?"

The male voice sounded confused. It also sounded familiar. I slowly looked up. Deputy Mayor George had a surprised look on him.

"I...I..." I had no words.

"We've called 911. They'll be here soon," he rambled, avoiding the awkward predicament I was in.

Soon we heard sirens. The Jaws Of Life were used to extract Danny from his seat. He was the first to leave in an ambulance. Holliston Hospital was a good thirty minutes away.

I felt a sharp pain on my right side when the first responders carefully pulled me out of Danny's crushed brand new Nissan. My body was mostly on the floor of the backseat, with my legs on the seat. The second ambulance at the accident transported me to the same hospital Danny was heading to. The paramedics in the third ambulance tended to the scrapes and bruises George and his friends suffered from. The fun they had at the recently-opened golf course nearby was now overshadowed by an unfortunate accident. All because I wanted to excite Danny.

CHAPTER

♂

My left tebia was broken, as well as three fingers on my right hand. Surgery was performed. The pain was excruciating. Morphine was administered. I.V.s were hooked up. I was in and out of consciousness for God knows how long. I had no idea what had happened to MJ in all this. I never saw Tina arrive, but I got blurry visions of her being at my side whenever I'd wake up. She deserved so much better than me. She deserved a loving, faithful life partner. I was no longer it. But that was the last thing on my mind at the moment.

I just wanted the pain to stop. Or at least decrease. Eventually my morphine drip turned into oral painkillers. That's when I was given the go-ahead to go home and rest until my casts came off next month.

The day after I got home, Tina went straight for the jugular. Our accident had made the local news. Putting two and two together, Tina found out about my affair with MJ. She was angry. She was hurt.

"Who is she?"

I remained silent.

"I knew you'd been seeing someone else. I saw it in your face. I saw it in your eyes. I could hear it in your voice when you'd pretended to be stuck in a meeting. Am I not good enough for you anymore?

"Is she prettier? Richer? Or is she just sluttier than me?"

"Can this wait?" I asked. My painkillers were wearing off. I showed tremendous discomfort. Dutifully, Tina tended to my needs.

"Why her? Why now?"

"I met her at work."

"Is she better than me?"

"We fought the attraction for so long. I'm sorry it's come to this, Tina."

"I want you out."

"Not like this, Tina. Be reasonable."

"Let your little hussy take care of you. I'm done. I want you gone tomorrow."

Tina walked away. I felt sad for her. But I also finally felt relief. My secrets were out, no longer haunting me. I had to live with those consequences...but I'd survive.

I called my sister Denise, hoping she'd take me in. I was hoping she'd be willing to nurse me back to health before I start looking for new digs. With some hesitance, she came over. She packed me a bag under the watchful eye of Tina. Denise drove us to her condo downtown where I would stay until further notice. My life, as I knew it, would never be the same.

I was reprimanded by Juno for conducting personal business under the guise of Juno meetings. Once I'd return to work, they were going to put me on probation for up to a year.

I was charged with distracted driving, not yielding to traffic, and public indecency. Fines were given. Points removed. I however fared better than MJ.

CHAPTER 61

♀

I left the hospital a few days later with a broken right shoulder and a few cracked ribs. I also suffered a mild concussion. The neurologist suspended my driver's permit in three-month intervals until he saw fit to let me drive again. I was sent to recover at home. Alone. Except it wasn't home. It was a condo. With no memories created in it. Nobody to share it with. I never felt so abandoned. Alone.

I received one visitor during the first week home. It was Deputy Mayor George.

"Are you feeling better?" he asked. He sounded concerned. Yet, I knew why he was visiting. Maybe it was his way to formulate the right words.

"I'm making progress every day, George. Thanks for asking. Can I offer you coffee or tea?"

"No thanks," he answered. "I'm not here for long."

"I know," I sighed. "Give it to me."

"I hate doing this, MJ. But you know you've breached the Conflict of Interest clause in your contract with the City. We have no choice but to terminate your employment with us."

"I understand," I smiled, defeated tears welling in my eyes. This is not how I wanted my job to end. But after all this time of sneaking around with Danny, my actions had finally caught up with me. Defeat and relief. They mingled together that day.

"The Legal Department will be sending you a formal termination letter by registered mail. It's been a pleasure working with you all these years. It's too bad it had to end this way."

I said nothing. George got up and left without saying goodbye. Without even shaking hands. I was put out like yesterday's garbage. Just like that. But that's not what hurt the most.

How could you, Mom?! Was the first text I received once I got a phone replacing the one destroyed in the accident. The message came from Nicole. *What a fool you've made of yourself...of our family.*

Wow...just wow, Rick wrote. *You've laid this guilt trip on me for such a long time. How long has your affair been going on?*

And I thought Dad was the perv, wrote Marcel.

The only decent one I received came from Annie: *I'm sorry this happened to you.*

And then I received a surprise one, leaving me speechless: *I've read your messages. You can have him.* Without question, I knew it came from Tina.

Our secret affair was no longer secret. Our whole world knew. There was deep healing to be done. Communication with my children would need repairing. What a mess I'd created. Only I could fix this. But for now, I simply needed to hire some medical help for a few weeks. I couldn't do anything by myself with an arm in a sling and unpredictable headaches.

A few weeks later, feeling brave, I texted Danny, wondering if he'd like to see me. I hadn't spoken or seen him since the accident. It was past a month since Danny had lost control of his vehicle and had swerved into the other lane, bumping the SUV Deputy Mayor George was in, along with three of Holliston's Members of the Legislative Assembly.

I taxied over to Danny's new address: his sister Denise's condo behind City Hall. I buzzed her unit's number. With reluctance, she let me in into her home. What an awkward way to meet someone for the very first time.

"Hello. I'm MJ Noël."

"Yes. I know who you are," Denise replied as she led me to her living room. She showed no expression. "Please sit. I'll go get Danny."

Moments later, Denise returned wheeling Danny in. He remained in a wheelchair, still wearing a cast on his leg and his hand. He'd lost weight. His face was gaunt. His belly even seemed to have shrunk. His eyes had lost their sparkle. They no longer radiated. His sapphire colour had changed into a storm cloud grey.

I felt nervous. I felt drained. My energy was sapped from simply sitting next to him. I felt broken looking at him. Maybe I'd come too early. I'd hoped he'd missed me as much as I had missed him. There was no hint of that as we sat in silence. I had to take some responsibility in the state he was in. Hadn't he suffered enough?

I got up to look out the picture window, but was distracted by a lively colourful painting hung next to the patio door.

"It's an Alvin Richard original," Denise smiled from the kitchen as she loaded the dishwasher.

"Denise," Danny addressed his petite sister. "Could you give us some privacy?"

"I'll go get the mail," she answered, respecting his request.

"Come here," Danny sighed. It reflected the strength he'd lost since our accident.

I sat closest to his chair at the end of the sofa. "How are you?" I asked, my eyes welling.

"Getting there," he smiled weakly. Silence followed. "MJ?"

"Yes?"

"I'd do it again."

"Do what?"

"I don't regret these last years. I'd do it all over again, just to be with you."

I smiled. He was still mine. Life *would* resume.

"Have you contacted Cathy, yet?" I asked hesitantly.

"I..I..What if I don't want to know?" he asked, sounding like a child.

"I suppose it's your choice." I felt sad for him. For Luke. But respect had to be given. I had opened a can of worms. He was putting the lid back on..for now. It was his life, not mine.

"I noticed you're wearing that polka dot dress. My favourite," he grinned, looking at my exposed cleavage.

"I bought you a gift, but I left it at home," I grinned, trying to change the subject. "It's a book."

"Cool!" he expressed. I knew he wasn't much of a reader. "What's it about?" he feigned interest.

"It's the Kama Sutra," I whispered in embarrassment. He laughed out loud.

His left hand squeezed my knee. "I'm not done with you, just yet, Ms Noël. Just give me some time to get back on my own two feet."

"And I was thinking," I exhaled, "when you're more mobile, you can move in with me. I just can't give you the level of care you need, right now. I'm still recovering myself."

"Something to look forward to," he smirked. My Danny was getting back to his old self. "I have a gift for you, too."

"Oh?" I was surprised.

Danny reached under the knitted throw covering his legs, and came up with a velvet-covered box. "These were my mother's. My father gifted her these when I was born."

I took the box and opened it. A pair of sapphire earrings awaited my touch. They were absolutely gorgeous. I was shocked. I was speechless. I looked at a smiling Danny. His eyes were getting their sparkle back.

"I may never be ready to give you a ring. But would you settle for these?"

ACKNOWLEDGMENTS

To my patient husband who has spent endless hours alone while I wrote this book...thank you for letting me be me.

To my fabulous daughters M & J. You've inspired me to be the best person I can be and chase my dreams. Here it is!

To my exceptional editor Lee D Thompson. Your talent has made my project a beautiful reality, and your professionalism has been unwavering. I value every minute you've spent polishing this story with me.

To my parents (posthumously). My hunger to read came from Papa, my writing from Maman. Merci. Vous étiez des parents exceptionnels.

To my YW ladies. You are the push I needed. You've guided me through every step to make the Danny and MJ living in my head become the **Danny & MJ** in print. Your love and support is amazing.

To my friends who have been there from Day One, I salute you. Your long term dedication to my art has not gone unnoticed.

CPSIA information can be obtained
at www.ICGtesting.com
Printed in the USA
LVHW020755171219
640715LV00001B/1/P